ESCAPE to
DESTINY

Enjoy

Jim Laughton

ESCAPE to
DESTINY

Can an orphan boy from an obscure
planet make a galactic difference?

JIM LAUGHTER &
VICTOR J. BRETTHAUER

TATE PUBLISHING & *Enterprises*

Published by Tate Publishing & Enterprises, LLC
127 E. Trade Center Terrace | Mustang, Oklahoma 73064 USA
1.888.361.9473 | www.tatepublishing.com

Tate Publishing is committed to excellence in the publishing industry. The company reflects the philosophy established by the founders, based on Psalm 68:11,
"The Lord gave the word and great was the company of those who published it."

Book design copyright © 2007 by Tate Publishing, LLC. All rights reserved.
Edited by Brianne Webb
Cover design by Janae J. Glass
Interior design by Kellie Southerland
Jim Laughter photo courtesy of Lifetouch Portrait Studios, Inc.
Victor J. Bretthauer photo courtesy of Chuck Robinson

Published in the United States of America

ISBN: 978-1-60462-288-1
1. Juvenile Fiction: Science Fiction, Fantasy, and Magic: Series
2. Fiction: Futuristic and Science Fiction: Series
07.12.28

DEDICATION

To our loving wives, Wilma and Niki, without whom this project would still be just an idea in a file folder. You encouraged us, stood beside us, threatened us, and nagged us. And when we needed someone to proofread our pathetic scribbles, you endured a constant barrage of us asking, "Well, what do you think about it?"

Thank you, our loves, for your everyday presence in our lives. We are nothing without you.

Jim and Victor

PROLOGUE

We are not alone. But you already knew that. It is the way in which we are not alone that is the question, isn't it? If you are expecting this book to be about silicone-based aliens that look like green Jell-O, you will be sorely disappointed. If, on the other hand, your mind is open to the unexpected possibility that whoever is out there is more like us, and that we, in fact, are the odd ones, then hang on tight.

Welcome to Galactic Axia! Sorry. That's what it calls itself, and only dusty ancient history books on some planet suggest it was ever otherwise. Using an accidentally discovered drive system that doesn't warp anything other than the mind of someone trying to explain it, Axia ships travel faster than light. Much faster. And considering the Axia spans much, if not all, of the Milky Way galaxy, that is a good thing.

The humans of Galactic Axia (yes, they are our parent stock here on Earth) are not very different from ourselves. They have the same needs and wants as we do, and some have noted similarities between Axia culture and some societies here on Earth.

Oh! I forgot to mention that Earth isn't the center of anything in Galactic Axia. In fact, our planet is "closed," as Axia puts it. Quarantined. Seeded with threatened species of plants and animals from other similar worlds and then later used as a safe place to exile criminals and malcontents, Earth was then left to its own devices. The Axia keeps watch over Earth (or Sol-3, as they call it) hoping for the day when we'll mature.

But someday we will come out when we grow up a bit and aren't a threat to civilization out there. In the meantime, we are being prepared. This book and its companions are but one way that is being done. So journey on, dear reader. It is not by happenstance that this book came into your possession.

1

The house was silent in the predawn darkness, except for the raucous snores coming from the room down the hall where his older brother slept. In a small corner bedroom, a teenage boy woke in a cold sweat, shaking and nearly nauseous. *Not again!* he thought. An involuntary shudder racked his body and he desperately tried to push the unbidden nightmare from his recollection. But the more he tried, the stronger it became. "No!" he hissed in a harsh whisper while those fateful images replayed in his mind.

The air was crisp—a beautiful spring day. Along with the other kids in his class, the ten-year-old was enjoying a field trip to a local museum. That it was to the new wing dedicated to the military branch of the Axia and its far-flung personnel was of special interest to the boy, Delmar Eagleman. Ever since the day that two service troopers had arrived at the Eagleman farm wearing their formal dress uniforms, his mother had become withdrawn; she had a haunted look in her eye. He knew she wasn't telling him something—something about his father, a trooper himself. Now maybe Delmar could find out something at the museum! He was barely able to contain his excitement!

His older brother, Dorn, almost a man himself, looked at Delmar sullenly and mumbled something about being a stupid kid. He had been roped into replacing their mother as chaperone for this bunch of brats when she was called to Keeler Field for something to do with their father's disappearance. She would pick them up at the school after the field trip. *I could be out with my friends instead of babysitting these brats*, Dorn thought. He was mad, and he didn't care who knew it. But Delmar didn't care. He was going to find out what they were keeping secret from him. That was enough incentive for him to put up with a lot from his brother.

Since the school was reasonably close to the museum, the teacher and chaperones decided to have the kids walk to the museum rather than use a bus. The weather was good and it would help burn off some of the excess energy from the gaggle of ten year olds. The plan worked well, although more than once the teacher thought it was akin to holding back wild horses.

The new museum display was everything Delmar hoped it would be; however, in recollection the visit seemed to fly by in a flash. As was usual, when the memory scrolled, the day's event seemed unimportant. It was what happened later that mattered.

The boy saw himself as a ten year old walking in single file back to the school, his older brother walking directly behind him, prodding him on with an occasional push or poke. Delmar knew what was going to happen next and found himself powerless to stop the awful memory. The afternoon was warm and traffic was growing heavy. Mindful of the adults, the students kept to the sidewalks. Everything was going well. Even Dorn's persistent scornful remarks could not dampen Delmar's spirits.

Approaching one of the major intersections, the lead element of the class stopped and waited under supervision for the light to change and for the crosswalk to clear. The traffic signal changed and cross traffic started up again when suddenly, before the students could move, the blare of a truck air horn split the air. As if in slow motion, Delmar recalled the monstrous runaway truck looming suddenly in the intersection where it smashed into several cars just starting to move toward the students.

Metal and glass flew everywhere as the truck careened onward, barely slowing even though it had a small car crushed under its front bumper. Everything ground to a halt, and the air froze for what seemed like an eternity. Then Delmar heard someone scream. It was him. He was screaming, his eyes glued on the crushed car. It was his mother's car. She was still inside it. She wasn't moving. Still screaming, someone picked him up and carried him away from the accident.

The youth shuddered again, reliving the horror as if it had happened only yesterday. What followed next Delmar could not forget although he desperately wanted to—the hospital, the funeral, the court, and most of all, his brother. Shaking young Delmar while angry tears streamed down his face, Dorn had told him that both his mother and father were dead and it was all Delmar's fault. It had something to do with him being too wimpy to walk home from school and her having to pick him up, but Delmar was sure that wasn't true.

"Dorn wanted the ride, not me," Delmar muttered to himself.

And that was the beginning of Delmar's daily nightmare. Appointed legal guardian of his younger brother, Dorn never let a day go by without letting his anger and resentment be known. The brothers took two different routes dealing with their grief. Dorn essentially crawled inside a bottle. Delmar crawled inside himself.

Delmar must have fallen back asleep because the next thing he knew, Dorn was dragging him out of bed and screaming in his face.

"Get your mangy hide out here and fix me some breakfast!" Dorn screamed as he drew back to cuff his younger brother. Delmar wisely ducked and scrambled out of Dorn's grasp. Running down the dirty hall to the kitchen, Delmar started pulling out pans while his brother laughed behind him. But Delmar knew he was safe for the moment when he heard Dorn turn and stumble into the bathroom. *Probably throwing up again!* Delmar thought. Listening while he pulled out meat and potatoes, Delmar was rewarded by hearing Dorn pay the drunkard's price for the previous night of drinking. *That should keep him busy for a few minutes*, Delmar thought with relief. Pushing back his ragged hair, Delmar concentrated on making something edible. Quality wasn't a big concern at this stage of their relationship. All he wanted was a temporary reprieve from Dorn's ever-present anger.

About the time his brother arrived, Delmar was shoveling the food onto a plate. After putting the plate in front of Dorn, Delmar served himself and started to take his plate to the far end of the table. But before he could dodge, Dorn lashed out and knocked it out of his hand.

"That's what you get for being late!" Dorn growled. "Now clean up this pig sty and go get busy on your chores! I've got to go find you another job!"

Delmar swept up the food and broken crockery and then, in silent hunger, headed to his room to dress. Fortunately, he had a stash of food hidden out in the barn where Dorn would never find it. Such subterfuge had become necessary in the months since Dorn had pulled him out of school. Prior to that, Delmar could count on at least one hot meal at the cafeteria. But no more; now he had to fend for himself or starve.

The relief Delmar felt when he heard his brother leave in the truck was palatable. Nevertheless, he did not dare slack up on the chores. All too soon, Dorn would return and find something Delmar had not done. It was almost a pattern etched in stone. Taking only a couple of minutes to consume some of his hidden rations, Delmar quickly got back to trying to clean up the yard around the tired farmhouse. Delmar saw repairs and chores everywhere begging for attention, but out of survival, he concentrated on the ones Dorn had specified. He would work the others into his routine as he got a chance, assuming Dorn would allow the time, which was doubtful.

After raking up the worst of the mess, Delmar took what trash was burnable and started the burn pile. His lips tightened when he spotted the corner of a burned book near the edge. Painful memories came back of the day Dorn had taken the correspondence material the school had sent and threw them onto the burn pile. Dorn was always demanding more work out of Delmar, and this was yet another way to enforce it. The only consolation had been when the school authorities had shown up unexpectedly to find the burnt remains.

After that, Dorn had not touched the material that arrived regularly by the postal carrier. Unfortunately, Delmar hardly had time to touch them either. Dorn kept him so busy that Delmar had almost no time to study and complete the work.

It ended up piling up in a corner of Delmar's room, another heap in a house full of heaps.

Delmar had just finished turning their few animals out when he discovered that Dorn had returned home. Stepping into the house, Delmar found his older brother in another one of his signature rages. Obviously, Dorn's efforts had not gone as well as he expected. That meant trouble for Delmar. *Uh oh!* Delmar thought when he noticed that Dorn had already started drinking again. At the same moment, Dorn spotted his younger brother. That was all the provocation Dorn needed.

With an almost instinctive dodge, Delmar avoided the thrown bottle as it smashed against the doorframe. *I'll probably have to clean that up as well!* he sighed to himself. He watched his older brother drunkenly grab for another projectile. Delmar noticed that in spite of his inebriation, Dorn spared the full bottles and grabbed an empty to chuck at his brother.

"Get your worthless hide out to the barn and start shoveling!" Dorn screamed and made ready to throw again. Delmar wisely slipped out the door, hearing the next bottle break against it seconds later.

Stepping quickly around the garbage his brother had thrown in the general direction of the empty garbage can, Delmar scrambled across the side yard toward the tired barn beyond. Behind him, Delmar could hear the muttered curses as his brother settled down to drink more of the cheap alcoholic beverage in which he always seemed to be immersed. With luck, Delmar would find

Dorn passed out on the floor the next time he dared to venture into the house.

Entering the dilapidated barn, Delmar mentally ignored all but the most pressing repairs that begged for attention. There was simply too much to do, and being the only worker (since his brother considered himself management), Delmar had to be selective with his endeavors, not that they would ever come to the attention of his brother.

And that brought him back to the disgusting task now facing him: that of shoveling out the manure and chicken droppings. Delmar would prefer to use the scoop on the tractor. His long-dead father had designed things that way. But the money needed to return the tractor to serviceability went to more important things, such as Dorn's habits.

So rigging up a crude facemask against the stench, Delmar pulled on a pair of old patched work boots and waded into the task. *At least Dorn won't bother me here!* Delmar thought as he started forking the first layer of waste into a wheelbarrow. Neglect was actually helping him now. Over time, most of the ammonia had leeched out. And doing the monotonous task allowed Delmar to think on things—many things.

To Delmar's surprise, he heard Dorn storm out to the truck and leave in a shower of gravel and mud. *Wonder what he's up to now*, Delmar thought while he continued forking manure into the wheelbarrow. Whatever it is, Delmar was sure that he would find out soon enough. Bending to the task at hand, the youth concentrated on getting the odorous chore finished.

Just as Delmar was dumping the last load of manure into the compost pit, Dorn pulled back into the driveway. Hoping that his brother would just go inside and drink himself into a stupor, Delmar started washing down the stall area with buckets of soapy water. Using a hose would have been preferable, but it had split months ago, and Dorn did not deem it necessary to replace.

In the midst of sloshing another bucket into the back of the stalls, Delmar heard his brother yell from the barn entrance, "Get your lazy hide out here!" Without a word, Delmar set down the bucket and walked toward the entrance. He noticed that Dorn was avoiding the mud around the main barn door. Getting dirty was not part of Dorn's management style. That's what little brothers were for. Delmar stopped and waited just beyond Dorn's reach.

"Get yourself cleaned up!" Dorn ordered. "You got a job. You start working down at the Hassel farm in an hour." Without another word, Dorn turned and stormed off into the house. Delmar went to a side shed and stripped off his filthy outerwear and headed into the house via the door farthest from where Dorn was likely to be. The move paid off since the only evidence Delmar heard of his brother was the usual sounds of his drinking in the front room.

In short order, Delmar headed down the road toward the Hassel farm. He didn't consider asking Dorn to give him a lift in the truck. It was better to be alone on the road than trapped in a vehicle with his angry, drunken brother. Besides, the fuel in the tank had more important uses, such as driving Dorn to see his friends, or going to buy more supplies that Dorn needed to quiet his inner demons.

Arriving at the Hassel farm, Delmar stepped up onto the porch and knocked on the front door-frame. He had no idea what the Hassels were like. He only knew of them in passing as an older couple with a farm down the valley. Delmar did note with approval that the place was well maintained. Some heavier work obviously needed doing, and Delmar suspected that was why he was here.

The door opened to reveal a pleasant-faced elderly woman in work clothes.

"You must be Delmar," she said as she opened the screen door and invited the youth to come inside. As Delmar stepped into the simple but clean farmhouse, an older man with an evident limp came from beyond the front room. His face reflected both strength and humor. Delmar decided right then that he was going to like this job.

"Glad to meet you, Delmar!" the man said, taking Delmar's hand in his own. "I'm Robert Hassel, and this is my wife, Agnes."

"I'm pleased to meet both of you," Delmar said formally.

"Come on back to the kitchen," Agnes said as she led the way. "We're about to sit down and eat."

"Join us," Robert said. He motioned for Delmar to go ahead of him.

"I better not," Delmar protested suddenly, remembering his brother. "If Dorn—"

"We won't tell if you won't," Robert said with a wink.

"You look as if you could use some chow," Agnes added from where she was setting the last of what appeared to be a feast on the table. Delmar looked up into Robert's eyes and detected that the man probably suspected what kind of person Dorn was. More importantly, Delmar saw in that look that he was safe here.

"I guess it's okay," Delmar said awkwardly. "If it doesn't keep me from getting the job done."

"Don't you worry 'bout that," Agnes said from where Robert helped her be seated. Following his hosts, Delmar waited until Robert was seated before taking the extra chair at the table. He could not remember the last time he had enjoyed a home-cooked meal other than the hash he usually cooked for Dorn. Actually, he could, but Delmar avoided thinking about his past that was gone forever.

The mealtime went by fast for the youth, who felt a bit awkward around this couple. Delmar found himself feasting, not just on the good food, but also on the good company of honest adults, which was quite a difference from what normally happened at Delmar's house. Delmar relaxed and only occasionally detected that the couple was slowly feeling him out. Instinctively, Delmar became defensive and gave evasive answers to any queries about his home life.

The meal finished, Robert led Delmar out to the barn. In contrast to the barn on the Eagleman farm, this one was well kept and neat. By comparison,

Delmar could not see anything in immediate need of repair. Mr. Hassel quickly disabused him of that notion. Together they started on what Mr. Hassel called preventative maintenance.

By the time the afternoon light began to fail, Delmar had already worked up a good sweat. It was obvious to Robert that Delmar was used to hard work, but it bothered him that the boy showed a hidden fearfulness concerning any task they set out to do. Robert made a mental note to quietly check into what was going on down at the Eagleman farm.

Agnes suddenly appeared at the barn door.

"You two ever going to quit?" she asked. "I've almost got supper ready." Delmar seemed to jump at the mention of mealtime. He knew he had to prepare the evening meal for Dorn or he would receive a beating for his neglect.

"Almost done, honey," Robert said as he straightened up from where they had been working on the hay conveyor. "Ready, Delmar?" Robert called up to where Delmar was greasing and tightening the top sprocket assembly.

"Uh…I better not," Delmar said defensively. "I've got to get back home. My brother will be expecting his dinner." Agnes raised an eyebrow at her husband but said nothing.

"Good 'nuff then," Mr. Hassel said. "We'll finish this tomorrow. What time can you be here?"

"What time do you want me here, sir?" Delmar asked back as he climbed down from the loft.

"Soon as you finish your chores?" Robert asked, suspecting that there was more to this than feeding a few animals.

"I think I could be here by ten, sir," Delmar answered. "But I'll have to clear it with my brother."

"I'll take care of that," Robert said. Delmar's face suddenly blanched, but he said nothing. "You go clean up, and I'll give you a ride home. No need for you to be late."

"I'll be fine, sir," Delmar said. Before either Robert or Agnes could say more, the youth scooted off to the mudroom to clean up. The couple looked at each other knowingly. Agnes headed back to the farmhouse while Robert started buttoning things up for the night. Before he got back, Robert saw Delmar heading up the country road toward the Eagleman farm farther up the valley. *I better go make that call*, Robert thought as he headed for the house.

To Delmar's surprise, Dorn was in a halfway good mood when he got home. Almost as soon as Delmar stepped through the door, Dorn spoke up.

"I got a call from that old farmer down the road," Dorn said menacingly. Delmar tried to hold his fear in check but it must have shown on his face. Dorn roared in laughter. Delmar tried to ignore him and started for the kitchen to make dinner. "Forget that!" Dorn ordered. "I'm going out," he continued. "I ain't puttin' up with your slop tonight!" Delmar felt relief. As Dorn got up to leave, he spoke back over his shoulder, "I want you up early tomorrow so you can get the chores done. That old fool wants you down there by nine, so you better not be late!"

Dorn sped out of the driveway for another night of drinking and mischief with his friends. In the meantime, Delmar went through the motions of making himself something to eat. *Maybe I can get some study time in*, Delmar thought while he warmed a can of soup. He had already fallen terribly behind and the hope of earning a graduation certificate seemed more elusive than ever. But before he'd even finished eating, Delmar slipped into an exhausted sleep. The last thought he had was wondering what new trouble this change in Dorn could mean.

2

Dawn arrived much too soon at the Eagleman farm. Delmar pried himself up from the table where he had fallen asleep the night before. He managed to drag himself to his room. Even the noisy arrival of Dorn from wherever he'd gone had not penetrated Delmar's exhaustion.

The house was still dark. Quietly dressing, Delmar slipped back down to the kitchen where he quickly whipped up some hash for Dorn. He left it covered in the heavy pan so it would retain its heat until his passed-out brother could arouse from his drunken slumber. Taking his portion, Delmar slipped out the back door and ambled slowly to the barn. At least here he could eat in peace. It also gave Delmar time to think.

Delmar regretted that he hadn't managed to get any of the correspondence work done. He knew that if completed materials weren't submitted in a timely manner, the school would eventually terminate his enrollment. Delmar knew this could seriously limit any hope he had of getting out of here. Resolving to try harder, Delmar finished his plate of hash and washed it down with a dipper of cool water.

Further thought was interrupted by a roar and crash from the house. *He's up*, Delmar thought as he headed the other way to do chores. Irreverently, Delmar hoped his brother would start drinking again so he would pass out. Then Delmar would have some peace while he quickly got the necessary chores out of the way.

Evidently, his prayers were heard as the noise soon ceased. *I wish he'd stay that way!* Delmar thought uncharitably. As quickly as he could, Delmar turned the animals out and put what feed they had left out as well. Delmar hoped the money earned from his new job with the Hassels would go to buy more feed, but he had his doubts. Resisting temptation to just quit, Delmar finished his chores and then headed down the road toward the Hassel farm.

Surprised to find Delmar at their door early, Agnes led him back to the kitchen where she and Robert had been eating breakfast.

"Breakfast is ready," Robert said. Agnes poured the youth a cup of coffee from the pot on the stove.

"No, thank you," Delmar said. "I've already eaten." But Agnes caught the hungry look in his eyes. *He may have eaten, but it wasn't much!* she thought angrily. Without a word, she whipped up another stack of pancakes and soon set the steaming plate down in front of the boy. Delmar reddened with embarrassment.

"Eat up, son," Robert said good-naturedly. "Don't want good food going to waste." Delmar's gut rumbled in agreement and the matter was decided. Sheepishly, he started on the food. Agnes sat back down and silently slid the butter and syrup over as a suggestion. Delmar took the hint and generously spread the condiments on his tall stack of hot cakes. The look of delight and satisfaction was all the Hassels needed to get another glimpse into Delmar's home life.

Watching the boy eat, Robert came to a decision. "I have to make a run into town," he announced. "I want you to finish stacking that hay and then see what you can do to fix the garden fence. You know where the tools are out in the barn. If I'm not back by then, I'm sure Agnes can come up with more for you to do."

"Yes, sir," Delmar said after hastily choking down a bite.

"Don't worry, Delmar," Robert went on with a chuckle. "She won't work you to death. It may seem like it, but she won't!"

Robert pushed up from the table after draining his coffee cup and spoke to his wife. "I may be a while," he said as he stepped over to grab his jacket off the hook. "I'll call before I come back just in case you need me to pick something up for you."

"I'll try to keep the list short," Agnes said with a smile. Delmar watched Mr. Hassel limp out to the car shed. He wondered what could be wrong with the old farmer's leg. A minute later, Robert drove his car down the drive and off toward town.

"Yes, I know he limps," Agnes suddenly said in answer to Delmar's thoughts. "Combat injury."

"I'm sorry," Delmar said.

"Don't be," Agnes answered, "we aren't. It's an old injury. I'm sure Robert will tell you all about it eventually," she added with a knowing smile.

"Guess I better get started on these projects," Delmar said as he started to get up.

"You'll do nothing of the kind until I let you," Agnes ordered in a tone that brooked no argument. "Now finish your breakfast. You don't want it to go to waste, do you?"

"No, ma'am," Delmar replied as he dutifully took another bite.

Now that's the waist I want to see it going to! Agnes thought while she studied Delmar's too-thin frame. Pouring herself a refill of coffee, she decided to make good use of the time.

"You graduate already?" she asked innocently.

"Why do you ask?" Delmar asked defensively.

"No reason. It's just a boy your age would normally be in school about now," Agnes answered. "So since you're not, I suspect you've graduated in some accelerated program."

"No, ma'am," Delmar admitted. "I'm in the correspondence program so I can be at home more. I hope to finish soon."

"I see," Agnes said. *Not a very good liar,* she thought. "What have you been studying lately?"

"History and stuff," Delmar answered evasively.

"So how do you like living under a dictatorial monarchy?"

"It's okay I guess," Delmar answered.

"But what if the empress ordered her troopers to storm this place and take us all captive?"

"She wouldn't do that, would she?" Delmar suddenly asked, fear shading his voice. Agnes made another mental note. *This is very interesting*, she thought. *Either he's never studied history and civics, or he has no understanding of it.*

"How about the ongoing war with the Redtails?" she asked.

"What about it?" Delmar dissembled. "I mean, can't we just leave them alone? Why do we have to provoke them to attack us?" Agnes felt her bile rising when she considered the absolute ignorance and distortion of facts Delmar was spouting.

"You better finish up and get on with those chores," Agnes chided as she changed tact. "I don't want your parents calling if you get home late." Delmar's face suddenly went ashen.

"I don't have any parents," he mumbled. Agnes was stunned.

"What did you say?" she stammered.

"I said I don't have any parents," Delmar replied more evenly. "My dad was a trooper and died in space somewhere. My mother was killed when I was ten. Now my brother is my guardian, and we do the best we can."

"I'm sure you do," Agnes said, trying to bring her

own emotions under control. Of course, she knew Delmar's history, having been friends and neighbors of his parents so long ago. It just didn't seem possible that this boy could have grown up without any parental guidance on a farm just down the road from her and Robert. It was no wonder the boy was confused and even a little bitter.

"You best get busy," Agnes said as she got up. "I'd like to see those projects well toward completion when Mr. Hassel gets home." Delmar hastily finished the last bites of his meal and stood up as well. Without a word, he placed his dishes in the sink and headed out toward the barn. Agnes watched him through the window and found her own thoughts going back to the sons she and Robert had lost early in their marriage.

Hours later, Agnes heard Robert drive into the farmyard. Stepping out onto the back porch, she could see his weariness in the way he walked.

"How did it go?" she asked as Robert dragged himself up onto the porch.

"Not very well," Robert answered. Agnes stepped supportively under one of his arms and together they walked inside.

"Tell me about it," Agnes said. She poured them steaming hot cups of coffee while Robert sagged into his chair at the table.

"First off, where's Delmar?" Robert asked.

"He went home as soon as the projects were

finished," Agnes reported. "But not before his brother showed up to collect payment. Dorn sure seemed anxious to get the money."

"Didn't he give Delmar a ride?" Robert asked.

"No," Agnes said tightly. "Dorn seemed in a hurry. Just before he left, he eyed Delmar, and I saw Delmar's face go pale. I suspect that's why Delmar left in such a hurry as soon as I released him." She gave her husband his coffee and then sat down across the corner of the table from him.

"That fits in with what I pieced together while talking to people today," Robert said wearily as he took a sip.

"I figured you went to the school," Agnes said.

"Yes, but they were the least helpful," Robert answered. "Seems Delmar hasn't been turning in his correspondence courses for a while now. Much more and they'll drop him from the program."

"So what did you do?" Agnes asked, knowing Robert wouldn't leave things to get worse when he could get involved.

"I signed up to mentor Delmar through the Service Tutorial Program," Robert answered with a wry smile. "I arranged for the material to come here directly. Then when Delmar's not doing chores, he can get some study in without interference."

"What interference?"

"It seems his brother, who does have legal guardianship, keeps Delmar so busy that his studies are neglected. Since Delmar is old enough to leave school, there's very little they can do about it. Even the social agency claims their hands are tied."

"That fits in with what I learned just talking with Delmar," Agnes reported.

"Been snooping again?" Robert quipped with a tired grin.

"Just asking a few questions," Agnes confessed. "What little knowledge Delmar has in some subjects such as history and civics is either missing or twisted. For the son of a trooper, you'd think he'd know a lot more."

"His father was reported missing and presumed dead, and his mother was killed in that terrible accident when he was only ten," Robert reminded Agnes. "It must have been hard on both of those boys."

Agnes reflected on what her husband had just told her. She took his hand and squeezed it gently in her own. "The Eaglemans were our friends, Robert," she said. "We should have watched out for those boys these last few years, but we didn't."

"I know, honey," Robert answered. "I think that's why I feel responsible for Delmar now."

Agnes leaned into Robert's chest. "Those could have been our boys," she whispered, trying to keep her emotions in check.

"Now honey," Robert said. "Stepping in and trying to raise those boys would not have brought our boys back to us."

Agnes looked up into the caring face of her husband. "There's one more thing, Robert," Agnes said. "I also suspect that things at home aren't too happy for Delmar. He seemed very uncomfortable around his brother, as if he expected to be hit or something. He stayed just out of Dorn's reach."

"My sources confirm that," Robert said. "Off the record, more than one person mentioned they suspected abuse and neglect. That, and Dorn has quite a reputation around the area as a trouble-maker and a boozer."

"So you think we're up to tutoring this boy?" Agnes asked.

"I don't see why not," Robert answered. "And besides, the chores won't last forever. Might as well pay him to be a student as well."

"When will we start?" Agnes asked.

"Soon enough," Robert replied. "They have to notify Delmar first. Then the materials will come here if he doesn't object."

"What's worrying you?" Agnes asked, detecting hesitancy in her husband.

"I just hope Dorn doesn't interfere," Robert admitted.

The boy looked up as the shadow of the incoming ship moved across the field. He stopped hoeing the weeds around the cabbages and stared with unabashed envy as the ship glided silently out of his field of vision, heading toward the spaceport several miles away to the south.

"Hey! Dreamer!" Dorn yelled. "You better get your dreams back on those cabbages, or I'll thrash ya good!" Sure, Delmar had dreams. *They're certainly higher than the dirt and weeds surrounding these cabbages*, he thought. Definitely higher than anything that might be percolating in the lazy brain of his nearly thirty-year-old brother.

Noticing Dorn heading for the truck, Delmar got confused. "What about dinner?" Delmar asked as Dorn got into the vehicle.

"You're on your own, kid!" Dorn snapped back. "I can't stand the slop you call food anyway! I'm going to have some decent food tonight! And just because I'm gone, don't slack none on your work!" Without another word, he sped out of the rutted drive. Delmar watched silently while the truck drove away in the direction of town. He was pretty sure where Dorn would soon be and what would happen to the money Delmar had received from the Hassels. *Sure isn't going for supplies around here!* Delmar thought angrily as he went back to the hoeing.

After dark had finally fallen, Delmar herded the last of the livestock back into the barn and dragged his weary body into the house. Though it was pleasant not having Dorn around, Delmar felt the emptiness more than usual. Setting some potatoes on the stove to boil, Delmar retrieved one of the study books from the pile in his room. He set it where he could read it while he prepared some hamburger to fry.

Delmar tried to force his mind to understand the mathematical equations in the text, but the potatoes were demanding attention, and the meat needed cooking. Chopping in a little of one of the few onions they had left, Delmar tried to spice up the meat. He let it simmer and set the potatoes to drain and then started slicing up the soft-boiled tubers to add to the meat when it was done.

But food wasn't the only thing simmering at the moment. The resentment that had been building in the back of Delmar's mind for a long time demanded attention as well. His job at the Hassel farm had gotten Delmar's mind to remembering better times when he was young, and a time when this kitchen had been lit by the buoyant presence of his mother. Although his father was away on duty, the young Delmar had felt the safety of a home and those that loved him—a far cry from the shabbiness of his life now.

All too soon the meat was done and Delmar added the chopped potatoes to make a hash. Sure, it was monotonous, but it was easy, warm, and filling. Setting his plate in front of the book, Delmar tried to feed both his tired mind and body.

3

The morning dawned warm and early when Delmar saw his brother stagger out of the house toward the postal box on the road. Seeing Dorn this early in the morning after his usual late night carousing was a bit disturbing, so Delmar moved to a different part of the garden to avoid notice for as long as possible. The six months since he had started working for the Hassels had been relatively peaceful for Delmar. He knew that the wages of his labor were keeping Dorn in a steady buzz, but more importantly, it meant a respite from his usual outbursts of rage that were always directed at the younger brother. Even inebriated, though, Dorn knew better than to make it too hard for Delmar. After all, he did have to work.

Dorn finally made it to the mailbox and pulled out the previous day's offering from the rural postal carrier. He considered the gathering and perusal of the mail his personal prerogative and had beaten that point into his younger brother years before. It allowed Dorn to have yet one more measure of control over Delmar.

Sifting through the stack, Dorn was pleased to find the regular check from the Hassels for Delmar's labor. Tearing it open, Dorn grunted with satisfaction, noting that Delmar had kept his hours regular and high. The bonus they had included for Delmar would be spent on better uses than fixing up their old farm. Invested properly, Dorn anticipated the warm glow of liquid refreshment at his regular watering hole later that night.

Glancing at the rest of the stack of mail, Dorn also noticed an envelope from the school marked urgent in place of the usual packet of correspondence material for Delmar. His interception and destruction of their previous letter to Delmar had proven fruitful. Opening it, Dorn read with satisfaction that Delmar's enrollment had been dropped for lack of response to the previous missive or return of materials in a timely fashion. Dorn chuckled to himself. He was going to enjoy breaking the news to his brother. It also meant that Delmar now had more time to earn outside income.

"Delmar!" Dorn bellowed as he walked back toward the house with the incriminating letter clutched firmly in his hand. Having seen his breakfast waiting in the warmer, Dorn suspected Delmar was out somewhere doing his regular chores before he had to report down the road at the Hassel farm.

Delmar appeared around the side of an outbuilding from where he'd been working in the garden.

"Get over here, you loser!" Dorn yelled at him. Delmar dutifully came toward him, a wary expression on his face. He could see the glint of mischief in his older brother's eyes.

"What do you want?" Delmar asked evenly when he stopped close enough to hear but still out of range of Dorn's fists.

"Got a letter from those correspondence people," Dorn spat back. "You failed, you loser! They dropped you!"

"What?" Delmar asked fearfully.

"They canceled you!" Dorn laughed wickedly as he waved the incriminating letter. "You didn't stay in touch or turn in your work! I knew you were too lazy to make it work!" Dorn dropped the letter from the correspondence school in the mud and stepped on it with a twist of his shoe.

"But—" Delmar started to say but was cut short by another derisive laugh from his brother.

"Now finish whatever you're doing and get down to the Hassels'!" Dorn ordered. "This makes you more available, and I expect it to show!" Dorn said, waving the check. "You better have more hours next week!" he continued. "They're not happy, and you wouldn't want to get fired, would you?" Dorn said menacingly as he smoothly lied.

Delmar's face blanched. Leaving his crestfallen brother standing in the mud, Dorn headed back into the house still laughing aloud. Delmar steeled himself and left the muddy letter where it lay and turned back to his work in the garden.

The Hassels noticed the black cloud of despair hanging over Delmar's head when he arrived considerably early for work. The boy walked into the barn and started to do his regular chores just as he had done many times before.

"Looks like it's time to spring our surprise," Agnes observed while they both watched from inside the house.

"I'll call him in." Robert said. He stepped to the back door and onto the porch on the back of the house.

"I'll get the stuff ready," Agnes said behind him.

"Delmar!" Robert called. A moment later, the youth's head appeared around the barn door. "Come on inside," Robert continued and then headed back into the kitchen.

After leaving his boots in the mudroom, Delmar walked hesitantly into the kitchen. "Sit down," Robert said, waving him to one of the chairs. Agnes reappeared and after setting a bundle down, headed over to the counter. It was clear to her that Delmar thought that he was somehow in trouble here. His face paled at the thought of what he would face from his brother if he lost his job. Robert sensed the discomfort of the boy and sympathized. He'd tried to bring the abuse to the attention of the courts but was rebuffed by the social agency in charge of Delmar's oversight.

"I know you're wondering why I called you in here," the old farmer began. His wife set a piece of pie in front of the boy and served herself and her husband. Delmar's confusion was evident, but he kept his mouth closed.

While she poured the coffee all around, Mrs. Hassel scolded him, "Oh, come on, Delmar!" she said with mock seriousness. "You don't think we serve coffee and pie to someone we're about to fire, do you?" Delmar stared from one friendly face to the other, and for the first time that morning, dared to hope.

"As I was saying," Robert continued, "I wanted to talk to you about some things. The fields are done, and that pretty much finishes what I hired you for." Delmar's face paled again. *He looks like he's still expecting a beating*, thought the man disgustedly.

"Look, I'll be plain. I know your brother is little better than a cur and treats you like some kind of doormat," the man said angrily. "I don't intend to treat you the same." The old farmer paused for a moment. "The fields are done, but I expect you here every morning by nine," he continued. "I've got some heavy work I want you to get started on tomorrow."

"What do you want me to do, sir?" asked the boy, now more confused than ever.

"These!" said Robert with a grin as he hefted the school materials onto the table. Delmar was speechless for a minute and just stared at the books. "I know things are pretty rough at your house and that your brother has been preventing you from studying with extra chores until I hired you away," Robert said, "So starting tomorrow, I'm hiring you to come here and study!"

The room was silent while Delmar tried to deal with the shock. When he did try to speak, all that happened was his mouth hung open and stayed that way.

"Look, Delmar," Agnes said as she shoved a fork full of pie into the boy's open mouth, "we know you love to learn, and we want to help."

Delmar was chewing the bite when Robert spoke again. "Listen," he said, "your future is higher than that old farm, and we want to see you make it." Delmar was still blinking in disbelief when he swallowed the bite. Then with relief, he began to cry and laugh at the same time. After that, things brightened considerably in the little kitchen as the three enjoyed their pie and each other's company for some time.

Since that day, Delmar eagerly looked forward to going to work at the Hassel farm. That's not to say that the studies weren't work. Mr. Hassel took the position of schoolmaster seriously and drilled him diligently. He made sure the boy applied himself to the hard sciences and mathematics.

Mr. Hassel was surprised by the ability of his student, and Delmar made short work of the material. Using his own reference library, Mr. Hassel supplemented the correspondence courses and pushed (actually, it was more like holding back wild horses) Delmar to reach high.

But history and civics were Delmar's real problems—subjects that he just couldn't seem to grasp.

He knew Erdinata was a member of Galactic Axia. He just didn't understand the Imperial concept as a whole. Of course, he had never been off the planet, even though he knew his father had died in space. Nevertheless, Mr. Hassel understood the Axia and drilled Delmar unmercifully on it. But somehow, it just wasn't sinking in. All Robert could figure was that Delmar had some deeply ingrained preconceived notions preventing him from understanding his heritage. History and civics were both mysteries to Delmar, and there was no denying it.

Mr. Hassel pushed back from the table and examined the boy sitting across from him. These verbal lessons just weren't good enough. They needed something more. "Maybe what we need is a field trip," Mr. Hassel said. "Do you think you can get away from home tomorrow?"

"Yeah, sure," Delmar answered. "Dorn is off with his friends at some kind of race over at Keeler."

"Good," the old farmer said. "I'll pick you up at your house at six sharp tomorrow morning. We'll go have a day of fun."

Early the next morning, Delmar had just finished his chores and was getting dressed when he heard Mr. Hassel's ground car stop in the Eagleman front yard. The boy looked at the clock on his bedroom wall. "Six on the dot," Delmar said aloud. "Guess I better get a wiggle on."

A few minutes later, Delmar was securely strapped

into the front seat of Mr. Hassel's car, and they were speeding down the country road toward Keeler.

"Where are we going?" Delmar asked.

Mr. Hassel looked at the boy and smiled. "I've rented a flitter for the day," he answered. "We're taking a day trip over to Jasper Station."

"To the spaceport?" Delmar exclaimed.

"Yep, to the spaceport," Mr. Hassel answered. "I want you to see the Axia up close."

"Do you think we could take a ride on a real spaceship?" the boy asked.

"I really doubt it," Mr. Hassel answered. "But you can never tell. It just depends who's on duty."

Mr. Hassel was in the rental office for only a few minutes. Delmar had no idea a person could rent a flitter like renting a ground car. He had seen military flitters from time to time, and he knew there were sky cabs, but not personal rentals.

Mr. Hassel parked his ground car in a covered garage and motioned for Delmar to get out and follow him. "I didn't know you were a pilot," Delmar said to Mr. Hassel.

"Oh sure," the farmer answered. "You'll find out a lot of things about me if you'll keep your eyes open."

"Can you pilot the big ships too?" Delmar asked.

"Oh no," answered Mr. Hassel. "I was a combat infantry officer, not a fleet officer. But the opportunity to learn is always available for a person willing to apply and qualify themselves." Mr. Hassel looked over at the young boy. "Of course, not just anyone can walk in off the street and rent one of these things," he continued. "You have to hold a valid small-craft license, and you have to stay current with a minimum number of flight hours."

"How do you stay current out there on the farm?" the boy wanted to know.

"Mrs. Hassel and I go to Jasper Station four times a year for a week of refresher and qualification training."

"You do?" Delmar asked.

"Sure. Don't you remember when we were gone on vacation for a week last month?" the farmer asked. "We weren't out shopping for corn seed, you know."

"Do you mean to say Mrs. Hassel is a pilot too?" Delmar asked.

"You bet your life she is," Mr. Hassel answered. "She has more flight time than I do. She was with the fleet, you know." Delmar had no idea the old couple were flyers.

Delmar sat in the passenger seat of the flitter and strapped in while Mr. Hassel performed a preflight check of the flitter's systems. When he was satisfied the craft was flight worthy, he looked over at the boy and told him to hold on to his hat, and they were on their way.

It only took a minute for Mr. Hassel to receive departure clearance from Keeler operations. Then with a flick of his left hand on the axis ball and a gentle nudge on the throttle bar, the flitter shot straight up into the air. Delmar felt the ground suddenly fall away from him and soon found himself face to face with one of the most beautiful clouds he had ever seen.

Mr. Hassel looked over at Delmar and smiled. "This is a better classroom, isn't it?" he asked.

"You bet it is!" Delmar laughed. "I've never been in one of these things before!" Mr. Hassel advanced the throttle, and the flitter began to glide gracefully through the clouds.

"Anyway," Mr. Hassel said, picking back up on the lecture he had interrupted yesterday, "a byproduct of a ship's drive is both the canceling of inertia inside the ship and the creation of a repulsion field around the outside that prevents collisions with the debris of space. That's why you didn't feel the gravity pull against your body when we accelerated on take-off. The drive on this ship is different from the early ships, which used what was referred to as a bedsprings drive system, so called because of the array of rods sticking out the rear of the ship."

Mr. Hassel reached over and took Delmar's left hand and placed it on the throttle bar hanging from the ceiling of the flitter. "Control of the ships is through a simple throttle and axis-ball control system. The throttle consists of an iron bar hanging from the ceiling similar to what one sees in old steam locomotives. It's common in all Axia ships, from the largest cruiser right down to this simple flitter. Go ahead and give it a little nudge."

Delmar pushed the throttle bar forward ever so slightly. Mr. Hassel spun the axis ball and nosed the flitter down below the clouds. Delmar could see the ground far below them racing by at great speed.

"The axis ball is mounted next to the control

chair and is rolled by the pilot's left hand to change the attitude and direction of the ship," Mr. Hassel continued. "You can't reach it from there, but watch this." While Delmar watched, Mr. Hassel used the very tips of the fingers on his left hand to caress the axis ball. The flitter moved from side to side in a gentle sweeping motion, reminding Delmar of the swing on his own front porch.

"It must be dangerous out there in space," Delmar interjected. "How do they protect themselves?"

"Of course, this flitter isn't armed," Mr. Hassel answered, "but weaponry aboard line ships consists of various rays, from the small swivel-mounts all the way up to the large ray that runs along the axis of the ship."

A voice over the headset instructed Mr. Hassel to ascend to five thousand feet to clear the way for an incoming deep-space transport. He answered while at the same time rolling the axis ball back just a touch. The flitter nosed upward and leveled off at the requested altitude. Delmar watched his teacher operate the simple controls. *I could do that*, he thought. A few minutes later a large transport ship passed below them, apparently heading for the field outside of Keeler.

"Torpedoes, or torps, are also used," Mr. Hassel continued. "Both the rays and the torps are able to fire over a distance of better than ten thousand miles, although they are more effective at closer range."

It didn't take long for the flitter to reach Jasper Station, even though the station was several hundred miles from Big Valley and the Hassel farm.

Delmar had never been to the military installation before and was fascinated at the sight of hundreds of ships of all sizes and shapes. Military personnel in black service uniforms were everywhere.

"We're going right over there." Mr. Hassel pointed at a long low building at the edge of the airfield. "That's where my old unit is stationed. We'll see who's on duty."

After receiving clearance to land the flitter in a visitor zone, Delmar and Mr. Hassel caught a shuttle bus to the ground forces zone of the base. The building Mr. Hassel had pointed out seemed so small from the air but now loomed over them. It looked large enough to house a whole armored division.

Mr. Hassel showed his identification card at the reception desk, and after signing Delmar in on a visitor board, was waved through by a uniformed man with two stripes on his sleeve. However, this man was not wearing a service dress uniform like the one he'd seen before, but instead wore a simple black jumpsuit with his name on a leather nameplate over his right pocket. Delmar wondered what kind of name Hilipines was and where the man was from.

Delmar followed Mr. Hassel down a hallway in the massive building. *He sure seems to know where he's going*, thought Delmar. Mr. Hassel looked in at several offices along the way, but moved on quickly. He finally pushed through a set of heavy wooden doors where Delmar found himself inside a large hangar-like building. The room was filled with armored vehicles of every description.

"Robert?" a voice said from behind them. "Is that you?"

Delmar and Mr. Hassel spun around to find themselves face to face with a man of approximately Mr. Hassel's age. The man had short gray hair and stood well over six feet tall. He carried a clipboard in his left hand while he reached for Robert with his right.

"Kuba Trepp," Mr. Hassel replied with a smile. "I've been looking all over for you."

"Well, you found me," the large man answered. "What brings you to Jasper Station? You're not due to requalify your flight status for another couple of months. Where's Agnes?"

"She's back home. Kuba, I want you to meet a friend and pupil of mine," Mr. Hassel answered. "Delmar Eagleman, meet Kuba Trepp, an old friend of mine from the good old days."

"Let's just take it easy on the old part if you don't mind," Trepp said. "Pleased to meet you, young man," the man said, reaching for Delmar's hand.

"Yes, sir," Delmar answered, still a bit in awe of his surroundings.

"Delmar has lived his whole life on the farm," Mr. Hassel said to Kuba. "We're on a field trip, and I'm trying to enlighten him on the intricacies of the Axia."

"Then you couldn't be in better hands," Trepp said.

"Actually," Mr. Hassel said, "I was hoping you'd be willing to help."

"How's that?"

"We're at the point of our lesson now where we

discover that not all is peaceful and calm in the universe," Mr. Hassel answered. "And since you have such intimate knowledge of Red-tails, I wondered if you'd mind telling Delmar about them?"

Delmar looked expectantly at the large trooper, who in turn looked the young man over from head to toe. "Sure," he finally answered Robert. He reached over and put a large hand on Delmar's shoulder. "You listen real close, son," Trepp said. "You understand?"

"Yes, sir," Delmar answered.

"The Axia really only has one enemy, which comes from a neighboring galaxy," Trooper Trepp said. "They're called Red-tails. They are humanoid in appearance with thick, leathery red skin. They have vestigial horns growing from their foreheads and have a long pointed tail. The depredations of this enemy are enormous. Until the Axia mounted effective defensive fleets, the Red-tails would attack entire planets, destroying thoroughly and herding the humans aboard large transport ships, abducting them for later consumption."

Delmar looked dubiously at Mr. Hassel, then back at Trepp. He was sure the man was pulling his leg. "Aw, come on," he said.

"It's true," Mr. Hassel said.

"You bet your boots it's true," Trepp interjected. "And believe me, you don't want to tangle with one. The Red-tails are fierce opponents in battle, and no quarter is given. Many attempts were made to deal reasonably with these invaders, but without exception the Axia negotiators were taken captive and eaten. Understandably, the Red-tails are both feared and loathed."

The three men walked through the large hangar until they came to a set of steel double doors. "You ready for this, son?" Kuba Trepp asked.

"For what?" questioned Delmar.

"To face our enemy," the large man answered.

"You mean you have a Red-tail here in this building?" the boy asked with a catch in his voice.

Both Mr. Hassel and Kuba Trepp nodded. "Right here in this room," Trepp said.

Delmar swallowed hard; his throat had suddenly gone very dry. He wasn't sure he wanted to see the thing they were describing. But he couldn't chicken out, either. "Okay," he said. "I'm ready."

Trepp pulled one of the heavy doors open, and Delmar looked inside the dark room. He heard what sounded like a growl come from the darkness. Mr. Hassel and Trepp stepped through the door. Trepp grabbed Delmar by the elbow and pulled him in as well and closed the door.

Suddenly, Trepp turned loose of Delmar's arm and he found himself alone in the dark room. The growl sounded again, this time very close to Delmar. He felt warm breath on his neck and a cold chill ran up his spine. "Mr. Hassel," he said in a whisper. "Is that you?"

Another growl spun the boy around on his heels, and he tried to find his way back to the closed door but couldn't. Then something grabbed Delmar from behind and spun him around. Delmar screamed and lashed out hard at the thing that had hold of him, connecting with his fist against the thing's jaw. He felt the thing turn loose of him and stumble backward. Delmar also fell back and landed hard on his backside on the floor. He scooted backward until he came to rest against a wall.

"For cryin' out loud!" someone said from the darkness. "That kid really whacked me good. Trepp, where are you?"

All around him, men began to laugh. The lights came on and Delmar found himself facing over a dozen laughing men, Mr. Hassel and Mr. Trepp among them. Another man sat on the floor a dozen feet from Delmar. He was holding his jaw and seemed stunned. "Trepp!" he yelled. "You've had it, buster! You never said nothin' to me about this kid takin' a swing at me."

"I'm sorry," Delmar stammered. "I thought...I thought you were—"

"Don't sweat it, kid," Trepp said, reaching down to give Delmar a lift up. "Old Junior here never could take a punch."

"Mr. Hassel?" Delmar asked, still stunned. "You were in on this?"

"Yep," Mr. Hassel answered, "set it up from home yesterday. Figured you'd like to meet some of the boys."

Trepp lifted Delmar to his feet and then clapped him on the back. "You did real good, kid," he said. "Robert said you were made of good stuff."

"He did?" Delmar asked, still visibly shaken. "I thought I was going to wet myself."

Everyone in the room broke out into loud laughter and surrounded the boy, each one shaking his hand and introducing himself. Every man was at least fifty years old, so Delmar assumed these were friends of Mr. Hassel's from many years gone by.

"Delmar," Mr. Hassel finally said, "these are the boys from the old 653rd, my old unit. And these fellas have faced the enemy firsthand. Listen to what they have to say, just don't take any wooden coins from any of 'em."

The rest of the day went by without incident. Delmar and Mr. Hassel visited a memorial museum on the base and then they toured the spaceport. Mr. Hassel seemed to know everyone, and everyone seemed to know him. He was on first-name basis with many people.

The only disappointment Delmar had was that they weren't able to go up in a spaceship. However, he understood this was a military installation, not a recreational facility. But they did get to tour one of the large cruisers that was on station. Mr. Hassel knew the cargo master so they were able to go on board for a brief visit. While on board, Mr. Hassel showed Delmar how to operate the communications console and explained to him how the subspace transmitters, emergency beacon, and the ship's identity transponders worked.

All too soon it was time to catch the shuttle bus

back to the flitter parking area. Delmar was fascinated by everything he'd seen and wanted to learn more.

Before returning to the flitter, Mr. Hassel and Delmar stopped at the flight line café for lunch. "Did you enjoy yourself today, son?" the old farmer asked.

"Sure did," Delmar answered around a mouthful of hamburger. "All except for that Red-tail trick you played on me. I thought I was done for."

Mr. Hassel laughed aloud. "You shoulda seen the expression on your face when the lights came back on!" he said, tears welling up in his eyes. His laughter caused Delmar to start laughing, and before long he and Robert were enjoying each other's company more like father and son than teacher and pupil.

The flitter ride back gave Robert a chance to test his theory. "So what do you think of troopers now?" he asked as an aside.

"They just seem like regular guys," Delmar admitted.

"Not the blindly loyal boot heel of the empress, eh?" Robert jibed. Delmar blinked and looked at the older man. Robert thought he saw the beginning of comprehension on the boy's face.

"No, not really," Delmar finally admitted. "And I was surprised to find out that not only you but your wife was a trooper too."

"Not 'were,'" Robert corrected. "Though retired, we're still troopers at heart and in spirit. And more correctly, Agnes is what was called a Lady of the Fleet."

"So you're still loyal to the empress?" Delmar asked.

"Not so much to the person as to the throne," Robert explained. "We are part of a three-way trust between whoever occupies the throne and the citizens of the Axia."

"But I was taught that the Axia is spreading tyranny," Delmar admitted. "That's why Erdinata is independent."

"And who told you this?" Robert asked.

"As far back as I can remember, it was part of school," Delmar answered. "That's why I didn't care for the subject—too much bloodshed and oppression."

"And those troopers you met today, did they oppress you?"

"No," Delmar admitted. "But they sure know how to play a practical joke!" he added with a grin. Robert smiled but didn't answer. After a short silence, Delmar spoke up again. "So who runs the Axia anyway, if it's a trust like you say?"

"The empress is ruler by bloodline," Robert explained. "Assisting her is the Council of Nine. They act as advisors and can temporarily rule in case the ruler is incapacitated. Beyond that are the usual government agencies and the service, which is made up of troopers and ladies of the fleet."

"But if the troopers are so loyal, what keeps the empress from using them to subjugate other planets like ours?"

"As I said, the troopers are loyal to the throne. But more accurately, the trust that throne represents," Robert answered. "It is a system that counterbalances the different powers in the Axia. If a ruler gets out of line, the troopers can speak back. It's foundational in the constitution. Above all, they are the citizens of the Axia. This is a commonwealth of choice, not conquest."

"And the troopers are like the glue helping bind it together?" Delmar asked.

"Exactly!" Robert exclaimed. "The Axia is so big and has such a long history to guide it that it would be difficult in the extreme for any one person, even the ruler, to try to change it into something other than what it is. What we have here is the result of social evolution over the thousands of years the Axia has existed." The flitter grew quiet again while Delmar pondered these things.

"Can we study more about it?" Delmar suddenly asked after a long silence.

"Sure," Robert agreed.

"Good, cause I want to be sure of this for myself," Delmar stated. Inwardly, Robert smiled. *The door is open*, he thought to himself as he swung the flitter around to land at Keeler field. Robert was looking forward to telling Agnes about the breakthrough. *This is a banner day in more ways than one!* Robert thought happily.

4

Only a year later the courses in the mail were completed and the graduation examination scheduled. Delmar reported for work early that day, and as soon as he arrived, Mr. and Mrs. Hassel drove him to town in their ground car. Dropping him off at the examination site, they went to do some "shopping and such." Delmar reported for his exam and was assigned to one of the computers reserved for the process.

While he sweated through the various subjects on which the computer drilled him, Delmar wondered who programmed the demented machine. Several times, he noticed spelling and grammatical errors in the questions and became disgusted at the obvious sloppiness of the "expert" who had written the test.

Delmar handed in his scoring cartridge to the test monitor after only three hours. Inserting the cartridge into the scoring machine, the man looked crossly at the boy. His elapsed time to complete the test was definitely below average, and the test monitor was sure Delmar had failed.

A minute later the machine beeped and produced the graduation certificate. At the same time, it filed the actual score (which the students never get to see) with the central computer at the Education Department in the capital. Frowning, the man handed Delmar his certificate and the boy joyously left the building.

While Delmar had been taking his test, the Hassels were again checking on the legal status of the boy's living situation with Dorn. They'd waited for two hours, first in this office, next in that one, each time waiting while some bureaucrat consulted with yet another supervisor. Mr. Hassel's patience was wearing thin when they were finally ushered into the office of Ms. Prudence Hornbeck, the regional director of the social agency. Her assistant supervisor closed the door and the Hassels were left standing while a narrow-faced, hawkish woman continued to talk on the phone.

While he surveyed her desk, Mr. Hassel mused that it looked overly neat and little used. It was then that he noticed the indicators on the phone the director was using were not even lit. Recognizing the game, Mr. Hassel decided they could gain more by going along with the sham. Motioning his wife to follow his lead, and without waiting for the director to tell them to, Mr. Hassel sat down. Hornbeck frowned at them and then continued with her bogus call.

The standoff went on for several minutes, during which time he thought the woman should receive an acting award for her ability to fake a supposed two-way conversation. Pasting smiles on their faces, the Hassels continued in their efforts to outwait the director.

Frowning at them again, she finally concluded the "call" and turned her attention to the couple. "What may I do for you?" Ms. Hornbeck asked with poised sweetness. Feigning the forgetfulness of old age, Mr. Hassel acted startled at her question.

Assuming he was both hard of hearing and probably a little senile, the director repeated her question, this time enunciating the words louder with exaggerated lip motions. "I said, may I help you?" she repeated.

"You don't have to holler," answered Mr. Hassel. "We're not deaf. We're here to inquire about Delmar Eagleman."

At the mention of Delmar's name, Hornbeck's expression clouded and she spoke quietly into the intercom. After a minute, the secretary of her assistant supervisor brought in a file and placed it on her desk. She perched her glasses on the end of her nose and opened the file. Peering down through her bifocals gave her the appearance of looking at something distasteful on her desk. After a minute, she closed the file and looked up.

"I see that you've inquired before, Mr. Hassel,"

she said tartly. "You know what the court said. What brings you here today?"

"Well, I was just wondering if there had been any change in your agency's determination about the boy," Mr. Hassel replied.

"We thoroughly investigated your accusations against his older brother and found that the situation didn't merit change. According to our evaluation, he is an exemplary citizen and doing an excellent job of caring for his younger brother," she replied gruffly.

Mr. Hassel didn't care to be called a liar but held his temper in check. "Are you sure?" he asked evenly.

"I most certainly am!" Prudence Hornbeck answered hotly. "I have the report from the investigator right here in the file!" She flipped the file open and stabbed a page with her bony index finger.

The tension in the room was broken when the assistant to the director came into the office. After a hurried conference, she and the director left the room.

Mr. Hassel slid forward in his seat and scanned the report, reading it upside down. He noticed that the investigation had been made by telephone, with the investigator asking Delmar's older brother if anything was wrong. The response recorded was negative, followed by a comment from the investigator about nosy busybody neighbors. Mr. Hassel also noted that the report was dated over two months after he had filed the complaint. He slid back in his seat just as Hornbeck returned to the room.

"You're still here?" the director asked. It was obvious that she wanted them to leave as soon as possible.

"We were just leaving," answered Mr. Hassel. He and his wife stood. "Thank you for your time," he added as they moved toward the door.

"The matter is closed, Mr. Hassel," Hornbeck said curtly as the couple slid by. "Further interference by you will have serious repercussions!"

"I'm sure they will!" Mr. Hassel said, casting an angry glare at the director. He and Mrs. Hassel exited the building.

As soon as they were again in their ground car, Mrs. Hassel spoke her mind. "Of all the self-righteous, pompous, self-serving pinheads I've ever met!" she spat out. "What are you going to do about the way she treated us, Robert?"

"Exactly what I should have done a long time ago, Agnes," he replied. He pressed the starter switch on the vehicle and drove in silence to the post office. Once there, he asked the clerk for a special delivery Imperial packet. After paying for the packet and a tablet of paper, he returned to the car. He took his pen and quickly wrote several pages of notes about the situation and the treatment they received from the social agency.

At Robert's request, Agnes took some of the extra paper and detailed their treatment by the agency. When they finished, Robert took the notes and sealed them in the packet. Addressing the outside, Robert went back into the post office and mailed the packet. Back at the ground car, he got in and sighed happily.

"Where did you send the packet, Robert?" his wife asked.

"Where it will do the most good: the palace," he replied and then told her the addressee.

"She was certainly right when she said that further interference would have serious repercussions!" Agnes said with a smile.

Inside the post office, the clerk placed the packet into a special canvas pouch. Soon it would be outbound on a journey that would not end until it landed in a certain red box.

Floating down the street in happiness, Delmar was still staring at his graduation certificate. He brought himself back to the present and entered a small café where he and the Hassels had agreed to meet. He ordered coffee and sat just staring at the certificate. Without him noticing, the waitress brought his cup of coffee and set it down.

When the Hassels arrived, they found Delmar still staring at the certificate with a cup of cold untouched coffee on the table. They quietly slid into the booth across from Delmar without him seeing them. Finally Mr. Hassel spoke, "Well, I see it went pretty well!" said Robert in a voice loud enough to break the boy's concentration.

"Huh?" was all Delmar could think of to say, noticing them for the first time.

"We've been here for five minutes already!" Agnes Hassel said with a smile. Delmar looked from one beaming face to the other and broke into a grin himself. The boy was still speechless when the waitress came over and Robert ordered for all of them. After she had gone, Mr. Hassel nodded to his wife and she pulled a small package out of her purse. Robert took it and handed it to the boy.

"Here, son," he quietly said. "We want you to have this." Delmar looked at the package for a moment before unwrapping it. Inside was an old silver pocketwatch. The inside cover was engraved with the words: "From the boys of the 653rd unit to a fine trooper."

Delmar looked up at the Hassels, his question written on his face. "I received that watch when I was released from my old unit after being badly wounded," Robert said quietly. "My injuries never healed correctly, and though I could have continued to serve, my limitations could endanger my unit in a critical moment. Rather than take that risk, I accepted early retirement."

Pausing a moment, he went on. "The other troopers gave me that watch as their way of thanking me for keeping the faith and protecting their future. It was mine, and now it's yours." They soon fell into small talk until their food arrived.

When they finished their late lunch, Mr. Hassel looked at his watch and motioned Agnes and Delmar to the door. Robert paid the bill as they passed the counter. Soon they were speeding en route to the Hassel farm and arrived in time for Delmar to walk home without his brother being suspicious. Mrs.

Hassel had Delmar leave the precious certificate with them for safekeeping and with a hug sent the boy on his way.

"There he goes," Robert said as he watched the boy start for home. "If our boys had lived, that's what I would have wanted them to be." Agnes came up behind him and slipped an arm around her husband. Together they watched until Delmar disappeared over the rise.

When Delmar came through the door of the Eagleman farmhouse, Dorn hit him hard from behind and threw him to the floor. Dorn tried to kick the door shut but it sprang back open, breaking a pane from the small inset window as it slammed against the wall. Broken shards of glass fell to the floor, some of the larger pieces breaking again. Delmar could feel a trickle of blood running down the back of his neck. In the dim light of the room, he could see his brother, drunk and with a broken bottle in his hand, towering over him. The rage in Dorn's eyes was unmistakable, and Delmar slowly eased himself along the floor to gain a defensible position.

"Where you been, you little snot?" Dorn screamed drunkenly at him. "You went and tried to cause trouble for me with the social agency, didn't you?"

Delmar, confused by the accusation, knew that he had not seen anyone from the agency in several years. As his enraged brother came closer, Delmar prepared for the worst.

"Don't you try to run, you little son of a Red-tail! I'm gonna beat the tar outta you!" Dorn threatened.

Finally fed up with Dorn's abuse, Delmar kicked outward and connected with his brother's ankles, toppling the drunken man. Falling to the floor, Dorn was unable to get a good hold on the faster boy. Delmar twisted free of his drunken antagonist and leapt through the open door, running hard for the road. He dodged the thrown broken liquor bottle as he fled.

"You better run or I'll kill you!" his brother screamed at him and slammed the door. The rest of the small window in the door shattered with the impact.

Delmar ran, putting distance between himself and his dangerous brother. Fearing that Dorn might run him down from behind, he cut across several fields. He knew Dorn would look for him at the Hassels, so he decided to avoid their inviting sanctuary. Instead, he went deep into a nearby wood and found temporary shelter in an abandoned shack. He secured his makeshift shelter and sank to the floor. How could such a perfect day have gone so wrong?

Checking the outbuildings for the night, Robert Hassel was surprised to hear a ground car roar into his driveway and slide to a halt. He hurried around the side of the house and saw Delmar's older brother, drunk and enraged, pounding on the front door with the palm of his hand.

"Where you hidin' that no-good little snot?" the

man yelled at the door. Before he could intervene, Robert heard the door open and saw the drunken man stagger backward. In the light of the porch lamp, Robert saw Agnes standing firmly in front of the large man with her rifle pointed squarely at his chest.

"I don't know what you want, but you have exactly ten seconds to leave my property!" she said, her voice hard. His eyes wide with surprise, the man fell off the porch and lurched back to his truck. When he hesitated getting in, Agnes put a shot into the fence post beside him.

"Git, I said!" she yelled. "And don't ever come back!" The man leapt behind the controls and the vehicle spewed gravel as it reversed its course down the driveway. As soon as the truck was gone, Robert joined his wife on the porch.

"Good shot, Agnes," he said, "but now I have to repair the fence post."

Emptying the spent cartridge from the chamber, Agnes fed a fresh round in and cycled the weapon. "You know what I think, Robert?" she finally asked. "I think Delmar's in trouble."

"Well, it's obvious he isn't at home, or his drunken brother wouldn't have come here looking for him," he replied. "Wherever that boy is tonight, he's going to be awful lonely."

The couple remained quiet for a moment. In the distance, they could still hear the noise from Dorn's racing ground vehicle. After it finally faded, Agnes said, "We'll go look for him at first light before his brother sleeps off his booze."

"Sure wish I could help him tonight though," replied her husband as they walked into the house.

5

Early the next morning the Hassels were up at first light and ready to begin their search. Robert tried to think of how he would run if he were in Delmar's situation. Naturally, he would leave the roads quickly to avoid the danger of being run down. Taking to the fields would be a wise choice because of the difference in physical fitness between Delmar and his overweight brother.

The difficult part of the search would be determining how far Delmar would run before hiding. The boy had both good stamina and motivation, so he could have run quite a distance in a relatively short time. After several fruitless hours of searching, the Hassels decided to head for home.

Arriving back at the house, they silently went about fixing themselves some lunch. Their minds were still on the boy when they sat down to eat.

"Robert," Agnes began, "I don't like the thought of that boy being out there alone and hungry."

"I know what you mean, honey," replied her husband, "but there's not much we can do until he shows up."

Their conversation was interrupted by the sound of a ground car pulling into the driveway. Robert stood up and looked out the window to see a police vehicle in the lane. As the officer came up onto the porch, Robert opened the door and stepped out, Agnes just behind him.

"Morning, sir. Ma'am," the officer greeted them.

"What's up, officer?" Robert asked.

"Well folks, I have a complaint against you for threatening a neighbor with a gun last night," the officer replied.

"That's true, Officer," Robert returned. "He was drunk and acting in a threatening manner toward my wife."

"Is that true, ma'am?" asked the officer, looking at the small woman.

"Yes, sir," Agnes replied. "I told him to get off our property."

"Did you shoot at him, sir?" the man asked Robert.

"No, sir," Robert answered.

"I shot at him," Agnes spoke up. "When he hesitated, I put a slug into the fence post next to him," she said, pointing at the blasted fence post near the officer's ground car. The officer stepped off the porch and examined the fence post. He then returned to the porch and stood silently before the older couple.

"Well, ma'am," he began, "a complaint was

filed, and we're required by law to investigate. I'm going to have to give you a warning and charge you with assault."

"What?" the couple exclaimed together. "What do you mean?"

"That's right, folks," he said. "As investigating officer, I consider you, ma'am, as presenting a deadly hazard to innocent fence posts," he added with a smile.

When the couple remained speechless, the officer continued, "I hereby place you into the custody of your husband and require you to perform two hours of target practice." Robert and Agnes both let out a sigh of relief and smiled at the officer.

"What about the complaint?" asked Robert.

"We know the party who issued the complaint, and have for some time," the officer replied. "In fact, he was almost too drunk to file the complaint. Officially, we had to investigate his complaint, and I was the lucky one sent out to do it."

"Why do you say you're the lucky one, officer?" Robert asked.

"Because I'm the one who gets to ask for some of Miss Agnes' famous apple pie," he replied with a smile.

"Well then, let's go inside!" invited Robert, holding the door for Agnes and the officer. Agnes stopped abruptly and turned again to the officer, her nose buried halfway up his chest.

"What are you going to say on your report?" she asked as she stepped back, a worried expression on her face.

"I'm going to report that the shooting was justi-fied," he answered. "Half the guys down at the sta-tion would like to run that guy in, but can't. In fact, they're somewhat disappointed that you didn't bag the scum. How could you miss?"

"I didn't miss," Agnes replied. "If I'd shot him, there would have been a big mess to clean up and lots of paperwork afterwards. I thought hitting the fence post next to him would be sufficient."

"In that case, ma'am, I rescind the requirement about target practice," the officer said, and they continued into the house. "I couldn't have hit that close to the center of the post if I'd tried."

They went inside, and while Agnes cut the officer a large piece of pie, Robert poured them all cups of fresh coffee. Sitting around the table, they discussed the problem of Delmar's brother.

"He's been a problem to us for quite a while," the officer said. "He's had several run-ins with us, but nothing we can hold him on."

"He has?" said Robert with open surprise. "We spoke to the director down at the social agency yesterday and she claimed that he was an exemplary citizen."

"That's a laugh!" replied the officer. "But it figures, knowing that agency."

"We've had our frustrations with them too," said Agnes evenly. "We tried to get them to do something about the abuse that man is inflicting on Delmar, but got nowhere."

"You've got our sympathy, ma'am," the officer said. "How is Delmar doing anyway?"

"That's what we don't know," answered Robert. "After bringing him home from his graduation test yesterday, he went home, and we haven't seen him since. Then last night his brother came here thinking we were hiding the boy, so we suspect Delmar has run off."

"That is interesting news," remarked the officer. "You say Delmar didn't show up here?"

"That's right," Robert replied. "We went out and searched early this morning but couldn't find him."

The officer thought for a moment. "It's probably best the boy didn't come here, because this is where his brother would look first," he began. "And if the boy is classified as a runaway, the social agency would have him sought out and arrested."

"Do you think Dorn will report it?" Agnes asked, concerned.

"Don't think so," answered the officer. "If he did, they would cut off the financial aid they're sending him to care for his brother. I'm sure he won't jeopardize that."

"That's a relief," Robert said. "I wish we could find the boy and help him."

"Until he turns twenty-one, we can't do a thing about getting him out from under his brother," the officer added.

"There has to be a way!" Robert said hotly.

The officer thought for a minute. "There might be one way, if we can find him," the officer answered. "Of course, he has to be at least eighteen first." The trio fell silent as they thought through the situation.

"I just hope he can stay safe until his birthday,"

Robert said, shaking his head. "If he goes home, he's in for nothing but trouble."

"Well, he better not come here," the officer said. "The social agency will probably have you under surveillance for a few days, especially after your visit to their office yesterday. If nothing else, Dorn and his drinking buddies will be watching your place."

The light filtering into the cold interior of the dilapidated shack fell on the huddled form on the dirt floor. With a shudder, the boy stirred and raised himself up into a sitting position. The back of his head still ached, and he could feel the bruises on his knees from hitting the floor when his brother had attacked him.

A metallic taste in Delmar's mouth made him realize that at least one of his brother's blows had connected. Though he didn't recall being hit there, Delmar checked his teeth with his tongue and found everything as it should be. His stomach growled, and he ignored it out of necessity.

After looking through cracks in the wall to check for anyone waiting outside, Delmar unbarricaded the makeshift door and stepped out into the early sunlight. He washed and drank his fill at a nearby creek in an effort to quiet his stomach and to clear the bitter taste from his mouth. Rising up, he returned to the shack to consider his options.

He wouldn't return to the farm out of fear for his safety. Legally, he knew his brother was still his guardian until he turned twenty-one, but the thought of more than three more years like last night made him shudder.

He knew his brother would check with the Hassels, and Delmar refused to endanger them. From what Mr. Hassel had told him, he knew going to the social agency would only get him into more trouble, either with them or with his brother. This meant there was no other option. He would have to survive alone until he turned twenty-one. A deep sense of loneliness descended on Delmar at the prospect of hiding out for three years.

After the officer had gone, the Hassels started trying to figure out how they could find Delmar, much less help him. They'd found no sign of him, and although discouraging, it probably meant that his brother couldn't find him either. Robert figured that Delmar would avoid their place, and his brother showing up last night explained why.

Robert knew that Delmar would probably hide out for a while, and there were plenty of hills and hollows for that. Hunger would be a definite problem for the boy. There was little to live off of in the woods at this time of year. Anything from last season would be long gone, and it was still too early in the spring for there to be much new growth. Water would be no problem, and Delmar was resourceful enough to build or find some sort of shelter. *Food*, thought Robert, *would be the key*.

All day he tried to think of how to find the boy but came up with nothing viable. While he was feeding the stock, he realized that he'd been trying to figure it out backward. He didn't need to find Delmar. The boy would find him! With the glimmer of a workable plan in his mind, Robert hurried back to the house for supper.

After washing up, Robert sat down while Agnes brought the last items to the table. She took her place at his right, and after a brief prayer to the Unseen One, they served themselves.

Robert had just gotten a bite of roast beef into his mouth when Agnes spoke up. "Oh, Robert!" she began, "I just can't get my mind off of Delmar!"

"I know," he replied after hastily choking down the bite. "He's been on my mind all day too."

"What are we going to do?" Agnes asked. "How are we going to find him?"

"We're going to do nothing," Robert said. "When the time is right, he'll find us."

"What do you mean?" Agnes asked, her shock evident.

"Right now," explained her husband, "it isn't safe for Delmar to be seen, especially here. This is the first place Dorn will be watching. He's going to have to hide out until we can get this mess straightened out."

"But what about food?" she asked. "How will he survive?"

"I'm sure he'll do fine on all accounts except food," Robert replied. "That's where we come in."

"How?" she asked.

"What I'm thinking is that Delmar will contact us when and where we least expect it," Robert answered. "If we don't expect him, neither will his brother."

Thinking for a moment, Robert continued. "What we need to do is always be carrying non-perishable food with us so when we do meet, we can give it to him quickly."

"But we can't carry enough food like that to feed the boy, and large packs will attract attention," Agnes said anxiously.

"I know," he said. "For now, the first move is up to him."

The subject of their conversation was just returning to the shack from exploring the nearby hollows. Several caves in the vicinity looked inviting, but farther up in rougher country Delmar found an ideal cave in which to hide. Situated high enough that he could survey the approaches without being seen, it was still well concealed by surrounding trees and outcroppings of native stone.

Inside he found a small clear stream that showed signs of being a year-round source of water. He found several small vents in some of the deeper chambers of the cave, a couple of which with a little work would make excellent emergency escape routes. Tomorrow he'd move up there after he had done something about food.

It had been over twenty-four hours since Delmar had last eaten, and he knew from experience that he could go another day before it greatly hindered him. During his search, he'd found no berries or fruit ready to eat and had no tools or weapons with which to hunt. Delmar considered raiding farms down in the valley, but the thought of stealing from his neighbors was repulsive to the boy.

His only option left was to get food from someone like the Hassels. He'd thought of them often and knew they would understand his need. The problem was that going there might place them in danger of his brother, who would surely be watching.

"Watching!" the boy exclaimed aloud. "Watch!" Digging in his pocket, he found the old pocketwatch safe and unharmed. Delmar opened it and saw that it had run down. Looking at it hard, a plan began to form in his mind.

Early the next morning Agnes went out to put some letters in the mailbox. Opening it, she found the old watch, a twig of hickory, and a piece of limestone.

"Robert!" she cried. At first, she was afraid to touch the items, and then she hesitantly gathered them in her trembling hands. When her husband got there, she was holding them out in front of her.

"What is it?" he asked breathlessly as he ran up to her. She lifted the items toward him, and the realization dawned on his face. Without saying a word, he led her into the house where she laid the things on the kitchen table.

"We know he's all right!" Agnes said in a whisper.

"Yes," Robert agreed. "This is obviously from him. But why?"

"He's not rejecting our gift, is he?" she asked, suddenly fearful.

"No," her husband replied. "I think this is some sort of message." Robert sat for a while trying to unravel the secret of the three items. That Delmar had somehow wanted to communicate with them was a relief. The boy would have figured out about his need of supplies and he was appealing to them. Looking at each item in turn, Robert began to come up with an idea.

"Agnes, I think these might indicate a location of where we can find Delmar," he said.

"What do you mean?" she asked.

"Look at this rock," Robert answered. "It's unique to about three or four places up in those hills. Delmar knows about that because we covered it a few months ago in his studies."

Picking up the hickory twig, he continued, "This is from a hickory, which is also rare."

"Then if we could find some hickory near such an outcropping, we'd know his location!" Agnes said excitedly.

"Yes," agreed Robert, "and I think I know of such a place."

"Then we can take supplies to him!" concluded Agnes.

"Not yet," Robert said. "We can't just leave food out. Animals could get it before he does." Robert picked up the watch and carefully opened it, thinking there might be a note inside. He was disappointed when he found nothing. He stared at the face of the watch for a moment. Absentmindedly, Robert started to wind the watch when the idea hit him. Looking at the face again, he realized that it was set for exactly eleven thirty.

"That's it!" Robert suddenly cried.

"What?" asked Agnes.

"Delmar stopped the watch and set it for the time he wants to meet us!" Robert continued. Glancing at the kitchen clock, Robert noted that he had plenty of time to get ready.

"Agnes," he said, "start packing some foodstuffs in my old side pack while I gather some tools."

Agnes rose and entered her pantry while Robert laid the watch down and hurried to his workshop. A short time later, the side pack was ready. "When do we leave?" Agnes asked.

"We don't," Robert replied. "I'm going alone tonight."

"But why, Robert?" she asked pleadingly. "I want to see the boy too. You know I can still hike."

"It's not that I'm worried about your ability, honey," Robert said with a smile. "You always were athletic, even after you retired from the Ladies of the Fleet to be with me. It would attract too much attention if we both go."

Agnes looked crestfallen and then frowned. "What do you want me to do here?" she asked.

Robert thought for a moment. "Stay here and

make a distraction if anyone comes," he replied. "I don't want to be followed."

Later that night, Robert shouldered the pack and left out the back door. Crossing behind his barn, he was soon in the woods. Back at the house, Agnes closed all of the curtains and went upstairs to their room. She turned on a low light and put a cartridge in the player. The room soon filled with romantic music. All that could be seen from outside was the rosy glow of lamplight on the curtains.

Robert followed several of the game trails that ran deep into the hollows. Turning up one in particular, he reached his destination only an hour after leaving the farm. Pausing for breath after his climb, he was startled by the snap of a branch behind him. Turning cautiously, he saw the form of a man separate itself from the darkness.

"Delmar?" he whispered quietly.

"Mr. Hassel?" returned a whispered reply. "Am I glad to see you!" Embracing in a hug for a moment, Robert pulled back and looked at the boy.

"Not here," Delmar whispered. Motioning the older man to follow, the boy led him for some distance until they came to a thicket. He pulled back a tangle of branches and revealed a hole even darker than the night. Robert followed Delmar through the opening. Once inside, Delmar whispered again, "Okay, we're safe in here."

Robert opened his pack and pulled out a small hand lantern. He switched it on and the meager light he allowed to escape from his overshadowing hand revealed they were in a deep cave. He turned his eyes toward the boy and was shocked and disgusted by what he saw.

The young face that looked back at him was clean but bruised and suffering a few dried cuts. It was obvious that Delmar had received a few going-away presents at the hands of his brutish brother.

"We packed you some supplies," Robert said, opening the pack. "It should be enough to keep you for a couple of days."

"Thanks, Mr. Hassel!" the boy said as he eyed the food hungrily. Robert reached into his jacket pocket and pulled out the old pocketwatch.

"Here," he said, "I thought you might want this back." The boy's smile was more eloquent than words.

"You better eat, son," Robert said. "You look like you could use it." Just then, Delmar's stomach growled a reply.

Robert sat down next to the boy while he quickly ate two sandwiches Agnes had packed on top of the supplies as a decoy for Robert in case he was stopped by a roving patrol. That he occasionally went out at night to stargaze was no secret. Robert let Delmar eat while he filled him in about what had happened since they were last together. After he'd finished the sandwiches, Delmar told Robert about what happened with his brother. The older man gritted his teeth in anger. They discussed what Delmar should do and arranged to meet again for more supplies.

Neither wanted to part, but Robert knew he had best be going. After giving Delmar a hug, Robert went out through the concealed entrance and into the night. Inside, Delmar gathered the supplies and the lantern and stored them in a crevice deeper inside the cave. Rolling a sleeping bag out that Mr. Hassel had brought, the boy doused the light and settled in for the night.

6

Tumbling out of yet another canvas bag, a certain packet landed on the sorting table in an obscure back room. The duty clerk at the Imperial Postal Center in the palace on Shalimar, the home world of Galactic Axia, began sorting through the pile. After bringing order to the several hundred letters and packets, he began to read the priority stamps on each one and sort them accordingly.

Not everything went immediately to the empress' famous red box. Some had been marked for further research. He dealt with this first. Sorting to each department according to priority stamps, in a short while he had a smaller pile of material that would require unspecified research. He placed these items in another bin that would go to a department where each inquiry would be thoroughly studied before going to the red box.

Robert's packet nearly went into this bin until the clerk noticed the small blue seal under the return address. He pulled the packet back out of the bin and tossed it into his "In" basket.

The trooper sat down at his desk and sighed as he eyed his "In" basket that was nearly overflowing. He swallowed another slug of coffee, made a disgusted face, and set the cup down. Taking the top packet, he opened it and began to review the material inside.

An hour later, the trooper resealed another packet and tossed it into his "Out" basket. He had managed to get halfway through the stack. Pushing his chair back, he stood, stretched, and went in search of fresh coffee. He found a percolator singing its song in the breakroom, where he rinsed the sludge out of his cup and refilled it with the brew someone had recently made.

Returning to his desk, he sat down and pulled the blue-sealed packet from his "In" basket. He scanned the hand-written pages inside and then reread them carefully. Turning to a fresh page on his yellow tablet, he scratched several notes. A few minutes later he was satisfied that he had a grasp of the essentials noted on his tablet. He picked up the telephone on his desk and made several calls.

The weather turned warmer as spring crept into summer. Delmar had settled into the cave and set himself up pretty well. Among the tools Mr. Hassel brought him was fishing tackle, and the boy made good use of it. Early fruits were coming in, so Delmar was able to supplement the supplies his benefactor brought to him.

A routine of sorts developed whereby the Hassels left him caches of supplies in different places for him to pick up. This minimized traffic to Delmar's hiding spot by outsiders and kept Delmar's exposure to a random and minimal level.

The hikes in the woods by the Hassels were irregular enough not to arouse suspicion, and taking a pack along on such trips was easily acceptable. They had met a few other hikers on a few occasions but without any problems. Robert or Agnes would just change routes and drop off the supplies later for Delmar to retrieve after dark.

Delmar's only serious problem was loneliness, because they avoided contact with each other in case the Hassels were being followed. Robert suspected they had been followed once or twice early on when they heard the noise created by someone not wood-wise a distance behind them. By previous arrangement, they would not leave anything at the alternating drops if they suspected followers. Delmar would know to lay low a day, and the drops would resume two days later.

To ease the situation for the boy, Robert left an occasional book, and Agnes would write letters. Return of the books and replies to the letters from "home" were avoided because it increased the risk of exposure. When it was all over, Robert knew the materials would be returned. In the meantime, the Hassels had to content themselves with the thought that *no news was good news*.

Empress Ane was working through the material on her desk when a silent form came in. She looked up in time to see the trooper empty his carry pouch into her red box and collect the packets from the green one that she had finished. Sighing, she reached for the next packet. She made a game of trying to empty the red box before the trooper showed up with more. She occasionally succeeded. She had almost made it twice this morning but still had one or two packets left when he arrived. Ane suspected the trooper was peeking so he could get his timing just right, but she couldn't prove it.

Opening the top packet, she found several pages of handwritten notes, along with supplemental material gathered by one of her staff. She read the original petition and then picked up the packet itself and noted the blue seal under the return address. Setting these aside, Ane read the follow-up research, occasionally reviewing the original documents. She leaned back in her chair, closed her eyes, and tried to picture the situation in her mind. A hum filled the office.

"Hello, Mary," Ane said without opening her eyes.

"Hello, boss lady," Mary came back. "You look like you're taking things much too seriously again."

"I am, Mary," she replied. "This last packet bothers me some."

"Turn it and let me see," Mary said. Ane spread

the pages out and leaned back in her chair again, focusing the small video lens she wore on a chain around her neck toward the pages. After a moment, Mary replied. "I can see why."

"It just bothers me when people take more interest in their position than they do in serving the people they're supposed to help," Ane said, gesturing at the documents.

"What are you going to do about it?" Mary asked.

"I'm going to delegate one of our staff to investigate it and set it to rights!" Ane answered as she reached for her pen and tablet.

Taking a few minutes to detail her instructions, the empress signed the papers with a flourish and sealed it all back in the original packet. She addressed a routing slip, affixed it to the packet, and tossed it into the green box.

"That's it for this morning!" she said, pushing up out of her chair. "Mind if I come down for lunch?" she spoke into the air.

"Sure, boss lady!" Mary's voice answered. "Better hurry! Soup's on!"

Empress Ane briskly left the room and took the lift down to the spacefield to have lunch with her best friend. After she had gone, the trooper entered her office and again filled her red box and emptied the green box, the last packet going into his pouch along with the rest.

In the darkness, Delmar surveyed the area for signs

of observers but saw none. He carefully stepped out of hiding and retrieved the bundle of supplies from the thicket. There had been no bundle two nights ago near the old stump as there should have been, so Delmar had stayed holed up. Tonight was the night for the thicket drop, and he had come earlier than usual, anxious for the supplies and word from home.

Slipping the bundle into his carry pack, Delmar turned and started for the cave. He arrived at an outcropping above it and surveyed the area around the entrance for signs of visitors. Seeing none, he slipped inside and went deep inside before stopping. He'd grown accustomed to the blackness of the cave early on, so he'd gotten in the habit of entering by feel and sound to avoid use of the lantern near the entrance where it might be seen from outside.

Setting the pack down, he reached for the lantern and turned it on, the interior of his makeshift home illuminated by the yellowish light. As Delmar opened the latest bundle, he heard a cough come from the shadows.

"I thought you'd be here about now," Robert Hassel said as the boy whirled in preparation to flee. Delmar froze for a moment and then launched himself into the arms of the older man. They hugged fiercely for a minute and then pulled apart.

"Let me get a good look at you, son," Mr. Hassel said, holding the boy at arm's length. What met his eyes was a vast improvement from the last time he had seen the boy. The injuries had long ago healed, Robert noted, and the start of a beard gave his face a look of maturity. The boy was filling out into full manhood, and Robert was sure he had added at least an inch to his height since early spring.

"Boy, you look good!" Robert exclaimed as he clapped Delmar on the shoulders. "Here, take this and sit down. Now, tell me about yourself," he finished and handed Delmar the other pack he had brought tonight.

Delmar took the pack and sat down with it next to the lantern. Robert sat on the edge of the pallet and watched while the boy emptied the contents into his lap.

"How did you sneak in here without me seeing you?" Delmar asked, sorting through the new supplies.

"I came in just after you left for the bundle drop," Robert answered. "I knew since it was the night for the thicket, it would take you about half an hour before you could be back. So I just waltzed in and made myself at home."

Delmar chuckled and then looked serious. "You came for more than a visit, didn't you, sir?" he asked.

"Yes, I did," Robert replied. "Mrs. Hassel and I thought I better warn you about what's going on."

"Wasn't it risky for you to go into the woods twice in one day?" asked the boy, referring to the bundle.

"I didn't," said Robert. "Agnes set out that bundle while I stayed home. That way we can cover for each other if anyone comes to the house."

"Okay. So what's going on?" Delmar asked.

"Well, after the first two or three weeks things got pretty quiet," Robert began. "A social agency worker came once but didn't do more than ask if we'd seen you, which we hadn't that day. We never saw your brother again after Agnes scared him off, but figured something was up."

"So what's happening now?" Delmar asked, obviously puzzled.

Robert picked his tale back up. "Early this week we heard through Dorn's neighbors that the agency visited your brother. We think they finally figured out you were gone and came to investigate."

"Oh no!" the boy said. "If Dorn loses that financial support from the agency, he'll kill me for sure!"

"That's what we thought too, so I came to warn you and bring some extra supplies," Robert said. "We expect both the authorities and your brother will start hunting for you in earnest. He wants to find you for the money, and if they find you, they'll either send you home or put you in jail."

"But I didn't break any laws!" Delmar cried.

"No, you didn't," Robert agreed. "But you did break some of their policy guidelines, which is probably worse." They both grew silent while they contemplated the situation. Robert finally broke the silence. "Listen, Delmar," he began. "I want to tell you something, and then I'd better go. Remember the pocketwatch?"

"Of course I do," answered the boy.

"Well, I got that from my fellow troopers in the old 653rd after I was wounded. You remember meeting them when we went on our field trip to Jasper Station, don't you?" Delmar nodded. "They're a great bunch, and if you ever need help, you can count on them. Just show them the watch and explain that I sent you. They'll take care of things."

"But how will I find them?" Delmar asked.

"Just go to Jasper Station. The 653rd patrols this star cluster and you'll recognize their building."

"How will I get to them if they're not there?"

"In that case, appeal to any trooper unit," Robert answered. "We watch out for each other like one big extended family."

The cave grew quiet again, and Robert rose up to go. "I better go now," he said. "If I stay out too late, it might look suspicious."

The boy stood, and they embraced. Robert picked up his empty pack and walked slowly toward the entrance. Before he slipped through, they wordlessly shook hands, and Robert disappeared into the night.

The police ground car pulled up in front of the social agency office at the appointed time. Looking out of her window, Prudence Hornbeck, the director of the social agency, noted the arrival, and a glance at her expensive wall clock confirmed their punctuality. Efficiency pleased her, so it was with a satisfied smile that she greeted the officers.

After seating everyone involved in today's plans in the conference room, Director Hornbeck entered the room and strode to the front. "I want to thank everybody for coming today," she began. "We have a serious situation on our hands and our combined efforts today will bring an end to a dangerous set of circumstances." She paused for a moment and peered over her glasses at their faces while she pretended to check her notes. She made mental notes of which of her workers were reacting positively to this meeting, and also saw that the police officers looked bored.

Suppressing a frown, she looked up and continued, "I want to thank the officers for their cooperation in our effort today to apprehend this criminal. For those not familiar with our subject, here is his picture." She turned and pinned a large photograph of Delmar on the board behind her.

Returning to the front, she noticed that the police officers looked confused. "Is there a question, officers?" she asked condescendingly.

"Yes, there is," began an older man. "I thought we were going out to pick up this boy's older brother."

"You are definitely mistaken," she answered. "His older brother has been trying to raise this delinquent for many years. The boy has been nothing but trouble. He hasn't made any effort to care for himself or to help his older brother support him. The older brother reported to us that Delmar assaulted him and has run away and is now terrorizing the neighbors. Irate neighbors have reported numerous thefts and vandalism, and many are threatening him because of the actions of his delinquent brother. He has voiced concern for his personal safety. Our efforts today are to bring this vagrant to justice where he can be punished for his crimes."

A hand went up hesitantly. "Yes?" she asked one of her caseworkers.

"Ma'am, you mean we're to bring him in for counseling and rehabilitation, don't you?" he asked.

"Yes, that's what I meant," the director replied. She was pleased that the caseworker understood their policy.

The two officers had not said anything since her explanation, so the director adjourned the meeting and they dispersed to the waiting ground cars.

Arriving at the Eagleman farm, they all gathered around the front porch. Dorn was sitting on the edge of the step looking distraught. The view through the open door showed the living room had been trashed.

"You see what that monster did to me!" Dorn sobbed. "He tore up the house and then attacked me with a broken bottle!" The man held up his poorly bandaged arm.

"Why didn't you call the police?" one of the officers asked.

Prudence Hornbeck frowned at him. "Don't you see this poor man has been through enough?" she said angrily. "His brother threatened to kill him if he did, so he called us instead. I will not have you badgering our victim!" Everything grew silent again except for the pitiful sobbing of Dorn.

"Here's what I want you to do," Hornbeck said. "I want you to search the woods for this dangerous criminal while we stay here with this man. Now move out!"

The officers noticed that they were the only

ones to start toward the woods. The director and caseworkers gathered around the older brother, and someone said something about a grant request to pay for the damages supposedly caused by Delmar. Continuing into the woods, both officers were glad to be clear of the bureaucratic circus.

The fish had not been biting, so Delmar was checking his bait when he heard the crashing of someone in the forest below. He quickly gathered his things and silently slipped into a hidden viewpoint where he could observe the intruders.

Shortly after reaching his lookout point, Delmar spotted two police officers on the lower trail. Several minutes passed and he determined that there were only two of them. He suspected they were looking for him.

Carefully sliding back from his perch, Delmar edged along the trail toward the cave. He could still hear the noise below so he didn't unduly hurry. Rounding a bend, the boy was suddenly confronted by one of the officers. He froze as the man looked at him and grinned. "Don't worry, Delmar," the officer said, "we're not here to find you."

"But how did you catch me?" he asked. "I could hear you down on the trail."

"An old trick that you better learn, son," replied the officer. "We saw you watching us by the reflection from the metal in your hands," the officer said, pointing at the fishing tackle in Delmar's hand. "So as soon as we were out of your line of sight, we split up." Just then, the other officer came through the brush. He was also grinning.

The first officer continued, "After we split up, Joe here continued making noise like an army of greenhorns while I went up another trail to intercept you. Remember, it's not the obvious that you need to be wary of."

Delmar looked from one smiling officer to the other. "Are you going to take me in?" he asked fearfully.

"How can we take you in if we can't find you?" the first officer answered. "Now get going. We'll probably have to be back up here tomorrow with more searchers, and some of them don't understand."

Delmar took their advice and turned to leave. "Oh, by the way," Joe called, "happy birthday!"

Delmar stopped with surprise at the comment. In his many weeks in the woods, he had failed to keep an accurate record of the date. The boy turned, waved, and was quickly out of sight of the officers.

The two men sauntered leisurely down the trail and continued searching to give Delmar more time to conceal himself. If they arrived back too early at the Eagleman farm, more searchers would be called in immediately. By taking their time, they assured Delmar another night before they could mount a concentrated search effort.

"There! That should do it," said Director Prudence Hornbeck to the distraught man on the porch.

"There shouldn't be any problem with approval of this compensation grant."

After dispatching the officers to search, she had sent the rest of the caseworkers back to the office and stayed to help Dorn herself. Through the years, she had grown familiar with this case and developed a personal interest in it. She folded the completed grant, put it in her briefcase, and snapped the case shut. She looked up in time to see two officers emerge from the woods into the late afternoon sun.

"Well? Did you find him?" she asked as they approached the porch.

"No, ma'am, we didn't," the first officer answered.

"And why not?" she asked sternly.

"Ma'am, those woods are pretty big," Joe said.

"I don't see why that should present a problem," she replied. "I can see a couple of miles of the woods from here, so it should be no problem to find one little boy." The officers did not say anything. Why bother?

"Tomorrow we'll come back with some competent searchers!"

The two men refused to rise to the bait. Thinking for a moment, the director continued, "I want you officers to stay here and protect this man in case his brother shows up," she said, indicating Delmar's older brother. Dorn still sat on the porch, trying to look pitiful. "I'm going to go check out a lead you missed." With that she got into her agency ground car and sped down the driveway.

Robert had just finished with the cows and was carrying the milk into the house when the ground car pulled into their driveway. Agnes took the milk and set it in the cooler while Robert went out onto the porch.

"May I help you?" Robert said as Ms. Hornbeck strode up to the porch.

"Yes," she said. "Where are you hiding Delmar?"

"We're not hiding him," said Agnes. She came out onto the porch and stood beside her husband. The director looked up at them and frowned.

"I know you have him hidden here, which makes you criminals just like him." She then walked around the steps that lead onto the porch and headed back toward the outbuildings.

"And where do you think you're going?" Robert asked. He dismounted the steps and intercepted her.

"I'm going to search the buildings where you're hiding the boy," Hornbeck answered contentiously.

"No, you're not," said Robert evenly. "Now get off our property."

"You can't stop me from looking!" she said hotly as she glared into his face. Robert held his temper in check. This cretin wasn't worth getting angry over.

"I said, get off our property," he said with a firmness that set her back. She continued to glare at him for a moment, then turned and stalked back to her ground car.

"I'm coming back tomorrow with a search warrant and I'll tear this place apart! Then I'm going to have you arrested!" Director Hornbeck shouted. "They shouldn't let dangerous people like you out on the streets!" She climbed into her vehicle and slammed the door. Gravel flew as she sped down the driveway and onto the road.

Robert and Agnes just stood for a minute watching the ground car disappear out of sight. Robert climbed back up the steps, and together they went into the house for the evening. Tomorrow was going to be a busy day.

Back at the Eagleman farm, Prudence Hornbeck told Dorn and the officers about what had just happened. Assuring the pitiful man they would be back tomorrow, she and the officers returned to town. The privacy of the drive allowed the police officers to discuss the situation. Neither cared for the way things were going, and especially for the director's coddling of Delmar's brother. However, there was very little they could do. Their hands were tied by the local courts, which had given the social agency broad powers in these matters.

When they arrived back at the agency office, Ms. Hornbeck called another meeting. She and her minions planned tomorrow's search of the Hassel farm, and their subsequent arrest. A quick call to the judge secured the necessary warrants.

Calling the police chief, the director used the court orders she had just received to demand two dozen officers for tomorrow's action. Hamstrung by the court order, he reluctantly agreed.

7

Dawn at Jasper Station was bright and clear when the Axia cruiser set down. Its ramps extended and various details of the crew and the few passengers exited the craft. One particular passenger, a trooper-first, looked around and then spotted the groundcrew chief.

"Excuse me, Chief," the trooper-first called as he approached.

"Yes? How can I help you, Trooper?" replied the chief.

"I'm Trooper-First Michael Azor, and I need to find the liaison office," the trooper said.

"That would be over behind the ops office," answered the chief, pointing toward the operations building.

"Thanks a lot." Trooper Azor turned and strode toward the indicated structure.

Once inside, Mike Azor walked up to the counter. A clerk looked up from some paperwork and came over.

"May I help you, sir?" he asked.

"Yes," Mike answered and produced a packet of

papers. "I'm here under direction of Our Lady to investigate a situation." The clerk quickly scanned the papers and then looked up.

"Let me show you to the CO," he said. Mike followed him back to a small, overstuffed office where a lieutenant was seated behind a cluttered desk. The clerk made the necessary introductions and then left, closing the door behind him.

"What can I do for you, Trooper?" the lieutenant asked.

"I'm here under direction of Our Lady to investigate a certain matter," Mike replied. He handed the papers to the older man and waited. The lieutenant read the papers and then handed them back.

"It looks like we're going to be busy," he said. "When do you want to get started?"

"Immediately," Mike answered.

"I thought you'd say that." The lieutenant stood and took his hat from the rack in the corner. "Let's go."

Another meeting was just breaking up in Keeler. "Okay," said the director to the assembled caseworkers and reluctant police officers, "let's go."

It was obvious she enjoyed commanding such a large contingent of people. She was certain she was going to set things to rights before the day was over. The officers and the workers piled into their ground cars and the convoy wound out through the valley.

Arriving at the Eagleman farm, the cars carrying the caseworkers parked under a large tree. The police ground cars, along with the social agency director's car, continued up the road toward the Hassel farm.

Back in town, the ship carrying the lieutenant and Trooper-First Azor set down in a field across from the headquarters of the local police district. The nearly empty parking lot puzzled the lieutenant. Inside they also found a corresponding lack of personnel. The lieutenant approached the front desk clerk and asked to see the chief. After calling on her intercom, the bored-looking receptionist pointed to the door and asked the two men to enter.

As they stepped into the office, the chief greeted the lieutenant warmly. Introductions were made around and the three men sat down.

"So, Mike," began the police chief, "what brings you to our little neck of the galaxy?"

"I'm here on special assignment from Our Lady to investigate a matter that has come to her attention," he replied, handing the chief the papers. The chief read them for a couple of minutes, shaking his head occasionally. He finished with a grunt and handed the papers back to Mike.

"We've known about this situation for some time, but our hands have been tied by the courts," he finally said. "That agency and its director have undermined justice for quite a while. Today she used her friend the judge to force me to put twenty officers under her direction 'to apprehend parties hiding a criminal fugitive and search the premise of the same,'" he said, quoting from the court order. "She got the judge to issue arrest warrants against a neighbor who complained and also for the missing boy."

"Where is she now?" asked the lieutenant, apprehensively.

"I had to pull nearly every officer I had for her little expedition, and they went over to her office an hour ago," the chief replied. "If I figure right, they should be up the valley by now at the farm of Mr. Robert Hassel."

Trooper-First Mike Azor sat quietly for a minute. "Is this Robert Hassel the neighbor she intends to arrest?" Mike asked.

"Yes," answered the chief, "and his wife Agnes too. Something about reckless endangerment."

"I know those fine folks, chief. If Robert and Agnes say something happened, it did," Mike asserted.

"Well then, you better do something or she's going to make things pretty miserable for those people," the chief replied.

"Chief?" asked the lieutenant. "May I use your phone?"

"Sure, go ahead," the police chief answered. "I hope whatever you're thinking of doing works."

"I'm sure it will," replied the lieutenant with a grin. "I'm sure it will."

Agnes looked out the window to where Director Hornbeck was standing. The bullhorn was finally quiet, and now they waited. Robert watched the rear of the house from the back upstairs windows while Agnes covered the front. When the convoy of ground cars had pulled up in front of the farm, they had thought the police had come looking for Delmar.

Robert had gone partway out into the yard to talk with the director. When he refused to allow her onto their property to serve the warrant (none of the officers seemed inclined to do it), she became very angry, grabbed a gun, and threatened Robert. That was when Agnes put a slug into the headlight of the director's car while Robert ran for cover. Since that time, it had been a standoff with Director Hornbeck shouting threats at them through the bullhorn.

Agnes noticed some of the officers moving down the road. She saw them climb over the fence and fan out through the field in an effort to surround them.

"Robert!" she called, "it looks like they're going to try and cut through the side field to get to the outbuildings."

"I see them, honey," he called back. "Do you see any more going around the other way?"

"Just a minute, I'll check," she replied. Agnes slipped into the spare room above the kitchen where she could see the other side of the house.

"There go some more," she called to her husband. "It looks like a half-dozen or so sneaking through the oats." Returning to her viewpoint at the front bedroom window, Agnes observed Ms. Hornbeck talking into a portable radio.

"Looks like she's planning something, Robert," Agnes called out.

"Yeah," replied her husband. "The other bunch has spread out near the swine pens." Agnes saw the director talk again into the radio, and then a shot rang out.

"Here they come!" she yelled just as more shots careened off the house. Another shot was fired from the side field, and Agnes heard a downstairs window break. She stuck her rifle through the curtain and sent a round over the heads of the men near the front. She saw them all duck and then get ready to charge the house.

Suddenly the sky grew dark and everyone outside began to gesture wildly. Agnes ran to the side room again just in time to see an Axia cruiser land in the oats. Its hatches burst open and troopers in full battledress charged out. Many immediately covered the crouching police officers while most of the rest formed a protective barrier around the besieged house.

Another shadow indicated that a second ship had set down on the opposite side of the house near the barnyard. Robert joined his wife at the window just in time to see a trooper-first and a lieutenant exit the hatch and walk toward the director.

"Yahoo!" cried Robert. "That's Mike Azor!"

"It sure is!" said Agnes with a whoop. The Hassels descended the stairs and walked out defiantly into the front yard where the troopers had surrounded Prudence Hornbeck.

The lieutenant and the trooper-first were confronting the irate director. "How dare you invade my jurisdiction!" she screamed. "You have no right to interfere with the enforcement of our laws!" Suddenly she noticed the Hassels approaching.

"Stop those desperate criminals!" Hornbeck screeched. Lunging for a pistol, she tried to bring it to bear. Before either Robert or Agnes could react, two troopers leaped from behind and pinned the director to the ground.

The lieutenant looked down at the struggling woman and then turned to some of the police officers that stood nearby watching. "Gentlemen," he said, producing the Imperial warrant for them to see, "I think you should take this woman into custody."

"With pleasure, sir!" they answered. They relieved the troopers of the director, handcuffed her, and put her into one of their squad cars. Soon the vehicle headed toward town, the director's screaming face pressed against the window glass.

"What about the courts?" asked Robert, who had watched this entire episode take place. "Won't she be able to get free to harass us again?"

"I wouldn't worry about it, Robert," replied Mike with a grin. "I have an Imperial directive to investigate the whole mess and set it straight. She and that judge won't bother you or anybody else anymore."

Robert heard footsteps behind him and turned to see the troopers and police officers walking up together from the fields. There was the sound of good-natured laughter from both groups, and all the police officers were smiling.

Having stood watching silently, Agnes now spoke up, "Then the empress got our letter?" she asked.

"She most certainly did," Mike answered, "and I'm her reply."

"Well, we better go find Delmar now and tell him it's okay to come out of hiding," Robert remarked.

"Where is the boy now?" asked the lieutenant.

"He's been hiding from his brother and the social authorities for several months now up in the hills," Robert pointed.

"Do you think you can find him?" Mike asked.

"I know where to find him," Robert said. "But he may have moved after I warned him about the ruckus that crazy director woman was stirring up."

"We saw him yesterday up near Double Forks Hollow," one of the officers offered.

"That's near where he hides," remarked Agnes.

Mike thought for a long moment and then conferred with the lieutenant. Turning back to the officers, the lieutenant spoke. "Would you officers be willing to go search for the boy?" he asked. "You know those hills much better than my troopers."

The officers looked at each other and then Joe answered for the group. "Sure, lieutenant," he answered, "but I want to have a few of the guys go take care of some caseworkers and another little problem while the rest of us search."

"I see no problem with that," Mike replied. Then, addressing the lieutenant, he continued. "What they need to do is necessary, Lieutenant."

"Fine by me," the lieutenant replied. "Let's get things moving." The group broke up and a couple of police officers got into their ground cars and turned onto the road. The remaining officers and troopers paired up and headed toward the woods.

"Would you care to come aboard?" Mike asked the Hassels.

"I don't see why not," Robert answered. Taking Agnes' arm, they walked together up the ramp of the ship, followed by Mike and the lieutenant.

Delmar ventured out early, gathering extra fruit not far from the rise overlooking the Hassel farm. He knew it was safe to wiggle out where he could see things at this early hour, so he edged out onto an outcropping of rock so he could look down. The valley spread out beautifully below him, and he could clearly see all the buildings and equipment of the Hassel farm. An old familiar yearning to sit again at the Hassel's kitchen table filled him.

The summer mornings had been clear and crisp lately, and Delmar enjoyed them whenever he could. He stayed quite a while taking in the panorama as the sun rose higher, the shifting light detailing different things as they filtered into view.

Just as he was about to go, Delmar saw a number of police ground vehicles speeding up the road toward the Hassel farm, led by an unmarked government car. The cars skidded to a halt outside the Hassel driveway and the occupants quickly got out and formed a line in front of the property. Mr. Hassel appeared in the yard and the boy could clearly see the angry agitation of a woman in the line.

Suddenly, he saw Mr. Hassel run for the house and a few seconds later, he heard the crack of a rifle. Horrified, Delmar watched the scene unfold. He lay transfixed as the group broke up and began to surround the house. *It's like they're hunting hardened criminals*, he thought.

Soon after the men had surrounded the house, several more shots rang out. Delmar could see the glitter of broken glass as it flew outward from a broken window. He heard another shot and the group still at the front of the property dove for cover.

Just then, an Axia cruiser swooped down over the farm and landed in the field beside the house. Combat troopers spilled out and were quickly among the other men. The house was surrounded. Delmar felt terror seize him and he decided to slip back to the cave as the shadow of a second ship passed overhead. Forsaking quiet for speed, he ran for the cave.

Throughout the rest of the day, several teams of officers and troopers searched the hills and woods looking for the boy. Calling in via port-a-comm radios, they continued to have nothing to report. Robert and Agnes sat in the ship listening to the comm traffic and trying to aid the search with their knowledge of the hills.

Following Robert's directions, one team finally found the cave but not the boy. They retrieved the gear they found there, but when Robert later

JIM LAUGHTER & VICTOR J. BRETTHAUER

checked the stuff, he discovered the pocketwatch was missing. With the light of day fading into darkness, the lieutenant called everyone back from the search.

The police officers returned to town, and the troopers came onboard the ship. Agnes and Robert excused themselves and busied themselves with chores while a couple of troopers repaired the shot-out windows.

Mike told the Hassels he was going to move the ships back to the landing field near Keeler. Robert thought this might be wise, because he was concerned their presence might prevent the boy from returning. Mike mentioned that he would send another contingent of troopers out with the local police tomorrow to continue the search. He also said that he would be conducting an investigation hearing of the entire incident tomorrow and he would like the Hassels to be there.

As Mike walked up the ramp he turned and gave the couple the Axia salute, his right arm across his chest, palm down. Agnes and Robert returned the salute and watched the great ship close its hatches and soar skyward.

Huddled under a small cleft in the rocks miles from the Hassel farm, Delmar assessed his situation. In his haste to leave the cave, he had only managed to grab his sleeping bag, a few of the books, his pocketwatch, letters, and very little food. He had run for hours trying to put distance between himself and the people he saw attack the Hassel farm. It confused him to see Axia troopers surround the house, and he feared he had brought it all onto his benefactors. "This is not supposed to be a police state," Delmar muttered to himself.

Delmar was still too tense to sleep so he lay in the cleft and tried to plan his next move. He was sure they were searching for him, and eventually they would run him down. He turned over, looked at the stars, and rejected one plan after another. Finally, in the stillness of space, he saw the reflected light from a ship in orbit. The plan for his escape began to crystallize.

At nine the next morning, Trooper-First Mike Azor called the hearing to order. He had requisitioned one of the courtrooms in the town hall. Troopers standing at parade rest lined the walls while the gallery filled with civilian onlookers. Seated before Mike at the defense table were the social agency director and the judge who normally presided in this room. At the other table sat the lieutenant and the Hassels. After a brief prayer to the Unseen One offered by the chaplain, Mike ordered everyone to be seated.

From his chair behind the bench, Mike read into the record the original report and the instructions from Empress Ane. He handed the supplemental research material from Shalimar to another trooper who read it into the court record. Once completed, Mike called Mr. Hassel to the stand.

"Mr. Robert Hassel," he began, "did you submit the foregoing report for review by the empress?"

"Yes, sir, I did," Robert replied.

"Is the submitted report true and accurate to the best of your experience and observations?" Mike asked.

"Yes, sir, it is," Robert answered.

"Please tell the court about your dealings with the social agency and its director," Mike requested. Robert told of their efforts to report the abuse by the older brother and the way the social agency had blocked their efforts. Describing the visit he and Agnes had with Ms. Prudence Hornbeck months ago, Robert also told about the report he had read on her desk. He then related the threats and intimidation from the social agency, the director in particular, culminating with the attack the previous morning at the farm.

"Thank you, Mr. Hassel. You may return to your seat," Mike intoned. He then called Prudence Hornbeck to the stand. She looked pale, but defiant, as she was seated. Mike expected possible trouble so he had taken the extra precautionary measure of having troopers line the walls. He hoped their very presence would quell any possible outbursts. Mike asked the director to state her name and position for the record. He then asked her to explain the case history of Delmar and his brother. After many minutes of convoluted explanation, she finally concluded her statements.

"So after conducting a thorough investigation, we determined that Delmar is a dangerous delinquent who had endangered his brother and, as a threat to the community, should be apprehended," she said with conviction.

"Did you at any time check with local law enforcement personnel about Delmar or his brother?" Mike asked.

"Of course not!" she snapped. "What do they know?"

"Then on whose authority did you undertake your raid on the Hassel farm?" he asked.

"On my own authority, you fool!" Hornbeck answered. "I am the director!"

"Thank you, ma'am," Mike said evenly. "You may be seated." He then called the police chief to the stand.

"Sir," Mike began, "would you please tell us what you and your people know about Delmar and his older brother?"

The chief launched into a detailed description of their run-ins with the brother and the abuse that had been reported to them.

"Why didn't you act on these reports?" Mike asked.

"Because we were unable to get court authority to act," the chief replied. Mike excused the chief from the stand and called the judge. The man looked frightened as he came forward.

"Then please tell me, sir," began Mike, "what was your action on the request by the chief for warrants concerning Delmar's older brother?"

"I refused them," he answered.

"Why did you refuse them?" Mike asked.

"Because internal family matters are out of their jurisdiction," the man answered. "They fall under the authority of the social agency and its director."

"Tell me, sir," Mike continued, "what is the statute or law assigning such matters strictly to the social agency?"

The man thought for a moment. "There is no specific statute or law designating such, but it is the custom of the court to honor such requests from the agency," he answered quietly.

"You may step down," Mike said. After a moment, Mike picked up the gavel and held it suspended over the striking block. "By the power and authority vested in me by Imperial mandate, I find that the director acted in wanton disregard of the laws and policies of Galactic Axia. Without legal authority, she endangered a legal ward and other citizens. I also find the judge in violation of his oaths of office and party to travesty of justice. I hereby turn them both over to the district attorney for prosecution under the laws of the Axia at a trial commencing within thirty days."

Both the judge and Ms. Hornbeck looked stunned. "You can't do that!" screamed the director, jumping to her feet. Mike just looked at her as two troopers firmly returned her to her seat and then stood right behind her.

"I can, and I have," Mike said quietly. Then in a louder voice he said, "This hearing is adjourned." He banged the gavel.

Troopers escorted the former director and judge

out of the courtroom. Cheering broke out, and the lieutenant congratulated the Hassels. Mike stepped down, and together they went into the quietness of the judge's chambers.

"Good job, Mike!" said Robert, closing the door. "What do we do now?"

"The same as yesterday," Mike replied, "look for a missing boy."

Throughout the rest of the day, the reports from the search parties were all negative. They could find no trace of Delmar. As the sun set, Mike recalled the searchers and planned for another day of effort.

8

The lengthening shadows signaled the coming of another lonely night and slowly covered the brush of Delmar's hiding place. He had been watching the activity at the small spacefield for a couple of hours. Trying to determine the patterns of activity around the private freighters had proven to be a challenge.

Delmar lay his head down and rested his eyes. The ride he had managed to catch in the back of a poultry truck helped him cover the distance to the cargo field two districts over from the field in Big Valley, and gave his tired legs a much-needed rest. It also put him farther away from the terrifying scene in the valley. He'd traveled mainly at night to remain safe from those he feared.

Hunger had slowed him a bit after the third day, but he finally arrived at his destination. Now he just needed to wait a while before trying his plan.

"That's all we know so far," said Mike as he tossed the small stack of paper onto the desk. Robert and Agnes looked at the pile of reports with obvious disappointment.

The search for Delmar had gone on nearly continuously since the day Mike had arrived. It had been almost a week and they had turned up nothing. Mike had even ordered one of the ships to fly over the woods with its aura detector system tuned to humans. They had spotted several indications of humans and sent ground searchers to check them out, but each had proven to be hikers unaware of the search. Teams thoroughly searched all of the caves in the hills and found no trace. The local police chief also agreed to send out a planet-wide bulletin in an effort to get a lead on Delmar.

"It's like he just disappeared," remarked Robert.

"What if he's hurt?" fretted Agnes.

"Then we would have found him," replied Mike. "An injured man can't run."

"So tomorrow the bulletin goes out?" Robert said.

"Yes," replied Mike. "But in the meantime, I need to send an update to Our Lady."

Other matters in the case had not gone well either. Ms. Hornbeck and the judge had both been dealt with quickly. The new director cleaned house at the social agency. The staff, many of whom only dealt with inter-office paperwork, had been halved. Clients were happily reporting faster and better service.

However, in spite of the changes, some things remained the same. Delmar's brother had somehow managed to avoid prosecution, although Mike had been able to cut off his government payments for taking care of Delmar. The warrants against the Hassels were summarily dismissed, as well as several of the other legal suits the former director had initiated. As a result, the caseload in the courts had eased considerably, and morale among local law enforcement personnel was definitely high. Still, there was the nagging problem of the missing boy.

Using the cover of darkness to slide under the fence, Delmar slipped onto the field. He hid his small pack of belongings, straightened his clothes, and walked briskly toward the nearest freighter. The ship showed her years of service plying her trade, and though the paint looked new, it did nothing to hide recent repairs.

Delmar approached the men who were loading crates into the cargo bay and pitched in to help. No one seemed to notice him as the loading continued, except that the extra strong back was most welcome. The ship was finally loaded and the groundcrew sauntered back toward the buildings, leaving the regular crew and Delmar standing near the loading ramp.

"You better get goin,' boy," the cargo master said. "We're gonna lift off soon."

Delmar gulped once and spoke up. "I was wondering if you could use another hand. I'd be willing to do anything."

The cargo master eyed him suspiciously. "How old are you, boy?" he asked.

"Just turned eighteen, sir," Delmar replied.

"Well, let me go talk to the skipper," the cargo master said. "You sure proved you're willing to work." The master went inside. Delmar waited nervously for several minutes. Eventually two men came back out.

"Let me see some identification, son," the ship captain said. Delmar showed him the identification card he had received at graduation.

"Looks like you've learned something too," the captain said. "Why do you want to ship out? You in some kind of trouble, boy?"

Delmar paled but kept the nervousness out of his voice. "I've thought about space travel for several years since my mom died," he replied. "I've had some trouble at home with my older brother, and I want a new start."

The captain eyed him for a moment. The two men turned their backs to Delmar and moved out of earshot. After conferring a minute, they returned. "Okay," said the captain. "I'll take you on and assign you to Cargo Master Preston here. This is my ship, the *Malibu*. I'm in command, but Mr. Preston runs the crew. Now get on board and let's go."

Delmar sighed with relief. He ran over to the place where he had hidden his pack, grabbed it, and ran back just in time to follow the two men up the ramp.

"Now don't get your head full of no fanciful ideas, boy," Preston said as they entered the ship. "I can work 'em outta you before we break orbit." The hatch closed behind them and within minutes, the *Malibu* was streaking skyward.

Delmar learned quickly and adjusted to the daily routine aboard the ship. It became easy to tell morning from afternoon by which of the two levels he was scrubbing. The different patterns of flooring tile were all he needed for a timepiece. Preston worked him steady but not too hard, lest all the work be done and the boy should have some free time. Out barely ten days, the ship glistened from one end to the other. Delmar could see the tile patterns in his sleep.

However, scrubbing the *Malibu's* floors did not keep Delmar from learning. He kept his ears and eyes open and his mouth shut, the first advice Cargo Master Preston had given him after breaking orbit. From the disgusted tone of the skipper, he learned that there were problems with some of the rods of the bedsprings drive system and their power cells were weakening. They were also having trouble navigating and had to make frequent course corrections, and their communications array was apparently out of alignment. They were not making good time as they planet-hopped and would have to lay over at the next planet for repairs.

Beyond this, life was pretty dull. Even the food left something to be desired—namely variety. Their cook was singularly uninspired and it showed by what he served.

The Red-tail pilot could not believe his luck. He had been on patrol in this sector of space trying to find a likely spot for the cluster to open a new transit tube so they could make hit-and-run raids. This was one of the normal shipping lanes used by the humans of Galactic Axia.

The few Axia ships the Red-tail had seen were the large cruisers, and he certainly did not want to tangle with one of those. But this ship was different. From the looks of it, the ship should have been retired long ago. And though he wasn't familiar with Galactic Axia designs, he was sure the ship coming into his detector range was only running on partial power. The energy fluctuations emitting from its power source were intermittent at best.

The Red-tail pilot powered his scout ship down to avoid detection by the approaching ship. *You never know about these humans*, he thought. *They're full of tricks and capable of absolute treachery.*

The *Malibu* had taken off from Erdinata with a full load of iron ore and supplies for a couple of the inner colonies on Keltus and Olympia. The ship had handled well enough on the first leg of their journey, but the skipper knew he would have to put in at Mica for repairs if he hoped to stay in business. His green box power cells were running weak and intermittent, and he didn't like the way his communications arrays were acting.

Cargo Master Preston came forward to the control room and sat down heavily in the vacant comm chair. He had been recalculating the load weight and distribution variances in the cargo hold since dropping off their shipment of ore at Olympia.

"Something wrong, Preston?" the skipper asked.

"Naw. I just hate haulin' ore," the cargo master answered. "Seems to me like the Axia shouldn't put colonies on planets that don't have enough natural resources to mine their own iron."

"You'd think so, wouldn't you?" the skipper answered. "But ours is not to reason why."

"Ours is but to load and fly," Preston finished the old freighter idiom.

"Where's that new kid we took on?" the skipper asked.

"I've got him down in the cargo bay arranging pallets to get the weight right," Preston answered.

"He's a good worker. Too bad we'll have to put him off on Mica," the skipper said.

"Put him off?" Preston asked. "Why?"

"Because we'll be laid over for who knows how long getting this tub repaired," the skipper answered. "We can't afford to keep on extra crew just to sit in port."

"Sure seems a shame," Preston commented. "That boy really knows how to put his back into it."

The skipper wondered what kind of trouble the Eagleman kid was running from, but he didn't ask. *After all, I ain't the kid's father,* he thought. He'd left home when he was a teenager too, shipping out on one of the old solar sail ships. He remembered it took weeks just to get to the nearest moon, much less another star. So he wouldn't pry. He would just let the boy take care of his own problems and work them out the best he could.

"You're just lucky I don't put you off too," the skipper said to Preston.

Preston got up from the comm chair and poured a cup of hot coffee for himself from an old coffee pot, then handed a cup to the skipper. "Can't do it, Skipper," Preston said.

"And just why not?" the skipper asked. "You think you're something special around here?"

Preston sat back down in the comm chair. "Yep," he answered. "Seein' as'ta how I own quarter interest in this old tub, I'd say you'd have to either buy me out, which I know you can't afford, or knock me in the head, which I know you won't do."

"Got all the answers, don't ya?" the skipper asked.

"Not all of 'em," Preston answered, taking a sip of his hot coffee. "Just enough of 'em."

The panoramic view displayed on the main viewscreen of the freighter showed nothing but open space and bright stars. Regardless of how boring the time was on slow runs between the planets, the skipper never grew tired of space or the many wonders each star system held.

Cargo Master Preston sat with his back to the comm screen and detector panel, so he didn't see the red trace suddenly appear on the detector screen. The signal was very faint, and it took two more sweeps of the detector array to trigger the proximity alarm.

The red lights of the proximity alarm began to flash, followed by the shrill wail of the klaxon. Preston sat bolt upright in the comm chair and spilled the coffee he had just poured. The hot liquid seared down his right leg but Preston paid it no mind.

"What is it?" the skipper asked, moving to Preston's side.

"Don't know yet, Skipper," Preston answered. "Can't see nothin.'"

The skipper pushed Preston out of the comm chair and sat down at the controls himself. He hated making this run without a communications specialist. But the *Malibu* was a privately owned independent freighter and this was supposed to be a safe route. Besides, he had to cut costs somewhere.

The proximity klaxon continued to blare its warning, the shrill noise cutting through the skipper's brain. "Shut that racket-maker off," the skipper ordered.

Preston flipped a switch on the control panel and the klaxon went silent. At the same time, Preston glanced out the front portal and saw the Red-tail ship appear out of nowhere. Preston watched in horror as the Red-tail launched a torpedo at the *Malibu*.

"Incoming torpedo!" screamed Preston.

"Where?" the skipper asked more calmly than he really felt.

"Port bow. Twenty miles," Preston answered.

The skipper leaped from the comm chair and, as if by magic, landed in his control chair. With his left hand, he spun the axis ball hard to the left while throwing the ship into full reverse with his right hand. The ship lurched, and then seemed to stand still in space. Then with a great wrenching twist that even the inertial dampeners could not overcome, the ship fell away from the path of the incoming Red-tail weapon.

Preston fell to the floor with the first spin of the axis ball but was now back on his feet. He could feel, more than hear, the cargo in the cargo bay break away from its moorings and smash against a bulkhead. "I hope that kid got out of the way of that!" Preston exclaimed.

The skipper was too busy twisting and turning the ship to be concerned about what Preston was saying. "Get to the weapons console!" the skipper ordered.

Preston staggered across the control room to the weapons console on the old freighter. The *Malibu* had once been an active duty ship, but that was decades ago, so its weapons complement was very limited. She still sported the large heat ray that ran along the long axis of the ship. And she still had a few smaller swivel-mount heat rays. But torpedoes were rare, not to mention expensive to purchase in the private sector.

Preston hoped the one torpedo he still showed on the inventory was good and that the launch tube would fire it properly. They didn't run weapons drills on civilian freighters like they did on line vessels. This was a discrepancy he figured the skipper would rectify if they lived through this ordeal.

"I could use a little help here," the skipper called out, again giving the axis ball a spin and pushing the throttle bar forward, sending the ship on a parallel tangent from its previous course.

At just that moment, Delmar appeared at the control room door. Blood stained his face and shirt from a nasty cut on his forehead.

"What's happening?" Delmar yelled.

"Red-tail," Preston answered. "We're under attack." Preston saw the blood streaming down Delmar's face. "You all right, boy?"

"Yes, sir," Delmar answered. "It's just a little bump on the head."

"Get on that comm panel, boy!" the skipper ordered. "Try to get us some help!"

"Yes, sir," Delmar answered. Although he had never actually worked a comm panel before, he had seen one at the spaceport when Mr. Hassel had taken him on a field trip one day. Mr. Hassel had shown him how to use the simple device, especially the emergency beacon switch that would send out a distress call along with their coordinates in space and their identity registration. Any ship within a dozen elms would respond as soon as it picked up the signal.

Delmar sat at the comm panel and threw the emergency beacon switch. Then he picked up the headset and put it on. He pressed the switch on the mic and spoke clearly and calmly into it. "Mayday, mayday, mayday. Independent freighter *Malibu* declaring an emergency. We're under attack by Red-tails. Mayday, mayday, mayday."

This kid has moxie, thought Preston. *Cool, calm, ready for a fight. Kinda reminds me of me when I was a pup.*

"Good job, kid," Preston complimented the teen.

"Thanks," Delmar answered. "Mr. Hassel, uh, I mean, my school teacher told me about Red-tails, but I never expected to see one."

"That's one thing you don't want to see, boy," Preston answered. "If you see one up real close, the chances are you're already dead and fixin' to be his supper."

The skipper spun around in his command chair and yelled across the room at Preston. "Are you going to fire those weapons or just try to talk that thing to death?"

Delmar could not help but laugh out loud at the skipper's question. But now Preston was all business. He turned back to the weapons console, and with dexterity that belayed his gruff exterior, his fingers played across the weapons console like a seasoned professional. The axis heat ray fired, sending a searing blast of energy at the approaching Red-tail ship. Delmar could hear the sound of the swivel mount rays firing too, but the Red-tail continued to advance, twisting and turning out of the heat ray's path.

"Have you got a torpedo in your pocket anywhere?" the skipper asked.

"Sure do," Preston answered. "Can't tell ya if it'll light or not, but we got one."

"Then line it up and see if you can get us out of this jam!" the skipper exclaimed.

Delmar watched the cargo master activate another screen that was hidden behind a safety panel. A set of crosshairs like the one he had seen on Mrs. Hassel's old rifle appeared on the screen, along with a set of divergent coordinates. A red blip appeared on the screen that Delmar assumed was the location of the Red-tail ship.

Preston worked his fingers over the keyboard on the weapons console until he was satisfied he had the Red-tail ship locked into a good firing solution. With a quick press of a red button on the panel, Delmar heard the torpedo fire and watched it streak through space toward the Red-tail position.

In the meantime, the Red-tail had his sights set on a decent meal for a change. He figured the old freighter couldn't be carrying much of a crew, but just one of the humans would last him awhile. That is, if he could blow one out into space. Besides that, he had been spotted. The cluster commander would not be happy if he wasn't able to put a transit tube in this sector just because a single scout ship couldn't handle one old freighter.

The Red-tail saw the torpedo release from the freighter. By this time, he was only two or three hundred miles away from the Axia ship. He knew he had to act fast to avoid being hit.

The skipper, Preston, and Delmar watched the torpedo streak toward the Red-tail vessel. They saw the enemy ship twist and turn, trying its best to escape the incoming weapon. But it was no use. The torpedo was locked on. It was only a matter of seconds before the torpedo would find its mark. "Great shot, Preston!" the skipper shouted.

"Thanks," Preston answered. "Just like the old days."

The crew of the *Malibu* watched with elation as the torpedo closed in on its target. The Red-tail knew he had met his match. Then the torpedo struck the enemy vessel full broadside. Nothing. No explosion. No fireball. Nothing. The torpedo hit the Red-tail vessel and careened off into space. It was a dud.

"Uh-oh," Preston muttered. "I think we're in trouble!"

"You have an obvious talent for understatement," the skipper answered. "And we can't outrun this guy, so you better come up with something fast."

Delmar had an idea. "What if we jettison our cargo?" he asked. "That iron ore might confuse his sensors long enough for us to escape."

"Drop the load?" Preston asked. "You tryin' to bankrupt us, boy?"

"Do it!" the skipper ordered. "Create a debris field, and I'll try to buy us some time."

"Yes, sir," Preston answered. "Come on, boy!" Preston led the way out of the control room toward the cargo bay. What he saw when they got there did not make him happy. The cargo had shifted and broken loose from its bindings and was pressed against the cargo doors.

"Watch this." Preston pushed Delmar into a small pressurized room at the back of the cargo bay.

He reached overhead and threw a heavy switch that reminded Delmar of the electrical breaker switch in Mr. Hassel's barn.

Suddenly, the cargo bay doors began to swing outward, followed by an ear-wrenching blast of air. The cargo in the hold blew violently out through the open hatch along with everything else that wasn't bolted to the deck.

Preston closed the cargo hatch and waited for a minute while the cargo hold repressurized. "Come on," he said, pushing Delmar ahead of him. Then they felt the ship lurch as something hit it hard from the port side. "Heat ray," Preston said. "Must'a winged us."

The two men ran the length of the vessel back to the control room to find the skipper still in his control chair trying to out-maneuver the Red-tail ship. Preston looked out the front portal and saw their cargo floating freely in space, miraculously coming between them and the Red-tail.

"You still messin' with that critter?" Preston asked. "I figured you'd have us home sippin' coolin' drinks and eatin' apple pie by now."

"I was just about to order a slice for you and the boy there," the skipper answered. "But this guy just won't let go."

The three men on the bridge of the *Malibu* watched the Red-tail vessel close in on their position again. The debris field they had created wasn't working, and the enemy vessel was lining up for a clean shot at the old freighter.

Suddenly, the explosion of the Red-tail vessel lit up space. Unseen by either the Red-tail or the crew of the *Malibu*, an Axia heavy cruiser suddenly appeared out of nowhere and launched a devastating attack against the Red-tail ship. Two torpedoes struck the enemy vessel at the same time, scattering her atoms into open space. The last thought of the Red-tail invader had been that he wasn't going to taste any human flesh this trip.

"Axia heavy cruiser *Sanora* calling independent freighter *Malibu*," a voice said from the comm speaker. "This is Captain Michael T. Roseburg speaking. Do you require medical assistance?"

Delmar looked at the skipper, then back at Preston. "You're the comm operator," the skipper said to Delmar. "Answer the man."

"Yes, sir," Delmar replied, smiling at his sudden promotion. He crossed the control room to the comm panel and sat down in the comm chair.

"Independent freighter *Malibu* calling the *Sanora*," he said. "Negative on the medical assistance. But where…where did you come from?"

"You boys looked like you could use some help," answered Captain Roseburg.

"But how did you know we were here?" Delmar asked.

"Because you sent out an emergency distress signal," answered Roseburg.

"Oh yeah, that's right," Delmar answered. It seemed like so long ago since he had sent out the distress signal that he had forgotten he'd done it.

Preston and the skipper laughed at Delmar's lapse of memory. The skipper crossed the room to the comm panel and took the mic from Delmar's hand.

"This is Captain Arthur Norellen of the independent freighter *Malibu*," he said into the mic. Delmar realized at that moment that this was the first time he'd actually heard the skipper's name. He had just called him Skipper since leaving Erdinata, and come to think of it, so had Preston. "We sure appreciate you pulling our fat from the fire, Captain Roseburg."

"Nothing to it," Roseburg answered. "But from the looks of your ship, you're going to need some serious repairs. You have damage on both quarters of your aft port panel, and it looks like your drive system may have taken a hit. Where are you bound?"

"Next stop is Mica," Norellen answered.

"Do you require an escort?" Roseburg asked.

"No sir, I think we can make it," the skipper answered. "I've got a stout ship and a good crew. We'll make it."

"Roger," Roseburg answered. "Then if you don't need us any longer, we'll sweep the area for any more Red-tails."

"Thanks again for your help," Norellen said into the mic.

"Anytime," Roseburg answered. "Always happy to fry a Red-tail."

Delmar watched the giant cruiser vector away from them. *Wow!* he thought. *Wouldn't that be something?*

Preston clapped Delmar on the shoulder, and then poured the young man a cup of coffee. "Well, boy," he said. "Since we ain't got no cargo left, you might as well just stay here on the bridge and try to learn somethin.'"

"You mean it, sir?" Delmar asked.

"Sure he does," the skipper replied. "Soon as you get that knot on your head fixed up some, you can come over here and I'll show you how to drive this old boat."

After three weeks out from Erdinata, the *Malibu* was preparing to make planetfall at Mica when the skipper came into the cargo bay and pulled Preston aside. Delmar noticed that they kept looking at him, and he began to fear the authorities had found him. After a whispered conversation, the captain left and Preston walked over to Delmar. "Go put your things away," he ordered. "The skipper wants to see you in his cabin."

Delmar got up and took his scrub brush and pail to the storage locker. He walked slowly along the corridor to the captain's cabin and knocked.

"Come in," the skipper's rough voice resounded through the door. Delmar entered the small cabin and closed the door behind him. Trembling, he stood silent for a moment until the captain motioned for him to sit in the chair opposite his own.

"How's that cut on your forehead coming along, son?" the skipper asked. "Cook taking care of it all right?"

"Yes, sir," Delmar answered. He reached up and stroked the tender wound. He was sure it was going to leave a scar, but he had a feeling the injury wasn't really what the skipper wanted to talk about.

"Good," the skipper said, leaning forward slightly. "Delmar, I want to talk with you." Delmar's fear must have shown on his face. The captain leaned back in his chair and smiled at the young man.

"Relax," the skipper said, "you're not in trouble, and I'm not going to bite you." Delmar relaxed slightly but still felt apprehensive.

"The reason I had Preston send you down is I think it's time you and I discuss what your plans are once we reach Mica," the skipper said.

Delmar was taken aback by the captain's comment. He had grown so accustomed to life aboard ship that he'd forgotten there could be anything else. To think about possible changes when they made planetfall reintroduced uncertainty into his life.

"I hadn't really thought about it, sir," Delmar finally answered.

"Well, you better," replied the skipper. "Once we unload, we're going to have to put the ship in for some extensive repairs and I'm not going to need extra crew. You're a hard worker, Delmar, so you won't have trouble finding work."

The prospect that his tenure on the ship was definitely going to end shocked the boy, and his face telegraphed it. "But I thought I'd stay on, especially after our run-in with the Red-tail."

"Don't worry, son. You did real good," the skipper said. "I'll arrange some leads for you with a few friends of mine when we reach Mica. There's always a need for good workers. Of course, don't be looking for a berth as a comm operator. Those jobs are already filled."

Delmar turned to leave but the skipper stopped him. "You understand that I can't afford to keep you on, don't you, son?" he asked. "When we dropped our cargo, we lost our shipping fee. And it's going to be a long, expensive stay on Mica to get this old tub back into space."

"Uh...yes, sir. I understand, sir." Delmar finally answered. "And thanks for helping me when I needed it."

"No problem," answered the skipper. "I shipped out when I was a kid too. Just one thing though, Delmar."

"Yes sir," Delmar answered.

"When you get to port, be careful," the skipper advised. "There are all sorts of people in spaceports. Most are legitimate, and you'll find a good berth with them. However, others are pirates and use strong-arm tactics to recruit young men such as you. They'll take you on as crew and you'll never be heard from again."

"Pirates, sir?" Delmar asked. "In the Axia?"

"They're Galactic Axia citizens, most of them," answered the skipper. "But mostly they're old independent spacers that have no loyalty either way. They trade in whatever commodity they can, even human flesh."

"Slavery, Skipper?" Delmar asked, astonished.

"More like groceries," the skipper answered. "They sell human flesh to anyone or anything that will buy it."

The thought of an uncertain future on a strange planet scared the boy, and he certainly didn't want to run into any pirates. "Thank you, sir," Delmar said.

The skipper nodded at him and then returned to his books. He had to figure out how to make up for the load he had lost fighting the Red-tail.

Delmar let himself out and returned to the cargo bay and retrieved his bucket and brush and continued scrubbing, his mind again filled with terrifying images of uncertainty.

The mood in the Hassel farmhouse was glum as the three adults sat in silence. Pushing aside his near-empty coffee cup, Mike leaned back in his chair and looked at the couple.

"So that's the whole of it," he said sadly. "Except for minor signs, we've found no trace of the boy anywhere since they brought back the stuff from the cave."

Robert just looked at him for a moment, and then his face brightened with an idea. "If we haven't found Delmar, then obviously he's alive," he began. Robert paused and took a sip of lukewarm coffee. "An old space investigator once told me that if you eliminate all the possibilities, whatever is left, regardless of how unlikely, must be the answer." He took another sip of coffee. "If we eliminate all the possibilities of him being on Erdinata, there remains only one other place he can be."

"Space!" exclaimed Agnes, finishing her husband's thought.

"We covered the spacefields as a matter of routine, so if he's out there, someone had to help him," Mike replied. "We know it wasn't any of the fleet or I would have heard."

"That leaves only the independent freighters and passenger ships," Agnes said.

"We know it couldn't be a passenger ship, since Delmar had no money, that is unless he stowed away, which I doubt," Robert said. "He must have shipped out on a freighter."

"It's been over three weeks. There are a lot of ships to check up on," Mike commented. "I guess I'd better get some people on it."

With that, they all rose and the couple saw Mike to his ground car and watched it disappear into a cloud of dust. Robert looked up into the star-studded night. "It's going to be like looking for a needle in a haystack," he said to Agnes.

9

Delmar descended the ramp of the *Malibu* and headed through the gate off the field. He carried a small duffel bag in his right hand that contained everything he owned. In his left hand was a short list of people the skipper had recommended for Delmar to see.

The sudden change from living in an enclosed space with only a few other people to the crowds of the spaceport was overwhelming to the young man. The sounds of the spaceport were confusing and frightening and the noises and hustle and bustle of the freighters, transport ships, and military shuttle-craft added to Delmar's anxiety.

His flight out from Erdinata on the old freighter had been his first time in space. Now Delmar found himself alone on an alien planet. He didn't know anyone except Cargo Master Preston and the skipper back on the *Malibu*. Suddenly running from the authorities didn't seem like such a good idea.

Delmar threw his duffle bag over his shoulder and pushed his way through the crowd. He had never seen such a mix of humanity, nor heard many of the languages being spoken. Delmar paused for a moment beside a ground vehicle and listened to the conversation taking place between the driver and a prospective passenger. There seemed to be some dispute over the fare, but the boy could not understand a single word they said.

With conscience deference, Delmar walked along the breezeway of the spaceport. He figured the port was located outside of Mica City, the largest population center on the planet. At least, that was true of Jasper Station back on Erdinata. If this held true, he would have a long walk ahead of him. Delmar decided not to take the public transportation but instead to save his limited funds. "No need getting anywhere quick," he reasoned aloud. "I don't know where I'm going or anyone to see when I get there."

Delmar studied the short list of names the skipper had given him, so he decided to look up a few of them in hopes of securing an immediate berth. The cook onboard the freighter had insisted Delmar eat a good meal before leaving the ship, so he knew he could save the expense of at least one meal, maybe two.

Turning in at an open gate, Delmar spotted what appeared to be an operations building. He knew he had to avoid the civil and Axia authorities, but he hoped he could locate a few of the freighter captains at the flight line cafeteria. If he were lucky, he would have a job by the end of the day. If not, it was going to be a long, cold night.

The cafeteria proved to be little more than a large open-air gazebo with tables and vending machines. It did not take Delmar long to realize he'd have very little luck here. He did spot one grizzly old character that looked like he'd probably spent fifty years in deep space. His hair was long and unkempt, his dirty coverall uniform torn in several places, and Delmar thought he could smell the pungent aroma of pigs.

The old man spotted Delmar about the same time and motioned for him to come to his table. Delmar shook his head and started toward the exit. Before he realized it, the old man was at his side, his rough hand firmly gripping Delmar's elbow.

"Ya lookin' fer passage to the outer planets, sonny?" the old man asked. "I'm haulin' me a load of hogs, and I could sure use a strong young buck like you to swab out the pens." The foul odor emanating from the old man was nauseating to the boy. Delmar twisted right and left, trying to break the vice-like grip of the old man.

"What'cha fightin' fer, boy?" the old man asked. "I'm offerin' ya gainful employment."

"Just leave me alone!" Delmar exclaimed. "And turn loose of my arm." He twisted again, but still could not break the powerful grip of the old spacer.

A voice from behind Delmar startled him. "What's going on here?" the voice said. Delmar spun around just as the old man released the grip on his arm. Delmar stumbled and fell to the floor.

"Nothin,' Captain," the old man said, taking a step back away from Delmar.

Standing only a few feet from Delmar and towering over him like a giant tree was a man unlike any
Delmar had ever seen before. He was at least eight
feet tall, and Delmar guessed he weighed at least
three hundred pounds. There did not appear to be
an ounce of fat on the man.

Delmar still lay on the floor peering up at the
giant. He wore the blue uniform of the Mican Civil
Patrol. A heavy wooden baton swung from a leather
strap around the giant's right wrist.

"You all right, boy?" the giant asked.

"Yes, sir," Delmar croaked. "This man grabbed
me and wouldn't let go."

"Zeke?" the giant asked.

"Yes, Captain?" the old man answered.

"What have I told you about strong-arm recruiting
in this port?" the giant Mican patrol officer asked.

"But, Captain, sir," Zeke sputtered. "I was just
offerin' the boy a legitimate job."

"That's not what it looked like to me," the guard
said. "Now you get your things and get out of here
before I run you in."

"Yes, sir, Captain," the old spacer answered. He
then turned to Delmar and leered down at him with
menacing eyes. "I'll see you 'round, boy," he said,
then turned and walked away, leaving Delmar in the
presence of the Mican giant.

Delmar pushed himself up from the floor and turned
to leave, but the Mican guard placed his enormous hand
on Delmar's shoulder. "Hang on there a minute, young
fella," the guard said. "You here in port alone?"

"Yes sir," Delmar answered. "I just shipped in on the freighter *Malibu*, but they're laying over for repairs, so I'm just starting to look for another berth."

"How old are you, boy?" the giant asked. He did not seem impressed or convinced by Delmar's story.

"Eighteen, sir," Delmar answered.

"You in some kind of trouble?" the guard asked, seemingly fully aware that Delmar was on the run.

At just that moment, a commotion outside caught the giant's attention. He turned to get a better look at what appeared to be two kids scuffling on the ground, losing sight of Delmar for just a second. Delmar took advantage of the disturbance and took off running through the cafeteria and out onto the tarmac.

"Hey you! Boy! Stop!" the guard yelled after Delmar. But Delmar didn't look back. Instead, he darted back through the open gate and out onto the breezeway where he had been earlier. He looked up and down the street and decided to follow the general flow of outbound traffic.

Several hours passed, and Delmar was still walking toward what he hoped was a population center. His last meal had long since digested, and he could feel the grumblings of hunger churning on his insides.

The Mican sun hung low in the western sky. Delmar looked around to see if he could find a shelter of any kind. He was standing at the edge of a large field of what appeared to be some kind of grain he did not recognize.

A low structure that Delmar assumed was an equipment shed stood two or three hundred yards away in the field. Although it went against everything Delmar believed in, he decided to break into the shed and spend the night out of the elements. He walked carefully through the field, making sure he stayed between the rows so he wouldn't damage any of the grain. He remembered how Mr. Hassel hated it when anyone would cut across his fields and trample his crop. *I wonder what's he's doing right now?* he thought.

The shed was dark but dry. Delmar pried the hinge off the door and let himself in. A piece of farm equipment that resembled a tractor was all that was in the shed. Delmar had never seen a tractor with two engines and eight wheels before.

A low wattage light bulb hung from an exposed wire in the middle of the shed. Delmar stood on the fender of the tractor and cupped his hands around the bulb, trying to capture as much of its feeble heat as possible.

The floor of the shed was hard-packed topsoil, and there was no hay or anything else on which to lie. Delmar unrolled his sleeping bag, the same one Mr. Hassel had smuggled to him in the cave so long ago, and found a corner in which to sleep.

Delmar lay on the floor of the equipment shed and tried in vain to justify his situation. *Eighteen years old and a fugitive*, he thought. *But what crime have I committed? Why do I have to run?* "I'm not a criminal," he spoke aloud to himself. "I'm an orphan. Is that a crime? Why are the authorities after me? And why did Axia ships attack the Hassel farm?"

Delmar lay with his arm across his eyes and wept. *Were the Hassels still alive?* he wondered. *Or have they been arrested too?*

Sleep was a long time coming for Delmar that night. He knew he couldn't go back to the spaceport. The Mican guard had surely put out an alert for him by now. He didn't know anyone in town or even on the planet except the crew from the *Malibu*, and he could not go back there. Delmar lay in the equipment shed, alone and forsaken by everyone he knew, and silently wept himself to sleep.

The morning Mican sun filtered in through the cracks in the slat walls of the equipment shed. Delmar sat up and tried to stretch the kinks from his back. He missed his comfortable bunk on the *Malibu*, and even the mop he had grown so accustomed to using every day. Rubbing the sleep from his eyes, Delmar stood and rolled his sleeping bag into a tight bundle and stored it in his duffle bag.

Not wanting to draw any attention to himself, Delmar pushed the shed door open only slightly. He peered out cautiously, and not seeing anyone around, stepped out into the cool morning air. He tried to reattach the hinge he had broken off last night, but the hole was completely stripped out. An audible growl from his stomach reminded him that he would need to find nourishment soon.

Delmar walked back across the field to the road he had been on the evening before. Traffic was light, but no one stopped to pick him up. He used his right hand as a visor against the bright morning sun and looked to the east. Rising up from the ground only a few miles away was the first sign of the population center he had been heading for. The failing light had prevented him from seeing the buildings last night.

"I'll find something to eat there," Delmar said to himself. "Maybe even a job and a place to stay for a while."

Delmar threw his duffle bag over his shoulder again and started walking at a brisk pace toward the town in the distance. The closer he got, the larger the buildings looked.

It only took a couple of hours before Delmar found himself on the outskirts of a busy population center. He wandered around the streets of the city for what seemed like an eternity. A day and a night passed, then another and another. Every corner he turned led to dead ends and locked doors. He went from business to business asking for work and lodging but met a rebuff at every turn.

He soon came to realize that these people were accustomed to drifters from the spaceport seeking shelter and employment in their establishments. Delmar wondered how many times help had been offered, only to have the kindness returned by being robbed or taken advantage of. So, instead of finding employment and lodging, Delmar slept in whatever vacant corner he could find. A week passed very slowly.

Delmar had lost track of the days while wandering the streets and found himself stranded in an alien city on a Sabbath day of the planet. Most of the businesses were closed or would open later in the day. His meager earnings were dwindling fast, his clothes were filthy, and he was in terrible need of a bath. He was alone and afraid and desperately in need of someone to talk to.

Something inside of him seemed to say run, and he nearly did as a cold sweat trickled down his back. But he had nowhere to run to. He had no idea of how far he had walked, and he knew he could never find his way back to the spaceport now even if he wanted to.

Trying to fight back his fear, Delmar entered a building. He missed the sense of safety afforded by the confining walls of the *Malibu*. He found himself in a small temple to the Unseen One. A service was in progress, so Delmar quietly sat down on the back row so he would not be conspicuous.

He vaguely remembered going to temple as a very young boy. It had seemed dull and lifeless then to an energy-filled eight-year-old boy. Now it was quietly reassuring to him and his heart slowed down from its panicked frenzy. He decided to sit for a while until he could regain his composure.

The Holy One was standing at the front with several parents and their infants. He took each child in turn and held it before the parents while they all prayed together. He spoke about the overseeing eye of the Unseen One watching over each small life. After he had finished with the young families, they returned to their seats and he stepped back behind the Anointed Desk.

Opening his sacred book, the Holy One turned

to a passage and began to read. Delmar did not have a copy to follow along, so he sat still and listened carefully. The Holy One spoke of the faithfulness of the Unseen One and how his faithfulness extended beyond the atmosphere to all those on all of the planets. He spoke personally of the loneliness of space and its inherent terrors. He finished by reminding his flock of the personal care of the Unseen One, even when least apparent.

The Holy One stepped back from the Anointed Desk, and another man took his place. Everyone stood, so Delmar did too. They sang an ancient hymn about the Unseen One and keeping the faith.

The words of the song ended, but the soft soulful music continued as the Holy One prayed the dismissal. When the prayer ended, everyone turned to go. Delmar noticed that the Holy One had disappeared from behind the Desk. Turning to leave, Delmar saw the man was already at the back of the temple speaking with everyone as they were leaving. Delmar could not slip out because of the press of people, so he waited his turn to exit.

When Delmar reached the door, the Holy One shook his hand and looked him in the eye. "I saw you come in during the dedication," he said. "Please stay. We need to talk." Delmar didn't know quite what to do, so he stayed out of courtesy and waited while the Holy One finished greeting his congregation. After the last parishioner had left, the man closed the door and walked to where Delmar was waiting.

"Please come with me," he said. Delmar followed the man to his office. He noticed the man had a decided limp that had not been apparent when he'd been up on the platform.

They entered a small chamber behind the platform. The Holy One removed his robe and hung it on the back of the door. The man motioned for Delmar to sit. Taking his seat behind an old desk, the man let out a sigh and put his feet up on a stool reserved for the purpose.

"That feels better," the man remarked as he removed his shoes. Delmar noticed that his left leg and foot were artificial. The Holy One reached to a table beside him and poured himself a hot cup of tea from a steaming pot. He offered a cup to Delmar, who accepted. It had been a while since he had had anything to eat or drink.

"So, what's your name, young man?" the Holy One asked.

"My name is Delmar Eagleman, your holiness," he replied. The priest flinched, but the boy didn't notice.

"Don't worry about titles, Delmar," the older man replied. "My name is Jake Sender." The man's smile helped Delmar relax, and the tea didn't hurt either.

"I know that you're wondering why I wanted to talk with you," Jake began. "We've never met, but I knew when I saw you that we needed to talk about you."

Delmar was surprised at the directness of the man. In many ways, his manner reminded him of Mr. Hassel.

"I know it sounds presumptuous for me to start out so direct and all," Jake said, "but when you've been out there in space and seen how short a life can be, you learn to be direct."

"You were in space?" Delmar asked.

"Yes, I was. For many years," Jake answered. "I was a trooper chaplain and saw service both in ships and on planets."

"How did you come to be here?" Delmar said.

"About fifteen years ago my unit was detailed to route a Red-tail incursion that had managed to establish a base on one of the marginal planets near the rim. We sent their fleet packing and were starting to do pretty well on the surface when they suddenly and viciously counterattacked."

Jake paused as he recalled the event. He leaned back in his creaking chair and closed his eyes. "There were hordes of them, and they were taking out our infantry with heavier fortified weapons. We were being chewed up and had regrouped to a ridge. We tried to hang on until more troopers could reinforce us. The fighting had quieted down some when the ground opened up and poured out Red-tails through a concealed tunnel into our midst. The fighting was hand to hand and we were hard-pressed."

"Why didn't you use blasters?" the young man asked.

"Blasters are no good when you're that close," Jake answered, leaning back toward the desk. He picked up his teacup and continued. "If you fire at one Red-tail, you'll take out anything around him and behind. A blaster can't tell between friend and foe." Jake paused and took a sip of tea.

"Anyway, the fighting had become hand-to-hand

and we were using our swords. After a time, you just cut and slash at anything red, and there was more than enough of that. Finally, we were able to get the upper hand in the fight, and the few Red-tails left standing took to flight. That was when I found myself lying on the ground with a searing pain in my leg. I looked down and discovered ribbons of flesh where my boot had been. To this day I don't remember what got me, but it sure made a mess."

"Couldn't they repair your leg, or maybe even clone you a new one?" Delmar asked and stared at the artificial leg and foot.

"No, they couldn't," Jake replied. "Whatever got me damaged the nerves and poisoned the blood. They tried to save it but finally had to amputate. They gave me this artificial contraption, and I opted for release. They put me on reserve status with indefinite leave. I'd always liked Mica, even though it's an independent planet, so I came here with my wife and we've been here ever since."

Delmar did not quite know what to say, so he sipped his tea a moment while he thought furiously.

"So," said Jake, filling the void, "that brings us to you. How did a young man like you come to be here alone on Mica?"

Delmar wanted to fabricate some story but found that he couldn't do it. After all the time trying to avoid the subject, he had to tell someone.

"I had a bit of family trouble at home," he began. Pausing to gather his thoughts, he suddenly pictured Mr. Hassel and the scene at the farm. He felt himself choke. Then despite his best effort, the dam holding back weeks of grief and fear broke. He sobbed uncontrollably for a while, and then as he was able, haltingly told the entire tale.

Jake sat patiently and emanated comfort toward the boy as the long story unfolded. When Delmar finished, Jake poured them both some more tea and then spoke. "Delmar," he said quietly. "I have some good news for you."

Delmar looked up from his tea while Jake fished around in his desk and pulled out a folded scrap of paper.

"I received a starmail from an old friend of mine awhile back telling me about a young man he knew." Delmar was confused and wondered what this had to do with him.

"He told me about trouble with the authorities of their planet and how the empress had sent an emissary to straighten it all out. The only sad part was that he couldn't find his young friend to tell him the news."

With that, Jake handed the note to Delmar. He looked at the names at the bottom. It read, "Robert and Agnes Hassel."

Delmar's jaw dropped and he looked up at Jake and then back at the paper. He then took the letter and through tear-blurred vision read it from beginning to end. When he finished, he handed it back to Jake, questions in his eyes.

"You're wondering how I know Robert and Agnes, aren't you?" Jake asked. Delmar nodded. "We served together in the 653rd and were both wounded in the same fight with the Red-tails. Whatever they used on me also got several other troopers, including Robert. He opted out and retired to his home world, and I came here. We've been writing back and forth for years."

Delmar just stared for a moment and then got up and went over to Jake and hugged him. "I wish I had understood why the troopers landed at the farm," Delmar said. "I thought they were arresting the Hassels, or had killed them or something."

"No, Delmar," Jake replied. "Troopers don't work that way. I've never known of a trooper to be anything other than honorable and faithful, especially to another trooper like Robert."

Lifting his leg down with a groan, Jake leaned over his desk and picked up the telephone. "Now I have to make an important call," he said, grinning at the boy.

It was two in the morning when the telephone beside their bed rang. Grumbling sleepily, Robert picked up the instrument while Agnes buried her head under her pillow.

"Hello?" Robert said through a yawn. The voice on the other end spoke excitedly, and it took Robert a moment to comprehend what he was hearing.

"You mean Delmar is right there?" Robert asked. Agnes bolted upright when she heard Delmar's name. Looking at Robert for confirmation, she leapt out of bed and ran for the extension.

"That's right," they heard Jake say. "He's safe and sound, sitting right here in my office!" Delmar's voice was the next one they heard on the line, but Agnes was too overcome by emotions to speak. While Robert continued to talk on the upstairs phone, Agnes sank to her knees in the kitchen. With tears of joy coursing down her cheeks, she thanked the Unseen One.

10

It was decided that Delmar would stay with Jake and his wife, Sherry, for the time being. There were numerous legal ramifications involved concerning Dorn that Mr. Hassel would have to attend to before he and Agnes could possibly come to Mica.

According to the law on Delmar's home planet, he was a ward until he reached the age of twenty-one. Being on an independent planet changed things somewhat. Since Jake was working in the ministry and pastoring a recognized work, the court was able to allow him to act as temporary legal custodian of Delmar. Acting under Mican law, Delmar was eligible for their foster care system, and Jake and his wife were already licensed to do foster work. Before that could be established, however, the guardianship issue on his home world had to be resolved and jurisdiction transferred to the Mican courts.

"So that's the situation for the present," Robert said to Agnes and Mike. All three were sitting around the kitchen table having pie and the ever-present coffee.

"Let me get this straight," Mike replied. "Although we were able to get Dorn's financial aid revoked, because of local laws, we can't get his rights of guardianship nullified?"

"That's right," Robert answered.

"But why?" asked Agnes. "You've proven to the new judge that his brother was a threat to Delmar's safety."

"It doesn't make a difference," Robert replied, disgustedly. "By law, a guardianship can only be changed by the same judge who assigned it."

"But he's been removed from the bench!" exclaimed Agnes.

"Does the law have any exceptions?" asked Mike.

"Only two," Robert answered. "Death of the original judge or death of the current guardian. Fitness for office or dismissal aren't covered, and therefore excluded from consideration."

"Well, I for one don't like it!" snapped Agnes.

"You're not alone," replied her husband. "The new judge didn't like it either."

"Then the law should be repealed or amended," Mike said as he shook his head.

"That was agreed, but it takes time," Robert said evenly. "Even if it could be changed, it wouldn't happen in time to affect Delmar's case."

Billions of miles away, the focus of their discussion

had plans that did not concern the courts. Delmar wasn't letting all of the legal morass surrounding his status interfere with exploring Mica.

To be on a completely different world excited him. Everything was familiar, yet different. Although the major language was the same, and both planets were under the cultural influence of the Axia, there were still many subtle variations.

Today he and Jake were going to visit the Mica Science museum. Up early to be ready, they caught the tunnel transit, which would carry them the 250 miles to the museum. Using a variation of the basic drive system that powered the spaceships, the transit was able to make the trip in twenty minutes.

Anyone observing the train would say it was just a spaceship in a tunnel, and they would essentially be correct. The repulsion field that was a byproduct of the drive caused the transit to float in the tunnel. Because of the limitations created by the atmosphere and the structural integrity of the tunnel itself, the transit had a top speed of only about 800 miles an hour. Although that was standing still compared to the spaceships, it was fast enough to satisfy most transit patrons.

Delmar enjoyed the ride immensely. Although the freighter he'd traveled on had been infinitely faster, there had been no sense of motion. Inertia was canceled by the drive of the transit, but there was still the sound of air in the tunnel. Its whisper conveyed a feeling of the great speed.

Delmar and Jake disembarked from the transit and walked the short distance to the museum entrance. Jake used his pass to borrow a levitation chair so he wouldn't have to walk too much. Their tickets in hand, the two entered the marbled portico of the museum.

Because of the limitation on their time, they had to decide between several different wings and the categories housed in them. Since it was Delmar's first time, Jake allowed the boy to choose.

After deliberating for a minute, the young man chose the wing housing Computer History. Jake raised an eyebrow at Delmar's choice, taking note of Delmar's interests.

Unaware that he was being evaluated, Delmar gave their tickets to the clerk stationed at the entrance, and he and Jake entered the wing. They found themselves in a dark passageway in which the Mican royal seal was displayed. Also displayed were company and school emblems of the various institutions of the planet. A recorded voice played from hidden speakers.

Welcome to the Computer History wing of the Mica Science Museum. Computers and their history are part and parcel with Mican history. Mica has long been reputed as the dominant developmental center of computers and their application. Ships from every corner of the galaxy carry Mican exports to the outer edges of Galactic Axia. Within this wing are housed displays from the earliest mechanical computing machines to the latest developments. You will find guides stationed at various displays to answer your questions. Take your time and enjoy your visit.

Moving slowly along the hallway, Jake and Delmar came to a cased display of ancient rod-and-bead computing devices. On the counter were several hands-on replicas. A small vid-unit screen played a recording of a contest between an experienced user of the device and someone using a handheld computing unit. Of the twenty calculations, the man with the rod-and-bead device won nineteen.

Several children were trying their hand with the replicas and making some progress. A museum guide was teaching them the basics. Jake couldn't help commenting. "It basically teaches the user to think and only does the mechanical working of the numbers," he said.

The guide looked up. "You're right, sir," she replied. "The user has to frame the problem in their mind and plan how to attack it. This device only crunches the numbers."

Farther along, Delmar and Jake came to a display of early electro-mechanical machines. They watched as yet another guide input a simple long division problem into the unit. It immediately started to whirl and thump away. The rhythm it produced caused a couple of visitors to tap their feet. To the humor of his friends, one young man performed an impromptu tap dance to the rhythm of the clack and clatter.

Through the protective glass siding, Delmar

could see gears and cams moving as the machine worked through the problem. Laboriously, it produced one decimal place after another until it displayed the answer. A plaque stated that this machine was very advanced for its day.

The next display was a large alcove almost the size of a tennis court. Occupying almost the entire room was the first known electronic computer. The museum was extremely proud of this unique artifact and had carefully restored it to full operating condition. More than half a dozen museum guides acted as technicians on the giant. Another was explaining the history of the computer to a tour group of schoolchildren.

Delmar and Jake joined the group and listened to the lecture. "The computer you see here is several thousand years old. After being stored and forgotten for much of that time, it was discovered and donated to the museum. We have spent many years researching the history of the unit and restoring it to operation.

"First designed and built by Dr. Frustratus Murphy, this invention represented a major leap in technology. It took him almost fifteen years to perfect the design and make it operational. Numerous times during its development, Dr. Murphy was faced with nearly unsolvable problems, many of which were beyond explanation. His diaries document many instances where everything checked out, but nothing worked. The temptation to quit was a constant companion to Dr. Murphy, but he was determined to complete the work. As he wrote it in his diary, 'I'm going to finish this thing if only to inflict it upon the rest of humanity!'" A ripple of laughter swept through the crowd of listeners.

The guide continued, "The construction of this computer used the latest electronic components of its day. Instead of the circuit components we are all familiar with, Dr. Murphy had to use several thousand glass bulbs filled with inert gas and heated to affect the flow of electrons," she said as she pointed to a glass panel that had been installed on the front of the computer. Through it, her audience could see dozens of the glass bulbs lighting the inside of the machine with their orange glow. "As you may have noticed, it is slightly warmer in this alcove than anywhere else in the museum," stated the guide, continuing her lecture. "The heat generated by this computer is enough to heat the entire wing and would render the computer inoperable unless we constantly cooled it with conditioned air and controlled the humidity level."

"Why does it take so many people to run it?" a small voice asked.

"Actually, it takes only one person to run it. The rest are constantly monitoring the operation of the circuits and making adjustments to keep the circuits balanced. We had a great deal of difficulty making replacement bulbs, and with so many in such a small space, they tend to react in strange ways. Notes found in Dr. Murphy's journals mentioned the need for extra staff to maintain the computer, so we followed his advice." The guide paused and scanned the audience.

"Okay," she said, "we're going to run a sample mathematical problem, and I'd like for you to give it to me," she said, pointing to a little brown-haired girl of about seven. The little girl looked frightened by the approach of the guide and looked at her teacher with an alarmed expression. The teacher smiled at her and nodded.

The girl relaxed noticeably and turned to the guide who had knelt beside her. After a whispered conference, the guide wrote something on a notepad, thanked the girl, and stood up. She returned to her position at the front of the group and spoke to everyone present.

"Okay, here's the problem," she said as she handed the notepad to another technician. The man copied the simple equation onto a blackboard: $33 + 41(x) = 279$. He then handed the note pad to another technician who typed it into the terminal of the computer. He typed for nearly a minute.

"Why is he typing so much?" asked a boy near the front.

"Because he has to translate the problem into the language the computer uses," the first guide answered. "The early computers couldn't understand our spoken language, so they had to use a binary system."

"It sounds like computers were more trouble than they were worth," one of the teachers said.

"They still are!" blurted out Jake before he could

restrain himself. His remark drew a smattering of polite laughter. The technician at the terminal signaled to the tour guide that he was ready.

"Terry says he's ready to start," the guide answered. With that, the technician pushed the enter key. The computer began to buzz and hum. Numerous lights flashed, and the room temperature rose slightly. Somewhere a large ventilation fan whirled to remove the excess heat.

After a minute, a bell rang and a slip of paper ejected from a slot at the main terminal. The technician at the terminal took the slip of paper, read it, and chuckled. He handed the paper to the guide and signaled to the other technicians. Together they started checking other panels and meters on the computer.

The guide raised her eyebrows and went over to the blackboard. "I told you about the problems of keeping this thing cooled and the circuits stable," she said. "Here's why." She wrote the computer's answer on the blackboard beneath the problem: $x =$ peanut butter. The audience broke into laughter.

"As you can see, the early computers weren't very reliable," the guide said, smiling. "I thank you for your interest. We'll have another demonstration in about an hour," she concluded. The schoolchildren and adults alike broke into applause and then headed down the hall to the next display.

For the next couple of hours, Delmar and Jake went from display to display, each exhibit showing either a further development of computer science or one of the many strange failures. The latter were more interesting to Delmar. Mr. Hassel had taught him that we could learn more from our mistakes than from our successes. Several guides explained how the failures actually furthered the understanding of the machines and led to better working designs.

Near the end of the tour, they came to a display showing a picture of an elderly man named Ebilizer. A group of patrons had formed, so the guide present at the display began to speak.

"This display is dedicated to Mica's leading computer scientist—Ebilizer," he began. "As the leading inventor and researcher in computer science that we have today, this man has helped Mica retain its place as the leader in computer development. This gentleman holds no fewer than 137 patents for original design work. Here is a brief biography of our leading scientist."

The guide pressed the play button on a vid-unit and played a short exposé on a display monitor. It covered the early years and projects of the scientist. It detailed the early years of the Ebilizer Institute on Shalimar and introduced the viewers to developments made over the past few years.

When the display finished, the guide spoke again. "If you folks will please follow me," he said and led them into another room. They found themselves in a mock-up of the control room of a space freighter. Wax figures of the royal consort, Captain Mophesto and Empress Ane of Axia, were there. Captain Mophesto was in the control chair, and his wife, Empress Ane, was standing beside him.

"You are now standing in an accurate replica of the bridge on the spacer, *Mary Belle*. As many of you know, this is the private ship registered out of Mica that carries the Empress of Axia and her consort, Captain Mophesto," the guide said. "Installed in this ship is the latest computer developed by Professor Ebilizer, a self-teaching, self-programming computer. Through the sophistication of this computer, Ebilizer has made it possible for the first time in history for a ship to be flown from someplace other than the control seat."

Pausing for the "oohs" and "ahs," the guide continued, "Professor Ebilizer's daughter, Mary Ebilizer, is permanently confined to a bed. Her father's computer enables her to pilot this ship by remote control. Her cabin is over here." He motioned for everyone to come over to a cutaway in the wall of the mock-up where they could see into a dimly lit room. A draped figure of a female with auburn hair lay on the bunk.

"It is by request of Mary Ebilizer that we keep her form draped and the cabin dimly lit," the guide said. "She has graciously presented us with a portrait," he continued, pointing to a framed picture next to the cutaway. It showed a handsome woman in her prime. Auburn waist-length hair and a mischievous smile were her most prominent features.

"Mary Ebilizer is the licensed pilot of the *Mary Belle* and personally flies the ship for the empress and Captain Mophesto. She is renowned for her ability as a pilot and her academic skills in the sciences."

The guide led them through what would have been the passageway to the upper mess of the ship. Many noticed the plaques on the cabin doors identifying the private cabins of the royal couple and the crew.

In what would have been the upper mess was a dark room lit with the stars as seen from above Mica. To one side was the planet Mica, its cities glittering like jewels on a velvet cloth. Suspended as if in orbit was a model of the *Mary Belle*, painted in Mican royal blue. On the side was the royal star, signifying her as the private ship of the empress.

Everyone was silent while they drank in the sight. The guide finally spoke. "It is a great honor that the empress flies a Mican ship," he said proudly. "In recognition of Ebilizer's value to all the people throughout the galaxy, the empress has provided complete research facilities on Shalimar for Ebilizer to continue his valuable work. Captain Mophesto has set up a perpetual trust to endow the Ebilizer Institute with all the funds it needs. He has also gathered leading scientists from throughout the galaxy to work both here on Mica and at the Ebilizer Institute. The breakthroughs come on nearly a daily basis." The audience murmured appreciatively.

Opening an exit door to one side, the guide continued, "We at the museum thank you for your interest and patronage," he said. "As further developments happen with both computers and the chronicles of the *Mary Belle*, we will try to keep our displays up to date for your enjoyment and education. I do hope you've been pleased with our efforts. Thank you again for coming, and please return soon."

The tour ended, and the group applauded. With a last look at the model of the *Mary Belle*, Jake and Delmar followed the other patrons and exited the display. Waiting at the exit was an electric rail shuttle to return the group to the entrance of the museum. Delmar and Jake got on along with the others. After everyone was secure, the operator smoothly geared the shuttle into motion.

Jake returned the levitation chair at the museum entrance, and he and Delmar walked the short distance to the transit station. The twenty-minute ride home seemed much shorter. Delmar was lost in thought and spoke very little.

At home, Sherry called the two to the table. Dinner was most welcome since the men had forgotten to eat lunch. Around mouthfuls of food, Delmar told Sherry all that he had seen that day.

11

It was still early afternoon, but the local watering hole was already busy with its regular customers. The noise in the bar did not diminish as Dorn strode in. Hailed by friends near the back, he stopped at the bar for a bottle and then strutted toward the back, stopping along the way to take a long pull from the bottle. Flopping into a chair at the table, his friends hooted with delight as he took another long pull and downed a third of the beverage. Grinning at them, he came up for air. He belched once and stood the container on the table.

"Hey, Dorn," one of his inebriated friends said, "what'cha doin' tomorra?"

"I gotta go to the social agency about that bratty brother of mine a'gin," he replied.

His words slurred and barely understandable, another of Dorn's drunken friends replied, "Thought you said you got that all took care of last time."

"Thought we did too, but that nosy neighbor got another hearing, so we have to fight again," Dorn answered.

"Then why don't we just go take care of Mr. Nosy?" the first friend suggested, rising unsteadily to his feet.

"Forget about goin' out there," Dorn said and pulled his friend back down. "That old woman of his is a crack shot and almost killed me the last time I was there."

"Well then, we need to get 'im alone, don't we?" one of the other drunken men added. "If she ain't 'round to protect 'im, it should be pretty easy."

"Yeah," replied Dorn. "You're right!" he continued, slapping the man on the back. "If we jump him when he's in the barn, she won't be around in time to bail him out!"

"If some of us create a diversion at the front of the house, she'll never hear you at the barn," the second man said, spittle coursing down his chin and onto the front of his shirt.

"Then what're we waitin' for?" asked the first friend. "Let's get goin.'" They all rose unsteadily to their feet and with bottles in hand, staggered out the door.

Robert Hassel had just finished repairing the back fence and was on his way to the barn when he heard cars slowing on the road. Hurrying toward the structure, his mind raced ahead, concerned about what could be going on. He and Agnes had been a little jumpy since the trouble with Delmar's brother some time back.

Entering the barn to drop off his tools, Robert's eyes did not have adequate time to adjust to the dim interior. Suddenly, something hit him hard on the side of his head. As he rolled across the floor, he heard a rifle shot resound from near the house.

Robert tried to regain his feet, but someone caught him in the jaw with a mind-numbing blow. Rolling again from the impact, Robert felt two men grab him from either side and hoist him to his feet.

Although Robert still couldn't see his attackers, the rancid smell of stale alcohol was strong. He sensed someone staring at him nose-to-nose and felt the spray of spittle as the man spoke.

"Old man, you better leave off causin' me trouble or you might not be so lucky next time!" the guttural voice said.

Robert's mind whirled, but he knew he recognized the voice. Suddenly someone punched him hard in the stomach and threw him hard against a wall. Slumped against the wall, he looked up at a shadowy figure standing over him just in time to see the barrel of a small caliber handgun aimed at him. He rolled to his left but not before he saw the flash from the barrel. A slug tore into his leg. Struggling around again, Robert saw the figure of Delmar's brother towering over him, the smoking gun still in his hand. "I knew I recognized that voice," he said. A vicious kick to his head sent Robert into unconsciousness.

Back at the house, Agnes pumped another round into the chamber of her rifle and maintained her aim on the driver of the first car in her driveway. With her sights trained on the man, she thought that Robert wouldn't like having to fix another fence post. The driver just sat there with his hands raised while he stared down the business end of her rifle barrel.

"Now git off my property!" Agnes said, her voice hard and flat. The driver reached down nervously and fumbled with the starter before getting the ground car to start. The blue car and the red one behind it backed out onto the road, Agnes' sights unwavering on the driver. As they roared off down the road away from the farm, she lowered the gun and clicked it on the safety.

Picking up the spent brass, Agnes walked back inside and stood her rifle beside the door where she could get to it easily. She glanced at the clock and wondered where Robert could be. She knew he was fixing that back fence, but the commotion up front should have brought him running.

Looking out the back door, she scanned the fields for her husband. Not seeing him, she went back to the front door, picked up her rifle, and ran down the back steps toward the barn, the gun cocked and ready.

Not far from the Hassel farm, the pair of cars skidded to a stop on the loose gravel road and picked up three men who had been hiding in the brush. "Did you get 'im?" asked the driver of the blue car.

"Yeah, we got 'im good," answered one of the men as he reloaded his pistol from an ammo pouch on his belt. His breath came in short, rapid spurts, caused by the exertion of running across the open field.

"Well, that old lady gave us trouble up front and just missed me," the driver said through a wicked grin framed by crooked teeth.

"You're lucky," said another. "You should'a seen the fence post she blasted!" A couple of the others had a good laugh at this. The driver grumbled something and threw the ground car into gear. Gravel sprayed as both vehicles sped down the lane and back toward town.

Not long after the attack, the siren of a hover-ambulance wailed along the country road. The vehicle pulled into the Hassel farm and settled down near the back porch. The medics bailed out and ran toward the barn. Agnes met them, and together they entered the structure. Within minutes, they emerged, carrying a litter between them. They loaded it into the ambulance, helped Agnes into the back, and shut the door. Siren screaming, they raced toward town and the emergency team waiting at the hospital.

The insistent ringing of the phone woke Jake and Sherry. He fumbled for the instrument and sleepily answered it. What he heard caused him to sit straight up in bed.

Sherry, alerted by her husband's sudden motion,

sat up, and at Jake's insistence picked up the extension in the adjoining room.

"Okay, now repeat it again for Sherry," she heard Jake say to whoever was on the line. Then she heard Agnes' voice.

"I wanted to call you and tell you that Robert has been attacked and shot. He's unconscious but will recover," she said evenly.

"Any idea who did this?" Sherry asked.

"As I was telling Jake," Agnes continued, "at the same time he was shot, I was having trouble with some drunks in the front yard. We think they might be friends of Delmar's brother, Dorn."

"How is Robert now?" asked Jake.

"They still have him in surgery to repair damage from the gunshot," Agnes replied. Jake could hear Agnes' voice break just a little. *Probably just these old transmitters*, he thought. "He was lucky," Agnes continued. "The bullet hit one of the reinforcing plates in his thigh and was deflected away from the artery."

"Did Robert say anything?" Sherry asked.

"No," Agnes replied. "He was unconscious when I found him in the barn, and was still out when they took him into surgery. The emergency room doctor said someone roughed Robert up pretty bad. He has a concussion and some broken ribs," she added.

"Do you want us to come?" Jake asked, Sherry echoing his question.

"You might have to," Agnes answered. "The doctors aren't sure how long Robert may remain unconscious or in the hospital. The next hearing is tomorrow, which can be postponed for ten days. But if Robert can't be there, I don't know what we'll do."

"We're on our way," Jake said. "You take care and contact the liaison officer at Jasper Station. He'll be able to help you until we get there, which should be seven or eight days."

"Okay," replied Agnes, her voice breaking a little.

Jake and Sherry could hear a commotion over the phone. "Listen, I've got to go," said Agnes. "The doctors need to talk to me about Robert."

"Goodbye," said Jake and Sherry together. "And Agnes?"

"Yes, Jake?"

"Our prayers."

"Thanks."

After hanging up the phone, Sherry returned to the bedroom and quickly dressed. While she went down the hall to Delmar's room to tell the boy the bad news, Jake made a call to his ministerial assistant to have him cover the temple services. "Shot!" Jake heard Delmar exclaim from down the hallway. "Is he alright?"

Jake put a call through to the liaison officer at the spacefield. While he waited for the second call to connect, Jake considered his options and knew what he had to do—reactivate his reserve trooper status.

A short time later, a military flitter, a low-level sky cab, settled down outside of their home and Jake, Sherry, and Delmar got in. Racing only a few hundred feet above the city streets, it was soon at the spacefield and parked near a fast cruiser painted Axia black. The three ran up the ramp and the hatch closed.

The sub-lieutenant on duty greeted them. "Welcome aboard, Major Sender, Mrs. Sender, Mr. Eagleman," he said. "Let me show you to your quarters." They followed the man down the passageway as the ship lifted off the pad and accelerated into the night.

The presiding judge gaveled the hearing to order at 9 a.m. Motioning the parties forward, he noticed that while the social agency had two lawyers, the petitioning party had only an old woman flanked by two troopers.

The judge was perplexed by this and asked, "Where is the petitioner, Mr. Robert Hassel?"

"He is currently in the hospital recovering from a gunshot wound and a concussion and remains unconscious, Your Honor," one of the troopers, a lieutenant, answered. "Mr. Hassel was the victim of an attack at his farm."

Agnes was amazed to see the original regional director, Prudence Hornbeck, sitting with the two agency lawyers. Agnes asked how this was possible and discovered that the director's job was secured by appointment, and that she had resumed her position after a short probationary period.

"Do you intend to withdraw the petition?" asked one of the lawyers representing the social agency.

"No, we do not," replied the lieutenant, curtly. "We petition the court to grant a ten-day extension of these proceedings until either Mr. Hassel is able to represent the petition, or his role is assigned to another competent party."

"This is most unusual!" protested one of the agency attorneys. "I move that we proceed as scheduled." The judge thought for a moment. He didn't care for lawyers who tried to run his court for him.

"Overruled," replied the judge. "I hereby grant the petitioner a ten-day extension on these hearings pending appointment of a substitute petitioner. However, these hearings will proceed as scheduled ten days hence whether or not the substitute has been qualified."

"Oh, by the way," the judge said, addressing the lead attorney for the social agency. "I will decide what is and what is not unusual during these proceedings. Is that clear?"

"Yes, Your Honor," cowed the lawyer.

Banging his gavel again, the judge added, "Case postponed." The court clerk announced the next case on the docket and Agnes and the two troopers left the courtroom.

"Will Jake be here in time?" Agnes asked the lieutenant. "The doctors said Robert is now in a mild coma, and they aren't sure when he'll come out of it."

"I understand that Major Sender, his wife, and Mr. Eagleman are already en route," he replied. "They should make it with a day to spare."

"I hope so," Agnes replied. "I can't stand those hotshot lawyers."

"Don't worry," the other trooper said. "Everything is being done as quickly as possible."

"Agnes?" the lieutenant asked. "Do you want to go home or back to the hospital?"

"I want to be with Robert, but I probably should go out to the farm to take care of the chores," she answered.

"Don't worry about the farm, ma'am," said the other trooper. "Several of the men have volunteered to take care of it for you so you can stay at the hospital with your husband."

"Thank you!" Agnes said wearily.

The troopers escorted Agnes to their waiting ground car. As they drove away from the courthouse, the lieutenant considered the mess that had developed and determined to put a call through to Mike Azor as soon as he could get back to the office.

———

Aboard the fast cruiser *Intrepid*, Jake consulted with the ship legal officer. "So that's the situation as I understand it," said Jake as he summed up the lengthy explanation. "Somehow that social agency is still side-stepping the laws of the Axia with their policies."

"It's obvious they don't play by the rules," the legal officer commented. "Using lawyers and the precedent of earlier rulings should both be prohibited in this kind of proceeding."

"Since when did the law ever get in their way?" Jake replied. "In spite of the efforts of Mike Azor using an Imperial directive, that agency still honors its own policies above that of Axia law."

"Well, I might have an idea, but I have to talk to someone first," replied the legal officer.

"Then I'll leave you to it and get back to my wife," Jake said as he rose. "Let me know if you have any luck."

Jake left the officer's cabin and returned to Sherry and Delmar. The legal officer called the trooper operating the comm and put in a request to contact Mike Azor. The last he knew, Mike was still en route back to Shalimar. If his luck held, he could intercept him in time.

Mike was relaxing in his cabin with a good book aboard a regular transport ship when the intercom buzzed.

"Yes, what is it?" he said into the wall unit.

"We have two priority messages for you, sir," the comm trooper reported.

"On my way," answered Mike. He laid down the book and shrugged into his uniform jacket. Winding his way through the passageways to the comm center, Mike was soon there.

"Here are your messages," the comm trooper said, handing two envelopes to Mike. Mike thumb-printed the register and then opened his messages.

Scanning the two slips of paper, Mike noted that one had come from the liaison lieutenant back on Erdinata, and the second from another ship. He read both messages quickly and then spoke to the trooper. "I need to speak to the captain immediately," he said.

"I thought you might when both came in with priority status," the trooper replied. "I signaled the captain, and she's waiting for you on the bridge."

"Thank you," Mike said. Leaving the comm center, he went forward to the bridge. The captain looked up from where she was consulting with another crewmember and came over to meet Mike.

"Trooper Thomas notified me that you were on your way," she said. "What can I do for you?"

"As you know, I just received two priority messages," Mike began. "Both messages deal with the reason Our Lady sent me out here in the first place. It looks as if I need to reinstitute the Imperial Directive and return to Erdinata as quickly as possible."

"I thought that might be the case," the captain replied. "I had my second lay in the new heading in preparation for such an event."

"How soon can we get there?" Mike asked.

"Running in the low red zone on the throttle all the way will get us there in about nine or ten days," she answered. "She's an old boat, so we don't have the speed of the newer ships."

"Well, we better do it. Time is of the essence," Mike replied. "With your permission, I need to send several messages to the parties involved, as well as to Our Lady."

"Go ahead," the captain answered. "Tell the comm trooper to give it priority status."

"Thank you, Captain," returned Mike. As he

turned toward the comm cabin, he heard the captain issue orders for a course and speed change. Entering the comm center, Mike felt the slight vibration of the deck as the ship strained forward with everything she had.

12

Agnes and the liaison lieutenant watched the cruiser touch down on the designated landing pad. The hatch opened. The ramp extended and the captain came out first according to safety protocol. Signaling to those in the ship, the captain stepped aside and waited while guards were posted. Then came the passengers who, together with the ship's captain, approached the waiting couple.

Delmar broke away from the group and ran straight to Agnes. Emotions ran high there on the tarmac—emotions of tears and joy, laughter and crying. Agnes could not contain her excitement as Delmar lifted her up in his arms, then hugged her fiercely, not wanting to release the woman he considered his new mother.

Words alone could not express Agnes' thoughts, but she knew she had to try. "We thought we'd lost you, boy," Agnes said to Delmar. "We looked everywhere, but . . ."

Agnes began to cry just as Delmar pulled her close to him again. "I know," he said. "I just didn't understand what was happening at the farm. I got scared when I saw the ships and the troopers, and all the police. I panicked," he said sincerely. "I'm sorry. I should have known better."

Agnes buried her face in Delmar's chest again, staining his shirt with her tears. "Oh well, all that's behind us now," she said. "And we have a long road ahead of us." After another long hug, the two parted and introductions were made all around.

Taking leave of his passengers, the captain ambled toward the operations building. Those remaining walked casually to the liaison building where they gathered around a table laden with refreshments.

After everyone was served, the liaison lieutenant spoke up, "I know you are all anxious to visit, but unfortunately we have a hearing tomorrow and had better be ready."

"I received your brief on the ship on the way in," replied Jake. "I still feel like something is missing. Could you please bring all of us up to date?"

"Certainly," replied the lieutenant. "With the permission of Agnes, I have temporarily assumed the role of petitioner so she can be with Robert."

"How's he doing?" asked Delmar, anxiously.

"When I left there an hour ago, there'd been no change," Agnes replied. "He's stable and recovering from his injuries, but he's still in a mild coma."

"Have they caught whoever attacked him?" Sherry asked.

"Not yet," answered the other trooper with Agnes. "They have no real leads, except the suspicions of Agnes. They found no evidence beyond the bullet in Robert's leg. Efforts to match the ballistics of the bullet with any known weapon have been fruitless. We suspect the attack on Robert and the confrontation with Agnes at the front of the house are related, but can't prove anything. What would be ideal would be Robert's testimony or identification of his attacker, but he's still comatose."

"Okay, what about the hearing?" Jake asked.

"It convenes at 9 a.m. tomorrow, sir," the lieutenant replied. "The guardianship issue is up for review with a petition by Robert to have it changed. By law, there can be no change without the death of the judge or the original guardian. The social agency is flexing its muscles again and has two lawyers presenting their case. How Robert ever got the court to consider his petition is beyond me. Normally, it would be rejected by the court since it doesn't challenge the current law."

"What about the references Robert made to the Imperial Directive that Mike Azor enforced?" Jake asked.

"Unless that's reactivated by Mike or the empress, we haven't a leg to stand on," the lieutenant answered. "I sent a message to Mike and he's returning as soon as he can. The best estimate is tomorrow evening, which may be too late."

"Then we'll just have to wing it tomorrow," Jake

replied. "I have an idea that may stall things, but I have to make some calls tonight before I'll know if it'll work."

"Then it sounds like we can't make any more progress here," the lieutenant said. "Why don't we break off and let you all go see Robert? We all need some rest."

"Sounds good to us," Jake replied. The meeting adjourned. Agnes, Delmar, and the Senders took a ground transport to the hospital while the lieutenant and his assistant shuttled home.

Arriving at the hospital, they were ushered into Robert's room. It unnerved Delmar to see Mr. Hassel lying there without response. Agnes put an arm around Delmar and they stood holding each other for several minutes. Jake and Sherry slipped out quietly to let them have some privacy.

Later, Agnes and Delmar rejoined the Senders in the waiting room and the four continued on to the Hassel farm. As they passed his old home, Delmar noticed that his brother was having a party of some sort. It disappointed the boy but did not surprise him to see how badly the farm had deteriorated since he had run away so many months ago.

Agnes showed everyone to their rooms and went to bed. Sherry suspected that Agnes needed someone, so she quietly let herself in to comfort her old friend. Delmar went out to check the farm buildings and stock while Jake used the telephone. Calling some fellow ministers, Jake inquired about their experiences with the social agency and the courts.

While they talked, an idea formed in Jake's mind: an idea of how to handle the court in the morning.

The morning weather was beautiful outside the windows of the courtroom, but the banging of the gavel brought everyone's attention back inside. The presiding judge called the parties forward and noticed that along with Mrs. Hassel and the trooper lieutenant, there now stood a trooper chaplain in full dress uniform, major insignia on his collar. Trooper chaplains were rare enough that the judge had trouble not staring at the combination of rank insignia and a clerical collar together. The two attorneys also noticed the judge's reaction.

"Mrs. Hassel?" asked the judge. "Who is this gentleman, and why is he here?"

"This, Your Honor, is Trooper Chaplain Major Jake Sender," she responded. "He is here to represent Mr. Hassel in the petition proceedings. By previous order of this court, he is temporary foster guardian of Delmar Eagleman and as such has legal standing in these petition proceedings." Jake was pleased that Agnes had gotten through the prepared speech flawlessly, despite everything she'd been through over the past two weeks.

"Major Sender, please approach the bench and present your credentials as substitute petitioner," the judge called. Jake approached the bench and handed the bailiff his service reactivation papers, along with copies of his ordination and the court decree concerning his status with Delmar. He also included Robert's latest medical report. The judge reviewed the papers and handed them to the court clerk for copying and entry into the court record.

"Your Honor, we object," interjected one of the social agency lawyers. "We insist that the original petitioner be present or the case be dismissed."

"Objection overruled," the judge answered without looking up. "May I remind counsel that I have previously ruled a petitioner representative may assume the case in light of Mr. Hassel's continued disability?"

Turning back to Jake he said, "I find all your papers in order, Chaplain Sender. I rule that you may represent Mr. Hassel in these proceedings."

"Thank you, Your Honor," Jake replied. He retrieved his papers from the clerk, who had finished copying them and returned to his seat beside Agnes.

As was normal in such proceedings, the social agency opened with its rebuttal to the already presented petition. The first attorney for the agency began by stating why the petition should be dismissed. Referring to the law concerning the designation of guardianship, he attacked the petition based on failure to address either of the two exception clauses.

Hearing this plan of attack, Jake smiled to himself and bided his time. The attorney brought forth the agency's own reports concerning the suitability of Dorn to continue as guardian of his brother, Delmar. Adding to the preponderance of papers, he then entered the agency report concerning the interference by the Hassels. Again, Jake smiled. Concluding his statements by reiterating the agency's assertions, the lawyer finally sat down.

The judge then called the petitioner representative to present their petition and any objections to the rebuttal. Jake rose and stood before the bench. "Your Honor," he began, "the petition is already recorded in the court record, so I will summarize it. The petitioner requests that the designation of guardianship of Delmar Eagleman be reviewed in light of events that transpired in recent months. The petitioner is aware of the limitations of the law but, in light of the Imperial Directive, asks that reconsideration of the suitability of Dorn Eagleman as guardian be reviewed. The fact that these proceedings are happening at all, and that the social agency is defending its original assessment concerning guardianship when the law would normally cause the petition to be dismissed, strengthens our argument that there is sufficient cause and grounds for the court to entertain our petition."

The courtroom erupted in murmurs, and the lead attorney rose and objected to Jake's assertions. The judge gaveled the courtroom quiet and overruled the objection.

"The court recognizes the assertions of the petitioner and rules that they are sufficient to support the petition," the judge announced. "Petitioner, please continue."

"Thank you, Your Honor," Jake replied. "As petitioner representative, I would also bring to the court's attention that the agency has submitted prior testimony and rulings as precedent to its request for dismissal. In as much as the court admitted such testimony and the cited reports, the petitioner requests that equal strength and stature be granted to any prior testimony or rulings we may wish to cite."

Again, the courtroom was abuzz while the lead attorney strenuously objected. The judge leaned back in his overstuffed chair and thought for a minute. Turning to his monitor of the court record, he reviewed the opening statement of the agency counsel.

Finally, he turned back and faced the courtroom. "It is the opinion of this court that the petitioner will be granted the same right to cite previous testimony and rulings that the agency has been given by the admission of their arguments into the record. The objection is overruled."

The courtroom again erupted and it took the judge several tries to silence it. Order restored, the lead lawyer requested permission to approach the bench. "We request a recess until this afternoon in order to consider the petitioner's position and secure needed records and witnesses."

"Does the petitioner representative have any objection?" the judge asked.

Jake was perplexed by the tactic of the agency but could find no solid reason to object to the delay. "No, Your Honor," he answered. "We have no objection if the petitioner is granted the same privilege."

"Granted," agreed the judge. "This court is in

recess until two o'clock this afternoon," he stated, pounding his gavel. Everyone stood as the judge left the room. Jake, Agnes, and the lieutenant left the courtroom, followed by Delmar and Sherry.

Gathered around the conference table at the liaison office, they began to plan their strategy for that afternoon. "I was surprised the judge accepted their use of prior testimony and precedents," the liaison lieutenant said.

"I was hoping he would," Jake replied. "I know it goes against Axia law, but by opening it up in court, it allows us to fully examine their records and challenge their assessments."

"What about your argument that their objection to our petition grants us legitimacy?" Agnes asked. "Wasn't that rather risky?"

"Yes, it was," replied Jake. "But I had to discern the playing field of the court. By admitting their objections, they leave themselves open to the suspicion that they have something to hide.

"What do you think they're up to with this recess?" the lieutenant asked.

"I think for one they're buying time," answered Jake. "For another, I think they're going to put Dorn on the stand to parrot their pretty lines."

"How do you plan to deal with it?" Agnes asked.

"By fighting fire with fire," answered Jake. "I might put Delmar and you on the stand." The room became suddenly quiet as they all looked over at Delmar, who had remained silent so far.

To break the tension, the lieutenant spoke up, "It would help if we had some of the local police officers ready to testify," he said. "I'll contact the chief and get him to release those men."

"Good idea," answered Jake.

"Speaking of good ideas," Agnes interjected. "I think we should break for lunch." Her suggestion was met with enthusiasm, and the group went their separate ways.

Agnes, Delmar, and Sherry drove to the hospital to visit Robert while Jake stayed at the office to make more calls. Checking in at the nurses' station, they learned that Robert had become more restless and was showing signs that he was coming out of the coma.

When they entered his room, it was obvious what the nurses had meant. The sound of Agnes' voice caused Robert to stir even more, and he began to moan. Agnes talked to him, but he was still too deeply comatose to respond to her voice. After a few more minutes, the three excused themselves and rode the lift to the hospital cafeteria. The afternoon session in court was quickly approaching. They ate fast and with little conversation.

Again, the judge gaveled the court to order. Jake noticed that the agency lawyers had indeed brought Dorn to court. He looked terribly hung over. Sitting behind Agnes were the police officers that had been involved in the disturbances weeks ago, both at the Eagleman farm and later at the Hassel farm. According to protocol, the judge allowed the agency to state its case first.

Citing their first evaluations of the Eagleman home, the lawyers painted a pretty picture of Dorn and his ability to act as Delmar's guardian. They referred to the very report Robert had read months earlier in the director's office about the "thorough investigation" conducted after the Hassels' first allegations. Agnes' actions defending her home from Dorn and later the director were brought up as evidence to discredit the petition. As further support, they put Dorn on the stand to deliver the obviously prepared speech he had hastily been taught.

The lead attorney for the agency cited several agency policies in defense of their actions and strenuously demanded that the petition be dismissed. All through the orchestrated presentation, Jake did not offer one objection. He was carefully trying to have objections associated with the agency lawyers and not the petitioner. Finally, the attorney retired and the judge turned the floor to Jake.

"Thank you, Your Honor," Jake began smoothly. "First of all, I want to bring the court's attention to the findings of the hearing by the Imperial Directive representative concerning the guardianship of Delmar Eagleman." Before Jake could continue, the lead attorney objected. He claimed that the directive was not in force at the time of the original guardianship hearing and thus inadmissible.

The judge considered the objection for a moment. "The objection is sustained," he said. "Since this hearing is not under Axia Directive, references to such are inadmissible." Agnes gasped, but Jake did not seem concerned.

"I accept the restraints imposed by the agency's objections," he replied. He noticed the judge frown a little. His agreement caught the agency attorney off guard. Instead, Jake turned and faced Dorn in the witness chair, who under Axia law was still open to cross-examination.

Carefully, Jake questioned the man and got him to elaborate on his previous testimony. Once the man's tongue was loosened, he went into great detail about all the trouble Delmar had caused and the suffering he had sustained as the guardian. After embellishing the details of his visit to the Hassel farm, Dorn was dismissed from the stand. The agency attorneys were obviously nervous.

Jake then called on Agnes to offer her testimony concerning Dorn's visit and her actions. She brought up the point of how the man had been in a drunken rage, and blushingly quoted the profanities Dorn had screamed at her. The agency's lead attorney rose to object, but one glance from the judge silenced him.

Next Jake called on the first police officer that had handled Dorn's complaint against Agnes. He related how intoxicated Dorn had been and told the court about the visit he'd had with the Hassels, which confirmed Agnes' testimony. Jake asked the officer to recall his visit to the Eagleman farm the day the agency attacked the Hassels. The officer told about what he had seen at the Eagleman farm, especially noting that Dorn's bandaged arm had been unharmed when Dorn had filed a complaint against his delinquent brother the previous day and reported that Delmar had been missing for several days instead of several months. He then related the events that occurred at the Hassel farm, including the involvement of the troopers.

Jake waited for the agency lawyer to object, but the man was clearly hesitant. Thanking the officer, Jake allowed him to return to his seat.

Summarizing the testimony offered and pointing out the inconsistencies of the agency's version, Jake gave his closing argument. He was careful to emphasize the conflicting testimony given by Dorn and restated the man's inebriated condition, both past and present.

After Jake sat down, the judge announced that rebuttals would proceed tomorrow when court reconvened at 9 a.m. Banging his gavel, the judge adjourned the court.

Jake waited for the press of spectators to leave and thanked the officers for their help. He herded the group out the door and to the waiting transportation.

At the liaison office, Jake and the lieutenant brainstormed for the next day's session. Agnes, Sherry, and Delmar took the shuttle to the hospital to be with Robert.

As they went over the points they had made that day, the phone interrupted Jake and the lieutenant. Answering it, the lieutenant learned that the ship carrying Mike Azor had been damaged by a Red-tail attack and would be delayed a week, maybe more.

"Well, there goes our ace in the hole," the lieutenant said. Somewhat deflated by the news, they continued to go over their strategy for the next day. Weary from hashing over the information, they got up and slowly walked to their ground car. They discovered that Sherry and Delmar were just returning and looked very excited.

"Robert is waking up!" Sherry announced to the men. "Agnes is with him right now."

"That's good news!" replied Jake. "Is he able to talk?"

"Only a little bit," Sherry answered. "When he found out you were here, he wanted to see you immediately."

"Well, I guess we'd better get over there!" Jake said. The liaison lieutenant excused himself while the others raced to the hospital. There, Robert told Jake who had attacked him in the barn and what they had said. After he finished, Robert drifted back to sleep, and the doctor ushered the visitors out of the room.

"He's had enough for one day," the doctor said. He allowed Agnes to stay the night while the others returned to the Hassel farm.

At the farm, Sherry cooked dinner and made coffee while Delmar checked the outbuildings and animals. Jake sat in the front room to think and to rest his leg. He reviewed all of the testimony again and was able to see their weak points, as well as their strengths.

Sherry soon called him to dinner. Entering the kitchen, Jake saw that Delmar was already finished with the chores. They sat down to the food and, after invoking the blessing of the Unseen One, made quick work of it.

Having eaten, they talked themselves out. Jake excused himself to place a call while the others went to bed.

13

Early the next morning they met with the lieutenant before going to the courthouse. Agnes met them there and reported that Robert was still improving, though slowly. Jake was heartened by the news but it would do little good today.

Although he had a way to break the case open completely, it wouldn't work without Robert's testimony. All he could hope for now was to hang on as both sides went through their rebuttals. Jake knew that this was the strong suit of the agency lawyers, and he was not looking forward to it.

The judge gaveled the court into session. Jake noticed that the attorneys looked very pleased with themselves and wondered what they had up their sleeves. Again, the agency led off the proceedings.

"I recall Delmar Eagleman to the stand," announced the lead attorney. Delmar came forward and sat in the witness chair. The judge reminded him that he was still under oath. The lawyer questioned

Delmar as to his age and current place of residence. As soon as Delmar stated that he was eighteen and staying at the Hassel farm, the attorney stopped him. The attorney then turned and addressed the court.

"Your Honor," he began, "let the record show that this boy is still a legal minor. Also, let the record show that he is now back in Erdinata jurisdiction and no longer on Mica. By our law and the previous rulings of this court, he is required to be under the guardianship of his brother or that of the Reverend Sender if he remains on Mica. Inasmuch as the boy is in violation of the conditions of the court, I present a warrant for his arrest for delinquency and request that he be taken into custody immediately."

The attorney handed the warrant papers to the judge and then continued, "I further move that any testimony he has offered in these proceedings be disallowed."

Everyone in the courtroom sat in shocked silence while the judge looked at the papers. After deliberating for a minute, the judge banged his gavel and ordered the bailiff to take Delmar into custody. The stunned boy was handcuffed, led to the back of the courtroom, and seated between two officers.

The agency attorney again addressed the court, "I call Mrs. Agnes Hassel to the stand." Agnes looked nervously at Jake, who nodded. She then rose and took the stand.

"Is your name Agnes Hassel?" the lead attorney asked.

"Yes, it is," she answered.

"Are you presently sheltering Delmar Eagleman in your home?" he asked.

"Yes," she said quietly.

"I hereby submit to the court a warrant for the arrest of Agnes Hassel for harboring a fugitive," the attorney announced as he handed the papers to the judge. Reviewing the papers, the judge again banged his gavel, and soon Agnes was led away in handcuffs to sit on the back row. The courtroom was stunned. The agency attorneys and Dorn looked pleased.

Jake was shocked by the action taken by the agency. Rising to his feet, he requested an hour recess. The judge looked at the agency attorneys, who had no objection. He granted the recess and adjourned the court.

Jake, Sherry, and the lieutenant left the courtroom and drove silently to the hospital. They were shown into Robert's room, but he had lapsed again and was unresponsive. Leaving Sherry at the hospital, the two men talked while they drove back to court.

"That move this morning pretty much shuts down the petition, doesn't it?" asked the lieutenant.

"I'm afraid so," Jake replied. "I was hoping Robert would be in condition to testify, but that's out. With Agnes arrested, and Delmar in custody, we have no case. They totally undermined our position."

The two separated, with the lieutenant going to the liaison office and Jake returning to court. Jake took his place as the sound of the gavel called the court to order. The judge asked the agency attorneys if they were finished.

The lead attorney rose and began his summation. He again attacked the original petition and the motives behind it. Pointing at Agnes, who still sat handcuffed in the back of the courtroom, he questioned the character of the petitioners and suggested that they were responsible for Delmar's criminal behavior. He concluded by demanding that the petition be dismissed and requested prosecution of the Hassels.

As he took his seat, it was obvious that he was confident of his position, and Jake could easily see why. The judge called for the representative of the petitioner to give his rebuttal. Jake stood slowly to his feet and approached the bench.

"Your Honor," he began, but did not get to continue. The courtroom was plunged into momentary darkness as the sun was blocked out. Almost immediately afterwards, a commotion developed at the back of the courtroom and a trooper-first entered, followed by several troopers in battle dress. Mike Azor strode to the front of the room and took up a position before the bench and handed the judge a sheaf of documents.

"Let it be recorded that these proceedings are now under the jurisdiction of Imperial Directive. All prior testimony and precedents are to be disallowed, and only current testimony and evidence will be permitted." Mike turned toward the judge, who rose and offered Mike his chair behind the bench. Mike nodded and addressed the court.

"This court is hereby in recess for ten minutes."

Mike and the judge then adjourned to the judge's chambers for a hurried conference. The judge apprised Mike of all the proceedings, including the warrants against Delmar and Agnes.

Outside in the courtroom, Jake conferred quickly with two troopers. The courtroom again came to order when Mike and the judge both resumed the bench, with Mike sitting in the center seat and the judge behind him to the left.

"This court is now in session," Mike intoned. "The bailiff will release the prisoners and allow them to return to their seats." Delmar and Agnes were released and resumed their places behind Jake.

"Further, the warrants are disallowed," Mike announced. The attorneys for the agency started to object. Instead, Mike motioned for them to stay seated.

"Will the petitioner representative and the agency lead counsel approach the bench?" Mike requested. Jake and the agency lead lawyer came forward.

"Will both parties please state their position briefly without reference to previous rulings?" Mike asked.

The attorney for the agency went first. "We contend that, according to the law, the petition be disallowed because it does not address either of the allowable grounds for changing guardianship," he said.

Mike looked at Jake. Jake said, "It is the position of the petitioner that the guardianship be reviewed as to competence of the guardian."

Mike thought for a moment and said, "Does the petitioner have any other grounds for requesting this hearing?" Jake knew then that their effort would be disallowed.

"As petitioner representative, I don't, sir," answered Jake quietly.

"But I do!" said a raspy voice from the back of the courtroom. Everyone turned, and there, wrapped in a hospital robe, stood Robert Hassel, supported by two troopers and followed by Sherry. Agnes immediately jumped up and ran to Robert, taking station by his side. The troopers continued to lead Robert to the front of the courtroom and helped seat him at the table. Jake excused himself from before the bench and went over to Robert. After a quick conference, he approached the bench.

"Sir," Jake began, "the original petitioner has asked me to continue as his spokesman and hereby amends his petition."

"What is the amendment?" Mike asked.

"That the rights of guardianship of Dorn Eagleman be revoked on the grounds that he will be unable to care for his legal ward, Delmar Eagleman," Jake replied.

"Would you explain yourself?" Mike asked, looking at Robert. Robert tried to stand but gave up and sat back down.

"With pleasure, sir," he rasped. "I hereby accuse Dorn Eagleman of assault and attempted murder of myself in an effort to prevent our petition from being considered." Robert almost toppled over but Agnes and Sherry caught him. Mike glared at Dorn, who had turned ashen.

"Do you offer a sworn statement to that affect and personal testimony to support it?" Mike asked Robert.

Robert raised his right hand. "Yes sir, I do," he said. The courtroom went silent for a moment and then erupted. Mike gaveled it quiet.

"The bailiff will take Dorn Eagleman into custody," Mike ordered. The bailiff complied.

Turning back to the attorney for the agency, Mike asked, "Do you wish to object to the petition and its amendment?"

"No, sir, we do not," replied the lawyer. "Furthermore, we withdraw our position if a means can be found around the exception statutes in the law."

"I think I know a way," replied Mike. "Would you gentlemen, along with Delmar and Agnes, please join me in the judge's chambers?" Both men agreed. Mike recessed the court for ten minutes, and they followed Mike into the judge's chambers.

A few minutes later, they returned, and Mike turned the court back over to the judge. "It is the considered opinion of this court and the parties involved that the guardianship of Delmar Eagleman be assigned to Robert and Agnes Hassel. This is allowable under the Imperial statute covering trooper personnel who have not reached their majority," the judge said. Turning toward Delmar, he asked, "Do you, Delmar Eagleman, hereby state your intention to apply for entrance into the Galactic Axia Trooper Service?"

"Yes, sir, I do," Delmar answered.

"Does the ward have a sponsor, which is required under the Axia statute?" the judge asked.

"Yes, sir, he does," said Jake, standing.

"Is this decision in agreement with the new guardians?" the judge asked.

"Yes, sir, it is," Agnes answered for both of them. Robert nodded his agreement.

"Then it is the judgment of this court that the guardianship of Delmar Eagleman is established under Axia statute. Let the record show that his new guardians are Robert and Agnes Hassel and that Chaplain Major Jake Sender is acting as Delmar's sponsor for enlistment into the troopers."

The judge banged his gavel a final time and dismissed the court. Mike, joining the crowd around Robert, noticed the police officers were smiling as they handcuffed Dorn and led him away. As soon as the room was clear, the troopers wheeled in a litter and lifted Robert onto it. Everyone followed and they returned Robert to the hospital and put him back in bed. His nurse, displeased with the sudden excursion, threatened to tie him down and then ordered everyone out of the room so Robert could sleep.

Later that evening, a much happier group gathered around the table at the Hassel farm. Agnes and Sherry had whipped up quite a feast. After the men had cleared the table and cleaned up, dessert and coffee were served.

"Well, tomorrow is going to be a busy day," remarked Jake as he pushed back from the table.

"I hear you," replied Mike. "First, I have to file

the charges against Dorn on behalf of Robert and then arrange for someone to look after the farm."

"Won't it go to Delmar in this case?" Agnes asked.

"Yes and no," answered Mike. "Until he's twenty-one, or while Dorn is still alive, we can't change the deed. Half of the farm is actually in his name, but under the management of the guardian."

"Well then, it should be no problem," Sherry commented.

"There's still the problem of a lien that Dorn took out against it to pay his debts," Mike replied.

"What if the new guardian took action against Dorn on behalf of Delmar for breech of trust?" Jake asked. "Then the lien would go against Dorn in court and be added to the criminal penalties he faces for attempted murder."

"That's a good idea," Mike said. "That should provide a clear title to Delmar's half."

"What are you going to be doing tomorrow?" Agnes asked Jake.

"Under the Axia statute that Mike invoked, Delmar and I have to go start his application process to enlist," Jake replied.

Agnes got up and went into the other room. She came back and handed Delmar a familiar certificate. "I thought you might need this," she said.

"My graduation scores are recorded downtown at the education center," Delmar added.

"If they're as good as Robert wrote, they'll definitely help," Jake said.

"By the way, Mike?" asked Sherry. "How did you get here so fast? I thought your ship was damaged by Red-tails."

"We were badly damaged in an attack, but we came out of it with few injuries," Mike answered. "Our bedsprings drive was mostly shot out, and it looked as if we were going to have to limp the rest of the way in. Then we got a call from a scout asking if we needed help. The captain of our ship asked if they could deliver me under Imperial Directive to Erdinata as soon as possible. After I transferred, they light-jumped here at maximum speed and set directly down in the square outside the courthouse."

"Where did you get the extra troopers who entered the courtroom with you?" Jake asked. "A scout only holds the captain and maybe two other passengers."

"We called ahead, and the liaison office had a squad waiting for us when we set down," Mike replied. "I was briefed by the liaison lieutenant as we came in and he made sure the troopers waiting understood as well."

"That explains why they understood why I wanted them to go to the hospital to get Robert," Jake said.

"I had very little difficulty with the nurse because someone had called her," Sherry interjected. "Robert had roused again, and when I told him about Agnes and Delmar being arrested, he almost climbed out of that bed. It took the troopers and me a bit of effort to convince him to at least put on a robe before we came to court." Everyone chuckled.

"Will he be all right after today's exertions?" Jake asked.

"The doctor said he would," Agnes replied.

"In fact, today's events seemed to have hastened his recovery from the coma."

"Well, that's good to hear," Mike said. "Now I for one want to get some shuteye before arguing over words tomorrow."

Everyone agreed and the discussion wound down. They broke up and went to their rooms. Later that evening, Delmar lay in his bed staring up at the stars. So much had happened so fast, and the next day things would happen even faster. With a contented sigh, he finally rolled over and went to sleep.

Morning came with its usual luster, and things at the Hassel farmhouse were more hectic than usual. Mike and Agnes left early to see Robert and then to waste a perfectly good day in court. Jake and Delmar shuttled to the enlistment office for an appointment to have Delmar tested and evaluated. Sherry got the enjoyable task of staying at the farm to care for the animals and straighten up.

At the hospital, Agnes and Mike found Robert up and alert. Most of the visible wounds of the attack had healed enough so that the doctor no longer worried about infection. After checking him over, his doctor arranged for him to start some physical therapy on the wounded leg. Although the reinforcement plate installed years ago had deflected the bullet, there was still considerable damage to some of the tissue and tendons. Agnes and Mike wheeled Robert into the therapy room.

When they entered the room, Agnes heard a familiar voice. "Long time no see, Crazy Agnes," said a deep female voice.

Agnes whirled around and found herself face to face with the physical therapist. "Well, if it isn't Bulldozer Betty!" Agnes exclaimed, and the two women embraced.

"I didn't know you were on Erdinata," Agnes said.

"Yep! Been here almost a month," Betty answered. "Just transferred up from the southern continent last week. I was planning to look you up as soon as I got settled."

Turning to Mike and Robert, Agnes introduced her old acquaintance. "This is my old drill instructor, Betty 'Bulldozer' Brown," she said affectionately. "We called her Bulldozer because she pushed us so hard. She heard the nickname and liked it, so it stuck."

"This," said Robert, looking up warily at the large woman, "was your drill instructor?"

"I sure was, deary," answered Bulldozer, "and I'm going to be your physical therapist!" Poking a stiff finger into Robert's chest, she added, "So don't give me no lip!" She took control of Robert's wheelchair and guided it farther into the room. Agnes and Mike waved goodbye. The last thing Agnes saw was Robert with very wide eyes.

In court, Mike formally presented charges against Dorn for the attack on Robert. The court accepted the charges and issued warrants so the police could bring in the rest of Dorn's friends for questioning and possible charges. The preliminary hearing was delayed until after Robert could be released from the hospital and certified by his doctor.

After court, Mike took the underground tube to the liaison office while Agnes went back to the hospital to be with Robert. The assistant to the lieutenant was able to help Mike arrange for a caretaker for the Eagleman farm. Just as they were finishing the paperwork, the radio squawked the report that Mike's transport would soon be touching down. The two men stepped outside to the landing zone to watch it come in.

Soon two ships appeared in the sky over the field. The retrieval ship hovered above the disabled transport, and the men could see the purple-gold levitation ray lacing the two ships together. After the workers had set a dozen landing cradles in place, the retrieval ship lowered the transport into them and cut the ray. An audible groan rumbled across the tarmac as the stressed metal of the damaged ship settled into the cradles.

The hatch on the ship opened and the captain emerged. She saw Mike and waved, which he returned. She turned and began to survey the damage to her ship. Mike noticed her shoulders slump as she took in the extent of the battle damage.

Across town, Jake and Delmar were at the enlistment center. After filling out the lengthy application, a trooper interviewed Delmar and took documentation from Jake concerning Delmar's status. Delmar also submitted his graduation certificate for copying, and his identification for verification. A trooper led Delmar to a separate room where he struggled through the evaluation and placement test. Three hours later, Delmar's head was hurting, and his eyes would not focus. He was never more thankful when the trooper announced it was time for lunch. After eating, they returned to the center to retrieve the results of the test and to find out the next step.

The test results came back very high, which surprised the boy. He could not remember half of the questions. A trooper-first came out to double-check some of Delmar's answers on the application and then signed off on it, then left Delmar and Jake alone in the waiting room for what seemed like hours.

"There's one thing you have to get used to, Delmar," Jake said. "In the service we have a saying: 'Hurry up and wait.'"

A half hour later, the same trooper-first asked them to accompany him to an adjoining room.

"Well, Delmar," the trooper began, "you've passed the application process."

"Now what happens?" the boy asked.

"Tomorrow morning you have to be here for a complete physical," the trooper answered as he handed Delmar an appointment slip. "If you pass that, you'll be sworn in within thirty days and scheduled for twenty weeks of basic and advanced training."

Suddenly the enormity of enlisting caused

Delmar's throat to dry up. Fortunately, Jake spoke before Delmar had to, "What time do you want him here?" Jake asked the trooper.

"I know the appointment slip says 8 a.m., but being here early helps a lot. I suggest he gets plenty of sleep tonight and has a plain but filling breakfast tomorrow. Lots of fiber! If things run long, he may not get out of here until late afternoon."

"Thank you," said Jake as he stood. "I'll have him here by seven-thirty." The trooper shook their hands, and they left the office. Jake steered the boy to the shuttle and they were already halfway to the farm before Delmar finally spoke again. After that, the questions came nonstop until they reached home.

In the meantime, Mike and Agnes had again visited with Robert and were on their way home. Robert looked pretty beat after his therapy, so they had not stayed long. Mike was still chuckling about Robert's comments about his therapist. "A bulldozer only pushes things around. This woman was more of a road grader and pavement smoother. Only my leg was injured. Why does every muscle in my body ache?" Bulldozer Betty had really worked him over.

14

The sun was just topping the horizon when the
ground car pulled up to the enlistment center. A
young man hopped out and briskly climbed the
steps and slipped inside. Reporting to the trooper at
the counter, Delmar presented his appointment slip.
The trooper signed him in and issued him a neck
chain on which hung a key to one of the personal
lockers. He then gave the young man directions to
the lower level where he found himself waiting with
a half dozen other young men in a locker room.

Too nervous to sit, Delmar paced around the
room and located his assigned locker. A plain jumpsuit that he had been instructed to wear instead of his
regular clothes was folded neatly on the locker shelf.
Underneath was a pair of shower thongs. Stripping
completely, Delmar stowed his personal gear and
wiggled into the jumpsuit. He noted that it appeared
designed to fit no one in particular, ever. The jump-

suit had a drop-down panel in the seat as well as the front. *I wonder what these are for,* he thought.

Hanging the key around his neck by its chain, Delmar then slipped on the shower thongs and sat down to wait. The clock on the wall read five minutes until eight.

He didn't have long to wait. At two minutes before the hour a crush of about fifteen young men of all descriptions crowded into the locker room. They started to search frantically for their lockers amid considerable commotion. At eight sharp, a deep, thunderous voice pierced through the confusion. "All right! Find your lockers and change! Now!"

The voice generated even more frenzied activity on part of the men still looking for their lockers. Delmar tried to stay clear while several young men attempted to change into their jumpsuits while balanced on one foot.

"Come on! Move it!" the voice of doom yelled. "You'd all be dead in space at this rate!" Delmar could see why the trooper at the front desk had advised him to be here early.

"Those who are ready, line up with your toes on the blue line!" Almost everyone ran for the line on the floor, which allowed the few recruits still madly changing to have room to finish. Within a minute, all of the young men were standing fearfully with their toes on the blue line.

In front of them stood a trooper-first who looked much too small to have such a commanding voice. He walked up and down the line looking over the young men, like a wolf selecting his dinner from the herd.

"Okay, listen up!" the trooper boomed. "Sound off when I call your name." The trooper then proceeded to call roll and seemed barely satisfied as each young man announced his presence. Again pacing the line, he looked as if he was daring any of them to break and run.

"So you want to be troopers?" he boomed. Delmar was beginning to wonder if the man was capable of speaking at a normal volume.

"I'm here to take you through the physical examination process where you will be examined by a battery of doctors and specialists, one for each type of exam. You will keep your mouths shut except when required to speak. Stay in line and step lively." The trooper paused. "Are there any questions?" The young men in line were too scared to speak. "Good! Now, move out!"

The trooper led them to the first of countless rooms. An hour later, Delmar exited a room and stood at another blue line along with those who had also finished. He didn't realize there were so many methods to weigh and measure the human body. Dignity was something best left back in the locker room with the civilian clothes. Now he waited at the line while the trooper again paced back and forth. However, after having every possible orifice examined by both doctors and machines, he did learn the purpose of the drop-down panels in the jumpsuit.

As soon as the last young man was at the line,

the trooper led them into another examining room where they stripped and carried their jumpsuits. One by one, each young man had to lie down on an elevated table while a scan was made of his bone structure. After that, additional tables followed where other scanning machines probed them for things Delmar had never heard of. Finally allowed to dress, they found themselves again at a blue line where the ever-present trooper eyed them while he paced.

Released after several minutes, Delmar joined those in front of him and they each went into a small room to have their teeth X-rayed, followed by a large examination room that held half a dozen dentist chairs with two examiners at each. The trooper had them sit down in small groups. Bright lights swung over their open mouths, and two dental examiners probed and poked Delmar's teeth and gums. Afterwards, there was the familiar blue line and the pacing trooper.

The next delight was the full examination of their eyesight. Another room with a half dozen separate booths, each with a vision technician, greeted the young men as the trooper sent them in. He checked their sight for visual acuity and depth of field. The usual full spectrum of vision and color-blindness tests followed. Lastly, the doctor examined their eyes as organs themselves. The bright lights they used left spots in front of Delmar's eyes for several minutes. It made finding the blue line a little more difficult.

The hearing test was next. Each young man put on a set of earphones and sat quietly in a soundproof booth where he signaled with a handheld button when he did or did not hear the differing tones playing to test his auditory sensors. Seconds seemed like hours while Delmar listened to an endless stream of different tones.

Delmar soon found himself standing at yet another blue line where the trooper-first ordered the group of wary young men to drop the panels in their jumpsuits. Internists that specialized in the reproductive and digestive systems examined each man. Fortunately, it didn't take long and they again lined up, desperately trying to button the panels back in place.

A specialist of dermatology collected skin and hair samples from various areas of their bodies at the next station. Another examiner took blood samples, and then they were ushered into the latrine to produce samples of other bodily fluids and solids. Allowed to dress again, their toes were once again at the blue line. Delmar was starting to think that blue lines were one of the constants of the universe.

Led by their bulldog of a trooper, the young men found themselves in a small gymnasium. There were several blue lines here and the trooper had them spread out among them.

"Now the fun part!" bellowed the trooper. "We're going to run you through some basic exercises. Assume the push-up position with your fingers and chin on the blue line." He waited a moment while they got ready.

"All right! On my count. Up one!" Quickly,

Delmar found himself doing a steady rhythm of push-ups with occasional pauses. Several young men had to quit after the first ten or so, but most kept going. Delmar decided that he wasn't going to let the trooper get the best of him. His arms began to weaken and shake at thirty and Delmar was glad when they stopped at thirty-five.

Next, the trooper had them do sit-ups with their heels on the infamous blue line. Fifty was the ending count on this exercise and seemed to be a favorite of the trooper as he had them go through a dozen more drills. Sweat soaked through their jumpsuits while he had them run in place for ten minutes.

Finished with the exercise ordeal and again lined up on a blue line, the trooper herded them back into the locker room and had them strip for a quick shower. Afterwards they dressed back in their civilian clothes and lined up again. The trooper had them file out, throwing their used jumpsuits, thongs, and towels in different bins by the door. As they walked past him, the trooper collected their locker keys.

Delmar looked at the clock in the reception area and was shocked that it was only four o'clock. He went to a pay phone and called Jake. While he waited, Delmar asked at the counter when he would receive the results of his examination. The trooper behind the counter told him that he would know in about twenty-four to forty-eight hours.

Walking back near the front, Delmar spied the trooper who had shepherded them downstairs. One of the other troopers was talking to him, and

Delmar was surprised to hear the trooper speak in normal tones. Another young man approached the trooper. "Excuse me, sir," the young man began. "How many push-ups can you do?"

"Left-hand, right-hand, or both?" the trooper asked.

The young man looked astonished, but persisted. "All of them, sir," he replied.

"I can do 115 with either hand alone and 240 with both," the trooper replied with a grin.

"But I could never do that," the young man said.

"Don't worry, son," the trooper said with a friendly smile. "You will by the time you finish basic."

The toot of a horn broke Delmar away from the conversation, and he looked out the window to see Jake waiting for him. Delmar ran quickly out the door to the ground car. On the way home, Delmar didn't say much about his day.

Jake looked at him and finally spoke up. "By your quietness, I suspect they got their pound of flesh," Jake said with a grin. Delmar flinched at the comment and looked up.

"Literally!" Delmar replied with a grin of his own.

"Don't let your experience today phase you any," Jake continued. "It was a way of testing you early to see who can take it and who can't."

"Really?" responded Delmar.

"Yes, really," answered Jake. "It's even worse in basic."

At this last comment, Delmar stared at Jake with abstract disbelief. Jake laughed at his expression and finally Delmar joined in while they continued out to the farm.

While Delmar was undergoing his physical, Mike was meeting with the legal team he and the liaison lieutenant had assembled. Having the Imperial Directive allowed him to call on resources that he normally could not use. A ship had landed the night before with the last of the specialists he had requested. Now he had his entire team of twenty assembled.

"I sent each of you a brief description of the legal situation that has developed here on Erdinata," Mike began. "I want you to pay particular attention to conflicts between local law and the Axia. As the brief stated, several agencies have developed and enforced their own policies that are contrary to Galactic Axia laws and statutes."

Mike paused, and the liaison lieutenant took over. "When we last dealt with one of these agencies a couple of months ago, we thought we had taken care of the problem," he said. "Unfortunately, the resiliency of this type of governmental management is quite strong."

"How far are we authorized to go?" asked one of the team members.

"As far as necessary to eliminate the problem," Mike answered. "Our Lady is displeased with the situation and wants us to restore the trust of the people who have to deal daily with these agencies. Restore the faith and return these agencies to a true and honest system."

Mike stepped down and allowed the liaison lieutenant to detail the first departments for investigation. In short order, the team dispersed and began its inspections.

"Do you think it'll do any good?" the lieutenant asked Mike.

"Yes, I do," Mike replied. "This isn't the first time this team has had to clean house. My only regret is I didn't do this when I was first called here."

"Don't let it bother you so much," the lieutenant replied. "I thought it was taken care of last time too."

"Well, this should do it," Mike said. "I received a message from Shalimar just after I received yours that there were several more complaints in Our Lady's red box about this kind of situation. That's when I received authorization to assemble the legal team. Fortunately, most were on nearby planets and able to come quickly."

"That's what I like about the Axia," the lieutenant said. "It always has a way of correcting its excesses and shortfalls."

"I have another problem for you," Mike said. "I need someone to be caretaker of the Eagleman farm until Delmar is of legal age to assume his half of the title."

"What's the legal standing on the deed?" the lieutenant asked.

"It was divided in half between the two heirs, Delmar and Dorn, at the time of their mother's death," Mike answered. "Dorn legally owns half and managed the other half as Delmar's guardian. Dorn took out a lien on the whole property to pay off his bad debts, but there should be no problem seeing that it goes against him for misuse of trust property. With him in prison, his lien will come due and be sold at auction."

"How soon will that happen?" asked the lieutenant.

"About the same time Delmar turns twenty-one and is able to assume his half of the trust," answered Mike. "It is my intention to see to it that Delmar has first-offer rights to redeem the lien and assume full undivided title. That's why I need someone to keep it up for him."

"Let me check my files," the lieutenant said as he pulled open a drawer. "I can think of several troopers and their families who might work out."

The two older men accompanied the young trooper and his wife, Daren and Rosemary Sabeti, around to the front of the Eagleman house. Mike was careful to stay on the left side of the young man in case the cane he was using slipped. It was obvious to Mike that the young lady was several months pregnant and would not be able to catch her husband should he fall. *This is going to be interesting*, Mike thought. *A disabled man and a pregnant woman.*

"So there you see the whole of it," the liaison lieutenant said. "Some of the neighbors have offered to come in with their equipment and get those fields in shape, and I heard talk of a work party forming to clean and repair the house. What do you two think?"

"We like it a lot, sir," the disabled trooper said and smiled at his wife. "It'll give me something useful to do while I recover and will help us stop living out of a suitcase. It will also give us a place to start our family."

"Your service pay will be unaffected, and you pay the rent by your efforts," Mike said.

"Where are the owners?" the wife asked.

"One is going to a penal colony for a long time and the other has enlisted in the service," Mike answered. "We're authorized to find someone to take care of the place."

"Why isn't the one owner here right now?" the young trooper asked. He sat down on the porch to rest his injured leg.

"Because," Mike continued as he checked his watch, "he's just finishing his physical exam for enlistment." The young trooper grinned at Mike and the lieutenant knowingly.

"If he approves of us, we'll take it," the wife said, looking at her husband.

"I'm not too worried about it," Mike answered. "Let's go back to the office and draw up the paperwork."

"Do you mean we could actually have a house of our own?" Rosemary asked Mike.

"Looks like it," he answered. "Do you think you're up for it?"

"Up for it?" Daren said before his wife could answer. "Just try holding her back!"

Daren Sabeti stood back up and they all walked to the ground car. The lieutenant noticed that the young man was limping pretty badly and his face was ashen. However, he also noticed the spark in the young man's eyes when offered the challenge. He wasn't too worried about the young couple.

Dinner was just being set out when Jake and Delmar pulled into the driveway. As they climbed up the steps, Mike pulled in and parked his vehicle behind theirs. Together the three went inside, changed, and washed for dinner. Everyone shared their news around the dinner table.

Agnes and Sherry had been to visit Robert and had gotten to see him walk a little. Agnes wasn't sure whether it was determination to get better or a desire to get out from under his drill instructor of a therapist. Either way, she was glad to see his progress.

Delmar told of his trials that day and received hoots of appreciation and sympathy while he described the trooper-first. The older generation winked at each other in anticipation of what the boy would experience in basic. Delmar was a little worried that something would prevent his enlistment, but Jake and Mike both assured him that his chances were good if he'd made it this far.

Mike brought up the subject of a caretaker for the Eagleman farm. He described the young couple he and the liaison lieutenant had interviewed and their reaction to the place as it now looked. He suggested that Delmar meet them tomorrow at the office and the boy said it would be fine. Agnes interjected that she thought it would be better to have the meeting here at the farm so she could meet them too.

Mike excused himself for a moment to make a call. Returning a few minutes later, he announced that the couple would come for dinner and Agnes' reaction was all the confirmation Delmar needed.

Finally, the conversation wound down and everyone pitched in to clean up. Delmar and Mike went out to check on the animals and settle things for the night. Afterward, everyone drifted to their rooms and called it a night.

Delmar found himself reviewing the physical exam in his head again. Tomorrow he would find out for sure if he had passed and when he could finish the enlistment procedure. With blurry-eyed visions of being a trooper, he drifted off to sleep.

Delmar had been anxious all day waiting for the comm-link to ring. It didn't help that Jake had him over here at his old farm cleaning things. The trash in the house alone was enough to discourage anyone. One of the neighbors lent them his large truck, and Jake and Delmar made good use of it. They had already made three runs to the trash center, and they had not yet started on the barn.

As he went through things, Delmar was surprised to find that he had very few happy memories of the place. He'd expected that his earliest memories of when his parents had been alive would come flooding back to him, but they hadn't. Instead, he saw his brother at every turn.

Anything of value was long gone to support his

brother's drinking habit and parties. The boxes Delmar brought for mementos remained pitifully empty. His old room had been used as a dumpsite after he'd run away, and all of his personal effects were trashed, stolen, or sold.

Jake made a point of staying near the boy while they dragged the debris out to the truck. The project was daunting, but Delmar dug in and made amazing progress. The fourth load finished off the trash in the house, and the two men broke for a quick lunch. The house was now empty and Agnes, Sherry, and some of the neighbor ladies were coming later to give it a good scrub.

Although a disaster of its own, the barn showed less of the effect of Dorn's neglect. Among the few broken-down pieces of farm equipment were bundles of tangled fence wire and shattered furniture. Delmar and Jake dragged it all out into the open and separated what might be salvageable from the hopeless. Three more trips to the trash center took care of the wreckage of furniture and other debris.

The old tractor looked repairable and the bailer available for parts. Rooting around in the shop area, Delmar found that his father's old tools had actually survived in fair shape. Apparently, the mountain of trash prevented his brother from getting to them. Jake helped him set them in order again for the new caretakers.

Up on the shelves above the bench were old partial bottles and cans of paints and solvents. A few were still good but most had long since dried up. Jake backed the truck directly into the barn so loading was easier, and they made short work of the mess.

On the top shelf behind some of the cans, Delmar found an old metal ammo box that Jake recognized as predating the boy by many years. Opening it, Delmar found a collection of old family photographs and mementos that his mother had saved. He pulled out an early picture of his parents.

Delmar found himself choking up for the first time in years. He let the grief he had buried explode from his tortured chest. Silent sobs racked the boy for a long moment while Jake comforted him, his arm around the boy's shoulders.

When there were no more tears, Delmar carefully replaced the precious portrait of his parents back into the box. Digging deeper, he found another picture of his father taken before Delmar had been born. There he stood, tall and lean wearing the uniform of Axia black. Scribbled below the image was a tiny tight scrawl that simply read *T1 John Eagleman*. Jake looked at the picture of Delmar's father but said nothing. He noticed that both father and son exhibited the same strong lines and determined expression.

They called it quits for the day, and the difference in the Eagleman farm was astonishing. They got back to the Hassel farm and found preparations were well underway for their guests that night. Jake and Delmar went in and washed. Sherry chased them upstairs to change into better clothes. Mike arrived from town, and the table was set when the young trooper and his wife arrived.

Seated around the table, Delmar was able to learn a little about these prospective caretakers. Daren and Rosemary Sabeti had been married only five years when Daren was injured. The doctors repaired what they could. Now it was up to Daren. A long convalescence, preferably outdoors, would serve better to heal the injury than any amount of medicine. Daren, frustrated by inactivity, had jumped at the opportunity to combine his recuperation with doing something useful, but this was more than he had hoped for.

Agnes and Sherry took to the young wife almost immediately and were likewise impressed with her husband. Delmar was concerned with the young trooper's ability to take care of the farm in light of his injuries, but as he got to know Daren, he saw that the challenge would be a blessing. Sometimes a person needs a challenge to help them overcome a setback.

After they'd finished off dinner and some of Agnes' delicious apple pie, they retired to the living room. The young couple told Delmar what they hoped to do with the farm. Their plans were ambitious but realistic, and Delmar felt good about leaving the farm in this couple's care.

Looking at Agnes, Delmar saw that she was also in favor of the couple. Finally, he stood and walked over to Daren and Rosemary Sabeti. He looked them in the eye and told them he would be pleased if they would accept the challenge of being the caretakers. The couple broke into smiles. Delmar shook hands with them and then returned to his seat.

Mike stood up and called for everyone's attention. "While everybody is in such good spirits, I have an announcement to make," he said. The group grew quiet and all eyes were on him. Mike noticed that Delmar's eyes were wide with apprehension. Pulling an envelope from his breast pocket, he opened it and removed several sheets.

"I picked this up on my way over," he announced. He then read the letter aloud.

Mr. Delmar Eagleman,

This notice is to inform you that you have passed all entrance requirements for enlistment into the Galactic Axia Trooper Service. You may report to the enlistment center at ten o'clock any weekday morning within the next thirty calendar days to accept the oath of office.

Mike finished. Attached to the letter was a sheet listing personal articles to bring, as well as prohibited things. The group exploded into cheers and congratulations.

15

The day was still showing some early morning clouds from the storm the night before when the ground car pulled out of the driveway and headed toward town from the Hassel farm. Delmar had been unusually quiet that morning and only managed to eat lightly. Although he was oblivious to the fact, he had considerable sympathy from the other adults. Agnes tried to get the boy to smile, but nothing would cause his gray mask to slip. Jake thought that he only saw that expression on a man's face two times in life: when he enlisted and when he got married.

Speeding toward town, Sherry noticed that Delmar carefully examined his old home when they passed the Eagleman farm. The Sabetis had only moved in a couple of days ago, but already the changes were beginning to show. Besides curtains, there were signs that someone had started attacking the well-developed weeds in the flowerbeds.

Delmar seemed satisfied by the changes, and his gaze returned to the front for the rest of the trip.

Delmar expressed his desire to see Mr. Hassel before reporting at the enlistment center, but Agnes convinced him that it would be impractical. Unknown to the boy, two troopers were picking up Robert from the hospital and taking him to the enlistment center. The doctor signed the release for Robert to go home the night before, but they had managed to keep Delmar from finding out about it to surprise him. They would meet Robert there for the ceremony and then take him home.

Arriving at the enlistment center, Jake parked the car and they all entered the reception area. Delmar saw several of the young men he had taken the physical exam with three weeks earlier. When he checked in at the counter, the trooper behind the desk told him to listen for the announcement calling the enlistees to the ceremony. Delmar returned to sit by Agnes and the Senders and tried not to fidget.

The small bag of personal items the notice advised him to bring lay at his feet. He considered taking inventory again just to pass the time. Mentally, he could picture everything in the bag. He had packed and repacked it several times the night before.

A voice on the loudspeaker cut through his musings calling all enlistees to assemble. As per the instruction on the sheet, Delmar handed his bag to Agnes and quickly joined the other young men in front of a double door.

They found themselves in a small auditorium

with a curtained stage. Standing together on the small open floor in front of the stage, a trooper-third quickly called them to form up in front of the stage. There were several familiar blue lines on the floor. A dozen tiers of seats also rose behind them. Out of the corner of his eye, Delmar could see people filing into the upper seats, Agnes and the Senders among them. The trooper-third gave the enlistees a brief rundown of what to expect and then stepped to the side of the stage.

The lights dimmed and the curtain opened revealing a large Galactic Axia flag and a small lectern. A spotlight highlighted each. A figure approached the lectern through the shadows. The trooper-third called the young men to attention as the figure stepped into the light.

The spotlight highlighted the silver in the hair of the speaker. Rank insignia denoting a major glistened in the light against the black of his Axia uniform. As he stepped fully into the light, Delmar caught his breath. He had hoped to see Mr. Hassel before the ceremony, but had never expected this.

Major Hassel addressed the enlistees. "Today you take the first official step into the brotherhood of the troopers. You have all passed the stringent entry tests and the demanding physical requirements to qualify for enlistment," he said.

"I want you to be proud of making the cut thus far. The road ahead of you through twenty weeks of basic and advanced training will test each of you individually and as a team. You will come to exceed your own expectations and discover strengths and weaknesses you never knew you had.

"Right now is your last opportunity to withdraw from the arduous task ahead of you. Any who withdraws now may still enlist within the allotted calendar year without recrimination. We do not want you to enlist without carefully considering the consequences of your actions. We highly value honesty and faithfulness, and if you can't be honest and faithful to yourself first, you have no place among the troopers. We will now dim the lights and any who wish to wait on their enlistment until they are confident in their heart of the rightness of their action may anonymously move out the exit and join the spectators in the gallery."

The lights went out except for a few dim aisle lights. Delmar heard one or two move out. After a couple of minutes, the spotlights came on again, and in the reflected light, the ranks adjusted to fill in the vacant gaps.

Major Hassel gazed out at them intently for a few moments. "I will now administer your first oath as a trooper trainee," he said, breaking the silence. "Raise your right hand and repeat after me. Speak your full legal name at the appropriate place."

The spotlight on Major Hassel dimmed and the light on the Axia flag brightened. With the others, Delmar raised his right hand and together they repeated the oath of trooper trainees. As soon as they were finished, Major Hassel lowered his right hand, followed by the trainees. He then turned toward the flag and rendered the Axia salute as the anthem played, his right arm across his chest, palm facing the ground.

Delmar and the rest of the trainees could not salute at this time. It was an earned privilege of every trooper or lady of the fleet. The trainees remained at respectful attention. Delmar could hear people in the gallery rising and he could see several, including Agnes and the Senders, salute the flag. They all held this position until the last notes of the anthem faded away. Delmar realized that in all the times he had heard its ancient strains, he had never heard the words.

When the music faded away, Major Hassel turned again toward the trainees and addressed them. "You are now officially trooper trainees," he said. "I now release you for ten minutes to visit with your families and sponsors. You will reform ranks in ten minutes with your personal luggage and will be under direction of the trooper-third." Major Hassel surveyed them one more time. "Dismissed."

The ranks of trainees dispersed and searched the gallery for their families, or stayed on the floor to say their goodbyes. Agnes and the Senders quickly surrounded Delmar. When he pulled back from hugging Agnes, he opened his eyes and found himself staring into the face of Major Hassel.

The older man clasped his hand and Delmar finally found his voice. "Why didn't you tell me you were an active trooper?" he asked. "And when did you get out of the hospital?"

"I'll answer the questions one at a time," Major

Hassel replied with a smile. "Any retired trooper is forever on inactive status as a reservist. You saw Jake reassume his rank and status to help in the court proceedings. I asked to be reactivated for today so I might give you the best send-off I could." He finished with a grin. "As for the hospital, I was released this morning to go home and finish recuperation under the command of Agnes."

Delmar was still a little dumbfounded at the surprise of seeing Mr. Hassel in uniform as his swearing-in officer, so he did not immediately respond. He then hugged Mr. Hassel fiercely.

"Before you go, I want you to take this," Mr. Hassel said as he offered Delmar the familiar old pocketwatch.

"I was afraid to take it for fear of it being stolen or damaged," Delmar answered.

"That's understandable," Agnes replied for the two of them. "However, it's safe to take with you," she continued. "At induction you will have an opportunity to have valuables secured by your drill instructor. Turn it in then, and no harm will come to it."

"We'd better let this young man go," said Jake, looking at his watch. The trainees were already starting to reform their ranks. Hugging all of them again, Delmar quickly rejoined his group. The trooper-third called them to attention and marched them out through the exit and into the waiting transportation behind the building.

Later that evening, the two couples gathered around the table at the Hassel farm. "Boy, it sure feels good to be home," Robert said with a sigh. "I was getting tired of that hospital food."

"I thought you came home to get away from Bulldozer Betty," Agnes remarked with a grin. "I heard from the nurses that you were rather reluctant to go to therapy." Robert looked at Agnes with a hurt expression.

"You know the reason they make the hospital food so bad, don't you?" asked Sherry. "It's their way of encouraging the patients to hurry up and get better and leave."

"Well, I heard about Bulldozer Betty from the girls, and I'm sure glad I didn't have her for basic," Jake commented.

"I don't think you had to worry about that," his wife said. "You wouldn't have met the physical qualifications to be a lady of the fleet," she finished with a giggle. Agnes joined the laugh. Robert wisely kept his mouth shut.

After the girls had finished their laughter, the kitchen quieted for a minute. "I wonder how our boy is doing about now?" Robert finally offered.

"Oh, I think he's in good hands," Jake answered. "I found out that he's going to the Freewater Training Center."

"Then he won't have far to go," Sherry said.

"Still, leaving one's home planet always makes the journey seem longer," Agnes added.

"If I read the schedule right, he should be arriving there about nightfall three days from now," Jake commented.

"Arriving at night always makes it more interesting," Robert said. "I arrived at night, and seeing my drill instructor for the first time on a dimly lit drill pad certainly added to the fear."

"You were afraid?" Sherry asked.

"You bet I was," Robert answered. "I came from a pretty sheltered existence, and the shock was pretty hard. I'd heard that drill instructors were special Red-tail agents, and seeing mine that night seemed to confirm it." The conversation lapsed again as they contemplated their own experiences. Agnes finally broke the silence.

"So, how much longer can you folks stay?" she asked Jake and Sherry.

"If you'll have us, we're going to wait until Robert is up and around," Jake answered.

"Hey!" said Robert indignantly. "I can get around fine now."

"Sure you can," replied Jake. "Shall I tell the girls what happened when you tried to swing down that bale of hay this evening?"

"Just because my leg is a little stiff," came back Robert as a blush climbed his cheeks.

"We'll be glad to have you stay for as long as you like," Agnes said, trying to give Robert a chance to regain his composure.

"Won't staying cause problems for your congregation?" Robert asked in an effort to direct the conversation away from himself.

"Sure it will," replied Jake. "That's exactly what my assistant needs." Sherry stifled a laugh at the thought.

"He needs a challenge to strengthen him," Jake continued. "When the pastor is gone, trouble seems to come out of the woodwork. I'm not too worried."

"Then it's settled," Agnes said. "I wasn't quite ready to let Sherry go home yet anyway." Another chuckle ran around the table.

"If I remember the timetable," Robert began, "we should be hearing from Delmar before you leave."

"The first postcard with his unit number should arrive in about a week or ten days," Jake added. "The rest of his mail will be by electronic conveyance, but that first postcard is the most interesting. The card will have his starmail address on it. I look forward to seeing what he thinks of his first week at basic."

"He'll think what we all thought," Sherry said, "that he's dropped into a different universe where Red-tails masquerade as drill instructors!"

The thought that he had dropped into a different universe had indeed crossed Delmar's mind. The idea that his drill instructor was a disguised Red-tail would not occur to him for another few days.

After leaving the enlistment center, a transport bus delivered the trainees directly to the spacefield. Arriving there, they were loaded onto an Axia transport ship and were soon blasting into space.

The trooper-third remained with them and was already disabusing them of the notion that this was a pleasure flight. He ordered them to stow their bags in a set of lockers, and before the ship broke orbit, they were getting their first lesson on the intricacies of a mop and pail. Delmar was glad for his "training" aboard the *Malibu* and realized that Cargo Master Preston had certainly been a trooper at one time. The mopping technique that the trooper-third showed them was identical to Preston's.

The hours passed quickly, and Delmar was surprised when the trooper-third called them to stow their equipment and form ranks. After everyone was in line, he marched them to the lower mess for a hasty midday meal. The food was better than on the freighter, but they had less time in which to enjoy it. "Eat now and taste it later," the trooper-third ordered.

After the meal, the trooper-third detailed three of the trainees to assist in cleaning the mess and two more to help with the dishes. Delmar and the rest returned to the equipment lockers and retrieved their mops and pails. While he mopped some obscure compartment, Delmar realized that the tile matched some of those on the *Malibu*. Thoughts of writing a definitive study on floor tile throughout Galactic Axia helped him pass the time while handling the business end of his mop.

Three days later the trooper-third again had them stow their gear and assemble in their original compartment. Reclaiming their bags, they formed ranks on the ever-present blue lines. The ship jolted slightly and creaked as the drive disengaged and the ship settled onto its landing skids. The trooper-third led the trainees up the corridor and out through the hatch into the misty night air.

Delmar caught a brief glimpse of a lighted landing area beneath a cloudy night sky. Following the trooper-third, the nervous trainees found themselves in a large auditorium filled to capacity with other recruits. A short and overly detailed info-vid played on a large screen a film that outlined their new lives. It quickly dispelled any myths about basic being a glorified summer camp.

As soon as the video was over, the lights came up and a trooper-second appeared in front of the screen. "*Atteeen-hutt*!" his voice boomed. The trainees leapt to their feet.

A lieutenant strode up the center aisle and stepped onto the platform. "At ease," he said with a quiet but firm voice. "Welcome to Freewater Training Center. As of this moment, the outside world for you has ceased to exist, and this facility is your entire universe. You are here for twenty weeks of intensive training. We hope to turn you into troopers. As you may have gathered from the film, we go to great lengths to assure success in this effort."

The lieutenant gazed around the room, taking stock of row after row of trainees. "Contrary to what you may later believe, we are not out to kill you. We consider you an investment and will help you bring out the very best in yourselves. We do not produce mindless followers, but men and women able to think for themselves and as a team."

The lieutenant paused for a moment. A half dozen troopers came in and stood evenly spaced in front of the platform. Delmar noticed that each held a placard with a number on it. The several hundred trainees eyed the troopers and shifted nervously.

"In a moment your names will be read off as we divide you into flights of sixty people," the lieutenant continued. "Answer loudly and clearly. As you hear your name, you will assemble yourselves into ranks with your toes on the blue line in front of the designated trooper. They will take you to your assigned barracks where you will meet your drill instructors."

The lieutenant stepped back and a trooper-second came forward with a clipboard. In a surprisingly clear voice, he called out names in rapid fire. Trainees hurried forward among calls of "Yes, sirs" and "Presents," and formed ranks in front of the first trooper as he held up his placard. The process was repeated three more times before Delmar's name was called and he rushed to line up with the others in front of the trooper holding the placard reading, "Squadron 3703, Flight 775."

Finally, with all of the groups formed, the lieutenant again came forward. "Trainees," he said, "I wish you good success in your training." He paused as he again scanned the young faces around him. "Dismissed!" he said sharply, and the groups were led out of the exits toward their new homes. As the lieutenant watched their ragged attempts at marching, he mused at how soon that would be corrected.

Approaching the two-story barracks, Delmar found that his heart was in his throat. He had heard stories about drill instructors and was not looking forward to meeting his. The trooper led them into the building and had them form ranks in an open area of the lower bay. Because of the late hour, the lights remained dim in deference to the sleeping trainees in neighboring barracks.

After standing at silent attention for an eternity, a large trooper-first came into the clearing. He eyed the tired young men through smoked-lens glasses. By his round-billed hat, a universal symbol of his position, Delmar realized that this was the dreaded drill instructor.

The inspection continued for another three minutes before the drill instructor spoke. "Welcome to your home for the next five months," he began in a quiet, yet powerful voice. "I am your drill instructor, Trooper-First W. Buckner. You will address me as DI Buckner, and you will address me and all other troopers as sir. I am now the center of your existence. Your lives will be much easier if you remember that. I expect your ears to be open and your mouths shut."

After nodding to his assistant, the trooper-second started passing out postcards and pens. "You are to address the front of these postcards with your home address," Buckner said. "You will write that you arrived safely and then sign your full name prefixed by the initials TT. This stands for trooper trainee, a designation you will be addressed by and will address yourself as while you are at Freewater. You will then copy down the unit and flight number you see on the sign behind me." DI Buckner pointed over his shoulder with his thumb, never actually turning around to look at the sign.

"You will have access to starmail while you are on Freewater," Buckner continued. "Your Galactic Starmail address will be the first letter of your first name and the first five letters of your last name, followed by a forward sign, the letters GSS, which stands for Galactic Starmail Service, followed by a dot, then your unit number, dot, your flight number, dot, and finally FWTB, which stands for Freewater Training Base. You will see a sample of a valid starmail address on the sign. When you are finished, my assistant drill instructor will collect these cards and they will be mailed to your families."

A trainee sitting near the front of the group raised his hand. "What is it, Trainee?" Buckner asked.

"Sir, most of us have starmail addresses at home," the trainee answered. "Why can't we just starmail this information home and save the trouble of regular mail?"

"Because you're men now, that's why," Buckner answered. "You're not schoolboys away on a weekend camping trip. Your momma and daddy can't come bail you out now, so shut up and fill out the card!"

The trainees quickly complied with the instructions after which another trooper collected the cards and pens. "My assistant is Trooper-Second H. Stoddard. You will address him as DIA Stoddard. You will accord him the same respect and obedience that you show to me. He will now assign you to your bunks. Welcome to the 3703 Training

Squadron, Flight 775. Hit the rack and get some sleep. Tomorrow starts early."

With that, Buckner left the room and Stoddard began assigning the bunks in both starboard and port bays. Delmar's bunk at the left-hand end of the starboard bay was a welcome sight indeed. The trainees stripped to their skivvies and crawled under the sheets. When the lights finally faded, the sixty young men tried to convince their tired, scared bodies to go to sleep.

16

The aroma of breakfast drifted up into the dorm from the kitchen somewhere below. Sniffing the smell of bacon and eggs, the boy rolled over and opened his eyes. A large dog bound into the room and stuck its face squarely into Delmar's. Opening its mouth, the dog barked, "All right! Get up! Get out of bed! Hit the deck!"

Delmar really opened his eyes to find himself staring into the face of DIA Stoddard. Electrified into action, Delmar burst out of his bunk, and his feet hit the cold floor. Grabbing his clothes, he hastily pulled them on. He then tried to straighten his bunk and then ran to the latrine.

Through all of this, DIA Stoddard and DI Buckner prowled through both bays motivating the trainees with their very presence. Barely three minutes after leaving his bunk, Delmar heard the DI bellow for them to form ranks in the outside assembly bay. The sight of sixty men trying to run down the stairs at the same time might have been humorous at another time, but not this morning.

"Hurry up! Hurry up! Move it!" bellowed Buckner. Soon the three score of young men were again in ranks on the lower asphalt. The two drill instructors shifted the men around until their ranks were even for progression of height.

"Remember your positions. This is how you will form up in ranks from now on," DI Buckner announced. "Now we're taking you to the chow hall. After breakfast you'll start in-processing. Anyone with unsecured valuables, raise your hand. DIA Stoddard will take you to the office to record and secure them. All right, move!"

Delmar, along with several other trainees, assembled and followed the assistant drill instructor. Soon his valuable pocketwatch was safely stored in the company safe. Back in ranks, the unit moved out toward the mess hall.

The differently clad, rag-tag group of trainees stood at disheveled attention outside of the mess hall for twenty minutes. DI Buckner and his assistant walked stealthily among their charges and encouraged no talking.

Five minutes after finally sitting down at a table in the far corner of the dining hall, the trainees were called again to ranks and took their trays to the disposal room. Soon they were marching toward the buildings where they would begin their transformation from a colorful rainbow of civilians to a uniform unit of trainees.

First, they stripped and carried their civilian clothes in net bags they had picked up at the door. A brief physical followed, along with long lines in which their arms, hips, and thighs were the target of many needles. Next, they received their basic clothing and uniforms. Dressed in light blue jumpsuits, they were soon again outside and marching in jerking formation toward their barracks.

Next followed an hour of instruction concerning the care and laundry marking of their uniforms and other clothing. They turned their bags of civilian clothes over to a trooper with a large cart, with an assurance of their future retrieval. Delmar found it hard to believe that he would not see his civilian attire again for another twenty weeks.

A less than leisurely five-minute lunch happened and they again continued their orientation by the drill instructors. Delmar didn't realize there was so much to learn about clothing or about the fine art of making his bunk. Before they again formed up for a short dinner, they had made and remade their bunks too many times to count.

Dinner was more relaxed, with ten minutes given in which to inhale their food. Delmar would never remember what the food tasted like because it was too briefly in his mouth on its way to his stomach.

After dinner, they resumed the basic instruction about their barracks and its care. Squads were formed within the unit and duties assigned. Delmar found that his immediate future would again involve mops. Lights-out finally came and the trainees gratefully crawled into their bunks. Exhausted sleep overtook them at the end of the first of many similar days of early training.

Delmar was gone eight days when the postcard finally arrived at the Hassel farm. Agnes had gone out to the mailbox each morning after the postal flitter had come in hopes of finding the card. Robert watched her and did not need to see the piece of mail to know that it had finally arrived. If she could have done cartwheels she would have, but her waving arm was sufficient to alert her husband.

Jake came in the back door at the same time Agnes came in the front. She nearly ran into him, and her excitement telegraphed itself to Sherry, who was busy preparing for lunch. Although it only said the expected—"I arrived safely and my star-mail address is Deagle>gss.3703.775.fwtb"—it still spoke volumes to those who received it. Many were the memories that the four could tell of their own experiences in basic. Sherry saw Agnes' reaction and knew what she would be doing after lunch.

"So I guess I'm going to be getting lunch ready alone?" Sherry commented to Agnes.

"Huh?" replied Agnes as she stared at the treasured postcard. Robert and Jake had a good laugh about it and helped Sherry set the table. After nearly stepping on Agnes twice, Sherry finally steered her to a corner chair and made her sit down. When lunch was ready, Robert led Agnes to the table.

She propped the postcard up in front of her and mechanically ate the food set before her.

As soon as she was finished, Agnes got up and went to her desk in the front room and switched on their home computer, which was very simple compared to the fancy models now available. Her fingers trembled as she typed her first letter to Delmar.

HasselFarm>gss.bv.er
Deagle>gss.3703.775.fwtb
Subject: Postcard received

Dear Delmar,

We received your postcard late this morning and are glad that you made it safe and sound. The Senders are still here with us, and Mr. Sender is helping Mr. Hassel with the chores. Mr. Hassel is doing better each day. I expect he'll be back to normal soon.

Mrs. Sender and I are really enjoying each other's company. Mr. Hassel is alarmed when we go into the kitchen. He says he has already put on ten pounds since he came home from the hospital. He blames our cooking!

We went down and checked on the Sabetis, the young couple that is taking care of your farm. They've been painting the house, and the difference is wonderful. Some of the neighbors are helping with the fields. They planted a modest crop that should be ready for harvest before the weather turns cold again in a couple of months.

Daren has been working on the old tractor and thinks he may be able to have it running soon. Two of the pistons need replacing. A neighbor up the road from us has a couple extras left over from an old rig he retired. After those are installed, Daren and Robert will try to get it started.

Well, I better close for now. I know you're busy and are having an interesting time learning new things. Take care and write when you can.

Love,
The Hassels

At basic, Delmar was learning interesting things all right—the correct way to mop a latrine effectively, for one. For more than a week, he had been steadily improving his skill level with his mop. At night his hands still curled from holding the handle, and he occasionally practiced mopping in his dreams.

The first starmail from the Hassels arrived two weeks into basic. That evening Buckner allowed them a half hour of free time before lights-out as a reward for their improved marching ability. Delmar took the precious letter he had printed from his starmail, read, and reread it several times. Then he took stationery that he had picked up at the unit store and composed his reply, knowing he would have to transpose it to starmail tomorrow.

Deagle>gss.3703.775.fwtb
HasselFarm>gss.bv.er
Subject: No hair

Dear Mr. & Mrs. Hassel,

It was so good to receive your letter today. DI Buckner gave us a half hour of free time, so I'm able to reply.

Life here at basic has been interesting. Initial orientation went fine, except that I'm still getting used to having no hair. I know that I don't need to tell you and the Senders about basic, since you've all been through it. I will tell you that I am, of course, homesick. But that's expected, I guess. Some of the guys are having it pretty rough adjusting to the constant "personal attention" by our DIs. But I followed your advice to "listen, obey, and keep your mouth shut." So I'm doing okay so far. I've lost some weight but find that my strength and endurance at calisthenics is improving.

I made a friend who bunks next to me. His name is Stan Shane. He and DI Buckner have had a few problems, but I hope it will get better for him soon. Stan has a real strange idea about what it takes to be a man. I'm not sure, but I think he has suffered some sort of a tragedy and has trouble releasing his feelings. He's very withdrawn and a bit of a loner. I could be wrong but I think the DIs are trying to help him see things clearly.

I'm glad to hear about the farm and the progress Daren and Rosemary are making. When I think about it, the farm seems like it was never really home. You folks have been my real family, and I consider your place "home." Since you are now my legal guardians, would you mind if I called you Mom and Dad? It would be an honor to be able to do it.

I love you folks (the Senders too!). Write soon. Delmar

PS—Please send me the Senders' starmail address, or give them mine.

Love,
D

His timing was about right. Delmar stuffed the letter under his pillow and was ready for the rack before lights out. Hearing from the Hassels was somewhat of a shock after being here for what seemed like forever. To visualize their farm took some effort, and it seemed like it had been in another lifetime. Delmar continued his musing for another couple of minutes before rolling over and going to sleep.

Robert and Jake helped Daren finish reassembling the tractor, and now they were ready for the decisive moment. Robert connected the jumper cables to the power cell of the ground car, which Jake had pulled into the barn to provide a little extra boost. When Robert felt the connections were good, he nodded to Daren, who pressed the start switch. The old tractor engine turned over several times before the first cylinder caught. With a bang and a cloud of black smoke, the engine started.

Rosemary, who had been watching from the back porch, heard the bang and then saw the barn disappear in a cloud of smoke. At first, she was afraid the barn had caught fire, but then she heard the men cheering. The smoke lifted and she was again able to see the three men. Daren kept the tractor running for another couple of minutes and then shut it down so they could check something under the hood.

While Jake and Robert peered under the hood, Daren limped to the porch to tell Rosemary all about it. The appearance of his sooty face out of the smoky gloom startled the young woman. Sensing that he wanted to hug her, she hurried back into the house while he made smudgy face prints on the kitchen door window.

Jake and Robert arrived about then and laughed at Daren's predicament. All three men went over to the outside faucet and scrubbed off the worst of the soot.

"I think we may need to retighten the flywheel bolts," Jake said. "We'll have to go get the breaker bar to have enough leverage."

"It's nearly lunchtime anyway," Daren replied. "Why don't we break for lunch and you guys come back after you eat?"

"Sounds good to me," Robert commented. "Let's go, Jake."

The two older men went back to their ground car and unhooked it from the tractor. With a wave to Daren on the back porch, they drove up the road to the Hassel farm.

Agnes completed her morning ritual by switching on her computer to check the mailbox. A shriek of excitement brought Sherry to the doorway, and she saw Agnes grinning from ear to ear, waving a letter she had just printed from her starmail. About that same time, Robert and Jake drove into the driveway. Sherry met them at the door and sent them to the laundry room to scrub thoroughly. Passing Sherry's inspection, she allowed the two men to enter the kitchen. Agnes was still holding the letter from Delmar as they all gathered around.

"Go ahead. Read it aloud, Agnes," Sherry said, sharing her excitement. "We want to hear it, too." Agnes looked at the two men who nodded their agreement. Taking a deep breath, Agnes read the letter.

After she finished, she looked up into the eyes of her husband. Jake and Sherry hugged each other. Robert and Agnes both started to cry.

"Well, what are you two going to say?" Jake asked.

Agnes looked at Robert, tears still trickling down her cheeks. He answered for both of them, "It's fine by us," he replied happily. "The boy is already our son anyway."

Jake and Sherry both laughed again, and then they all gathered at the table. Agnes managed to be of some help to Sherry, although she had trouble seeing through her tears of joy. Lunch made it to the table and they were soon eating and laughing at each other.

After lunch Agnes again sat at her desk, this time trying to figure out how to say what was in her heart. She finally decided on an approach and began to write.

> HasselFarm>gss.bv.er
> Deagle>gss.3703.775.fwtb
> Subject: re: No hair
>
> Dear Son,
>
> We received your letter today, and all of us were so glad to hear from you. As you may have guessed from the beginning of this letter, Mr. Hassel and I both happily agree to be your "Mom and Dad." We feel honored by your request.
>
> The Senders are still here but will be leaving soon to return to Mica. Dad and Mr. Sender have been helping Daren get the tractor started, and you should have seen how sooty they looked when they came home! They are going back this afternoon to adjust it some, and Daren is looking forward to using it around the farm.

We're glad that you are adjusting to basic so well. Dad says not to worry about losing your hair. He says it will grow back just about the time you lose it for good. We're glad to hear that you're making friends, and wish our best to Stan. Tell him that these old troopers say it takes more than being a superman to be a real man.

Mr. Hassel—oops!—I mean Dad, continues to improve and we should be able to start walking in the woods again soon. Having Mr. Sender around has helped keep Dad out of my hair, and his help with the chores keeps him from overdoing it.

The oats are about ready to harvest and have grown up enough to obscure the impressions left by the ships. After harvest, Daren is coming up to help us fill them in. The neighbors will have to watch it when they bring the harvest equipment in so they don't drop an axle.

Well, that's about it from here. The Senders send (Ha Ha. No pun intended.) their love. They say they'll write soon from Mica. Take care and keep making us proud.

Love,
Mom and Dad

Robert and Agnes drove the Senders to the spacefield

to see them off. "You sure you're going to be all right with me gone?" Jake asked Robert.

"Don't worry about him," Agnes replied. "I'll keep him in line!"

"Well, you take care of yourself!" Sherry piped in, pointing at Robert. "I don't want to have to come play nursemaid! Of course, we could just call Bulldozer Betty and have her move in with you." Everyone except Robert got a chuckle just as the loudspeaker announced that the flight was boarding. The women hugged each other while Robert and Jake shook hands.

"You two be good on the way home!" Robert called, watching the couple climb up the ramp. Jake and Sherry waved back and then passed through the hatch. Robert and Agnes stayed to watch the transport ship lift off and waved as it soared skyward.

On the way home, they passed the Eagleman farm. The Sabetis had painted the house a light yellow, and they could see Rosemary starting to work on the green trim. Robert honked and Rosemary waved with her paintbrush. A little farther on, they saw Daren in the field on the tractor. He waved when Robert honked and then continued watching where he was plowing as he pulled a cutter rig along.

Arriving back at the house, it seemed strangely quiet not to have either the Senders or Delmar around the place. Agnes made dinner while Robert walked to the barn. She watched him and saw that his limp was decidedly reduced. It was good to see him getting around so well, although the cane lent him a certain dignified air when he would use it.

The weather had graced the trainees with a mild downpour all the way back to the barracks. The unit was getting used to marching, and the steady rhythm of their boot heels on the pavement was almost hypnotic. Delmar managed to avoid stumbling when DIA Stoddard brought them to a halt. "You've got fifteen minutes to check your starmail," Stoddard reported. "Dismissed."

Sitting on the floor next to his bunk (he didn't want to wrinkle his dustcover in case there might be an afternoon surprise inspection), Delmar opened the two letters he had printed off the computer. The first was from Daren and Rosemary Sabeti. It was a report on how the farm was improving. Delmar was glad to see that it was working out for the couple, and the thought that the old farm was seeing happier times was welcome.

The second letter was from the Hassels. Delmar got as far as the opening address and stopped. The word "son" left him speechless. He felt a knot form in his throat and tears blur his eyes. After a while, he was able to finish reading the letter and then just sat there thinking about being a "son." He remembered being an orphan, and he remembered being an abused younger brother, but being a son seemed special somehow.

Finally, his vision refocused. He saw his friend

Stan looking at the floor, a single page held limply in his hand. "Hey, what's wrong, Stan?" Delmar asked. Stan looked up at him, his expression hollow.

"Ah, nothing," Stan finally answered. He crumpled the page and threw it at the trash basket. Delmar watched him walk out front of the barracks and sit down on the steps. Delmar retrieved the crumpled page and stuffed it into his pocket. Just then, DIA Stoddard came through the bay and told the trainees to wrap things up in five minutes. Delmar quickly stowed his precious mail in his locker, finishing just in time to hear the call to form ranks. As an afterthought, he also tossed Stan's letter into his locker. He would have to investigate it later.

"You coming, Trainee?" he heard Stoddard's voice boom from the end of the barracks bay.

"Yes, sir," Delmar answered, and ran outside to join formation with the other trainees.

17

Deagle>gss.3703.775.fwtb
HasselFarm>gss.bv.er
Subject: haircut with hair

Dear Mom and Dad,

Boy, it sure feels great to write that! Life here at
Freewater has been very busy. This morning we had
our second haircut since arriving. This time was
different though—I actually had some hair to cut!
DI Buckner has been working us hard on close-
order drill. I think we're finally getting the hang
of it. When he didn't think anyone was looking, I
actually saw him smile. The other guys didn't believe
me, and some have started a pool about how long it
will be before anyone else sees him smile again.

Our unit has pulled KP (Kitchen Police) seven
times since we finished the orientation, and I'm

getting pretty good at it. Several of us ended up in the dishwashing room and got a system going. Since that time, we've volunteered to work together in there, and DIA Stoddard commented that the output of that clipper room has gone up noticeably.

Stan continues to have trouble. He got some sort of letter a couple of days ago that really left him depressed. He threw it away, and even though I know it really isn't my business, I found it and went and talked to DIA Stoddard about it. I didn't have the nerve to read it. Stan can do things but seems to have lost any desire, like he has given up inside. I tried to talk to him, but he didn't want to talk about it. Me and a couple of the guys have been covering for him on some of his details, but I don't think we're fooling the DIs any. I hope DI Buckner or DIA Stoddard can help him.

I got a letter from Daren and Rosemary Sabeti. They told me about the tractor and what they've done to the farm. It's nice to think that it can be a happy home again. I hope he's not straining himself too much.

Well, I better close. It's almost lights-out and I still have to get ready. Tomorrow we start vacuum suit drill. Should be fun! Take care and write soon.

Love,
Delmar, your son

PS—What is happening with Dorn? You haven't mentioned anything in your letters.

Plenty of things were happening with Dorn. The police had some trouble with him while holding him for trial. He'd tried to attack one of the officers, but the officer's partner stopped him. Since then he had been confined to his cell, which he trashed in protest. When the officers refused to clean up the mess or move him to another cell, he launched himself into a hunger strike. Ten pounds lighter, Dorn realized that he wasn't going to change things that way and learned to cooperate.

Robert's health improved to the point that he was able to attend the trial proceedings, so the date was set. Agnes stood by him as the court came to order and the bailiff led in Dorn. It didn't take long to run through the testimony both for and against him. After both sides had presented their closing arguments, the judge recessed for a late lunch and to deliberate.

After the recess, everyone returned to the courtroom. The judge brought the proceedings to order and asked the bailiff to bring in Dorn. The judge announced that he had reached his decision. He found Dorn not guilty of attempted murder based on the fact that he told Robert that worse was coming if he kept interfering. That, said the judge, showed evidence that Dorn expected Robert to survive the attack.

The judge went on to further state that Dorn was guilty of aggravated assault and called for him to step forward for sentencing. The bailiff escorted Dorn to the front of the courtroom and removed his shackles, as was traditional on Erdinata. No man could be condemned while under restraints against his will, but was to stand and accept his sentence. Dorn stood passively while the judge read his sentence.

Unexpectedly, Dorn turned and fled down the aisle and out the door. Several officers gave chase, but Dorn had both surprise and a head start to aid him. They gained on him after several blocks. The officers restrained themselves from firing at him out of concern for the bystanders as Dorn wove in and out among them.

A few bystanders tried to stop Dorn, but he managed to squirm free. It slowed him enough that he dove through a store entrance just before the police could reach him. He grabbed a young woman and dragged her back, using her as a shield against the police advance.

As they passed a hardware counter, Dorn grabbed a knife and held it to the woman's throat, slightly cutting her in the process. That was enough for her and she drove her fist hard into his groin, causing him to release his grip. As she fell to the floor, one of the officers shot Dorn in the chest, and he collapsed. Despite all efforts of the emergency medical team, he died later that night at the hospital.

In court the next day, the clerk entered testimony of the event into the case record, and the case closed. Glad that the ordeal was over, but knowing the news would not be good for Delmar, Robert and Agnes went home where she sat down and wrote him a letter.

HasselFarm>gss.bv.er
Deagle>gss.3703.775.fwtb
Subject: Sad news

Dear Son,

It is with heavy heart and mixed emotions that I answer your inquiry about your brother. I've attached a copy of the court report on the trial about what happened. I know your brother brought his destruction upon himself, but I'm still saddened by a wasted life.

Dad and I offer you our condolences and love. We know how Dorn mistreated you, and frankly, we're amazed that you exhibited no bitterness. I'm so glad your parents never witnessed it. I know Dorn's end would have disappointed them terribly. Your mother told me of their hopes for both of you boys when you were still very young. At the time, she didn't want you boys to know that, and I have kept it from you until now.

Son, you must continue to keep the faith your parents had in you from the start. Dad and I are proud of you and your accomplishments and are honored to stand as your parents today. We feel your grief. We love you. Please write soon.

Love,
Mom and Dad

Delmar read both the court report and Agnes' letter. Afterward he laid his head on his hands and wept. Until then he did not realize how much he still loved his brother and hoped that someday he would change. Now it was too late.

Delmar wept quietly for a while and then felt a hand on his shoulder. Through his tears, he saw Stan looking at him with a worried expression. "What's wrong, Del?" he asked. Delmar handed Stan the report and letter and let him read them. When Stan finished reading, he looked wide-eyed at Delmar.

"I thought you had a happy family," Stan remarked. "I thought I was the only one with troubles." Delmar was surprised at Stan's comments, and it was his turn to stare.

"I've always had family trouble," Delmar said quietly. "I never told you because I figured it wouldn't do any good and that you had enough troubles of your own."

"Tell me now," Stan said earnestly. "You need to talk, and I want to listen." Surprised by Stan's reaction, Delmar found himself suddenly opening up.

After many minutes, Delmar fell silent, his whole story told. Stan sat quietly for a long moment and then went and retrieved something from his locker. Sitting back down beside Delmar, he handed him a framed picture. It was of a beautiful young woman a little younger than Stan. Delmar looked at the picture and then at Stan, puzzled.

"That," Stan began haltingly, "was my fiancée. She was killed a few weeks ago in a shuttle accident." Tears coursed down Stan's cheeks, something Delmar had never seen.

"I received a letter from her brother about it," Stan said quietly. "We were going to be married after I graduated from basic. When she died, I gave up."

"I knew something was wrong," Delmar replied. "Why didn't you tell me?"

"Because I was afraid to cry, and I figured no one would care," Stan answered hesitantly. Delmar reached over and squeezed Stan's shoulder.

"Hey! I care," he said, "and you should too."

"What do you mean?" Stan asked.

"I mean, you should care about yourself," Delmar answered. "Your girl loved you and had faith in you. You have to honor that faith and keep going. Keep caring; keep living."

"But what about our hopes and dreams?" Stan asked, tears still coursing down his face.

"We can't change the past, as much as we'd like to," Delmar replied. "Your dreams together are over, but her dreams about you as a trooper aren't. Keep her faith, even if she can't be by your side."

Stan sat silently for several minutes, tears still staining his face. Finally, he struggled to his feet. "I'll make you a deal," he said. "If you keep going, I'll keep going." Delmar grinned in reply at his friend. Stan gripped Delmar's hand, a lasting friendship beginning to form through their bonds of grief.

Robert and Agnes again found themselves seated before the judge. The image of Dorn's flight from justice was still impressed in their minds in spite of the later trial of Dorn's friends that had harassed Agnes and assaulted Robert. Now they were here in regards to their role as Delmar's legal guardians to adjust the title of the farm and deed it fully to Delmar.

"Would the guardians approach the bench and present their papers?" the judge intoned. Robert and Agnes came forward and gave the judge copies of their guardianship papers, Dorn's death certificate, and the petition for title change. They turned to retake their seats, but the judge motioned for them to remain while he leafed through the stack.

Looking up, he addressed the court. "The court is in recess for ten minutes," he said and banged his gavel. The Hassels were a little dumbfounded until Robert noticed the judge motion for them to follow him into his chambers. He waved them to chairs and sat down behind his desk.

"We've been seeing a lot of each other lately, haven't we?" the judge commented with a smile. "I thought after all the recent troubles, it might be more relaxing to discuss this thing in here." The Hassels nodded back.

"I was beginning to think I should have a reserved parking spot and invest in some white shirts," Robert replied. Agnes and the judge both chuckled.

"How's Delmar doing?" the judge asked.

"The last letter sounded good," answered Agnes. "He seems to be adjusting well to the service and even making friends," she added.

"Well, I knew the news about his brother would

hit him pretty hard," the judge said. "Have you heard from him since you sent the court report?"

"No, sir, we haven't," Robert replied for both of them.

"I was afraid of that," the judge said. "I'm uncomfortable doing this title change so close on the heels of the news about Dorn."

"I agree," Robert answered. "Maybe we should route this through his DI so the news comes from a different angle."

"We have to contact the DI in any case," the judge commented. "Since Delmar is still a legal minor, we need a witnessed statement that he understands what is happening."

"Sounds good to us," Agnes stated.

"Okay. I'll write the necessary letter," the judge agreed. "Now let's go out there and do the formalities."

The three got up and returned to the courtroom. The judge reopened the proceedings and then ruled a continuance in the case until Delmar could submit a statement to the court.

The bang of his gavel released the Hassels, but a wink at Agnes and Robert told them they might be seeing the judge before the next court date.

> Deagle>gss.3703.775.fwtb
> HasselFarm>gss.bv.er
> Subject: re: Sad news
>
> Dear Mom and Dad,
>
> Sorry I haven't written sooner. Life here has been hectic, as you both would understand.

First, I want to say that the news about Dorn didn't completely surprise me, considering his violence toward me. I realized how much I still loved him and had hoped that he would eventually change. Now he's gone, and what's done is done.

I was surprised that you knew my parents. I vaguely remember some other adults from my earliest memories, but can't remember any faces or names. It was comforting to know there is that connection. Thank you for your encouragement.

We just finished suit drill training, and I wish you could have seen it. As you know, these pressure suits shrink to fit after you get into them. A few of the guys had trouble getting them on quickly enough and got all tangled up when the suits started shrinking early. They looked like poorly wrapped chickens! It took several of us to get them untangled!

Stan is doing much better now, so I'm not worried about him anymore. His fiancée died tragically in a shuttle accident a while back. He took it pretty hard and gave up. We talked it out right after the letter about Dorn came, and we're both doing a lot better. DIA Stoddard seems pleased by the improvement and now pairs the two of us for most drills and duty.

Well, I better sign off. Lights-out soon. Take care.

Love,
Delmar

Agnes had just finished clearing the dinner dishes when a car stopped outside the back door. Robert looked out and saw the judge and his wife get out and walk toward the back porch. Greeting them at the back door, he invited them in. Agnes directed them toward the kitchen table while Robert poured coffee. Agnes served some pie with whipped cream.

"So what brings you out this way, Your Honor?" Robert asked.

"Oh, we just thought we'd do a little bit of personal investigating," the judge responded. "We were curious about how that couple you have taking care of Delmar's place is doing."

"Well, when I was down there the day before yesterday, things looked pretty good," Agnes replied. "I had a visit with Rosemary, and the two of them seem pretty happy."

"We noticed several improvements in the place when we drove past," the judge's wife commented.

"I see they got the barn painted and repaired," the judge added. "How did he manage with that injured leg of his?"

"He's had some help from different neighbors, including us. But he does a lot out of sheer determination," Robert answered.

"It's a good thing, especially with winter coming on," the judge remarked. "Did they manage to get in any sort of crop?"

"Yes, sir," answered Agnes. "I know they got one field of late hay and some oats. They moved in too late to have much of a garden, but I know some of the ladies are pooling together some of their canning to stock the pantry as a surprise."

"So the neighbors around here have taken to them?" the judge asked.

"Yes, they have," answered Robert. He then changed tack on the conversation. "Why are you so curious?"

"Oh, I was trying to figure out all the options Delmar has open to him," the judge replied. "A young man in the troopers doesn't have much time to take care of a farm."

"Daren is a trooper too," Agnes said, perplexed. "He's managing the farm pretty well."

"I know that," the judge replied. "But he's on medical leave from the service for now."

"When he goes back they'll be moving," Robert commented.

"I'm not so sure he's going back," the judge said. "I was talking with his doctor the last time we played poker. He said the bone injuries are permanent and the boy's trooper days are over."

"Does Daren know?" Robert asked quietly.

"Not yet," replied the judge. "I think the liaison officer will tell him soon."

"Why hasn't he been told yet?" asked Agnes.

"Because they wanted him to have a goal for the present to aid his recovery as much as possible," the judge answered. "If they told him outright, the boy might have just given up. Leaving the service is hard on a person."

"So that's why you came to us first," Robert said as

he started to see where this was leading. "We know what it's like to have to leave and how to adjust."

"I see you're starting to catch my drift," the judge replied. "The liaison officer, his doctor, and I want him to be fairly well established in the community before he has to face the letdown of medical release."

"I guess I can speak for the neighbors and say they're accepted all right," Agnes replied. "But what about Delmar? It's his farm now."

"That's why I'm waiting to hear from Delmar and his DI," answered the judge. "In my letter I asked Delmar his intentions."

"Trooper Trainee Eagleman reporting, sir!" Delmar stood at attention in the office doorway.

"Come in and shut the door, Eagleman," DI Buckner said. "Have a seat and relax," he continued. "We're going to be here a while."

Delmar sat down and waited nervously in spite of the admonition to relax. One wasn't ordered to report to the duty office without it being something serious.

"What I need to see you about is a legal matter back on your home planet," Buckner began. "I received a letter from the judge overseeing your guardianship. It includes the legal papers concerning the property title of your farm and a personal set of questions he wants me to go over with you." He handed the legal papers to Delmar first. Delmar quickly read them and looked back at his DI.

"Sir, if I understand these correctly, they need

my signature, witnessed by you, to affect the transfer of Dorn's half of the property into my name."

"That's the essence of it," Buckner replied.

Delmar thought about it for a minute. "But, sir," he began. "I don't want the farm. I always figured Dorn would have it."

"That's the other issue the judge wrote about," Buckner replied. "He wants to know your intentions."

Delmar thought about it for another minute. "What would you do?" Delmar finally asked.

"I can't tell you what to do," Buckner replied, "but I could offer you some possible options."

Delmar didn't reply, but instead looked at his DI expectantly, so Buckner went on. "You've been in training now for two months. I've watched you, and you're doing very well. I saw how you helped Stan Shane and how you and the other guys covered for him."

Delmar blushed to find out they hadn't fooled the drill instructors. "That's what we try to teach our trainees," Buckner continued, "to help each other and work as a team. I think you're going to make a good trooper by the time you graduate. At that time, you'll go to a technical training school or out on assignment with one of the fleets. Either way, you'll receive assignments all over the Axia for years before you have an opportunity to settle down. That can be rough on a man, especially if he has established a home somewhere."

"Then you think I should give up the farm?" Delmar replied.

"No, not exactly," Buckner responded. "I think

you should first sign the documents so you have control of the property. Then after the change is recorded, come see me again."

"Yes, sir," replied Delmar. He took the pen and signed the papers and then Buckner signed as witness.

"I'll dispatch these to the judge tomorrow," Buckner said. He folded the sheets and stuffed them in a return envelope.

"Thank you, sir," Delmar said as he rose from the chair.

"Oh, one more thing, Eagleman," Buckner said, not looking at him.

"Sir?" Delmar answered, wondering what was up now.

"You didn't call me sir a minute ago," Buckner said. "Drop and give me sixty."

"Yes, sir," answered Delmar. He dropped to the floor and did sixty quick, textbook-perfect push-ups. As soon as he finished, he again stood at attention.

"All right, Trainee," Buckner said without looking up. "Dismissed."

Delmar quickly left the office. DI Buckner took the extra papers the judge had sent him and filed them in Delmar's folder for later reference.

18

HasselFarm>gss.bv.er
Deagle>gss.3703.775.fwtb
Subject: News from home

Dear Son,

We were in court again yesterday. The judge will be sending you the notice soon about the transfer of full title of your farm into your name.

This winter has been interesting. We got more snow than we expected. It's unseasonably cold for this time of year. I'm glad we got all the major chores done before it hit. Right now we have two feet of snow on the level ground out front, and Dad says the drifts out back of the barn are head high.

Daren came down with the tractor and a plow arrangement he built and cleared our driveway. He cleared driveways for the neighbors all up and down the road. Robert had him come in and warm up some before going home.

I noticed Daren was limping bad and asked him what was wrong. He said the doctors were unable to repair his left leg and were afraid they were going to have to amputate it soon. The service is going to let him go with a disability pension. He was so discouraged. He tried to hide it until Dad confronted him. They talked for a couple of hours and then Daren went home. Dad told me they're going to fix Daren up with a cloned leg, but because of the nerve damage higher up, he won't be able to stay in the service.

Next day—sorry for the delay. I had to break off and go help Robert with the animals.

I went over and saw Daren and Rosemary this morning. You would be pleased with the nice way they've fixed up the old house. It looks so different. Rosemary sure knows how to pretty things up. They painted all of the interior and did a flower print border around the top of the living and dining rooms. The kitchen is now a nice yellow and white with checkered curtains. After we'd been sitting a while, Rosemary got up and asked me to come see something. She led me into Dorn's old room, and it was so nice and clean with the fresh paint and all. There's a border of baby animals around the top of the wall, and the curtains have little animals and toys on them. She's turned Dorn's old room into the prettiest little nursery.

I'd been back only a few minutes this afternoon when Rosemary called. Daren had fallen in the barn and was hurt. Dad and I rushed down and helped him into the house. His left leg had quit on him completely. Dad drove us all to the hospital, where they admitted Daren. The doctors say they're going to have to amputate his leg in the morning. An infection has set in, and it will threaten Daren's life if they don't. Dad took Rosemary and me to their home where I'm staying for the night. He'll pick us up in the morning so we can be there at the hospital before Daren goes into surgery.

Well, I can see this letter has turned into a regular journal. I better close and let you get something done. You take care and write soon. How is Stan?

Love,
Mom and Dad

"So let's review it one more time," the instructor said. "The enlisted ranks of the service are as follows: trooper trainee, trooper, trooper-third, trooper-second, and trooper-first. Then there's the Academy for officer training." The instructor eyed his charges. The trainees were showing signs of hitting saturation.

"Okay, now the officer ranks, and then we'll quit:

sub-lieutenant, lieutenant, major, commander, colonel, sub-fleet commander, fleet-commander, chief fleet-commander, and of course the royal family," he intoned. He noticed a hand toward the rear. "Yes, trainee?" he asked.

"Sir?" the trainee said, standing, "Where do the ship ranks fit in?" The trainee sat down.

"They are independent of the service ranks," the instructor answered. "The officers are as follows: captain and pilot, executive officer and sometimes a chaplain, legal officer, and medical officer. Anyone taking the training and passing the qualifying exams can become a pilot. A captain must also show proficiency in landing the ships as well as in-flight piloting. The captain is the highest-ranking individual on the ship, regardless of his service rank or the rank of service personnel on board. The higher enlisted ranks include a cargo master and a crew chief. Other ranks are simply crewmembers. Any more questions before we quit?" Fortunately, there were none, so he dismissed the trainees.

Delmar received two starmails that day, one from the judge and one from the Hassels. Delmar unfolded his letter from the Hassels and read it as soon as they were given free time after lunch.

The letter from the judge noted that the property was now fully Delmar's. It further stated that, considering his age, decisions regarding the property required joint concurrence with the direction of his legal guardian.

As soon as he finished the letter, Delmar went

to the duty office and requested to see DI Buckner. DIA Stoddard waved him into the duty office.

Buckner sat at his desk. Delmar reported and Buckner told him to close the door and waved him to a seat. "What's up, Eagleman?" Buckner asked.

"This, sir," Delmar responded as he handed the notification to DI Buckner, who read it and reached for Delmar's file folder.

"So, what's on your mind?" Buckner asked.

"I was thinking, sir, that I might want to see if the caretakers want to have it. The farm, I mean," Delmar replied. "I understand that he's being medically released from the service, and that they're also expecting a baby. Mr. and Mrs. Hassel think well of them, and it sounds like it could work out." Buckner held up his hand to stop Delmar. He opened Delmar's folder and pulled out two letters.

"I received this letter from the judge and another one from your guardian concerning that possibility two weeks ago," Buckner said. "Both are concerned about your career as a trooper and the situation of your caretaker. What they weren't sure about was your feelings about the property. They asked me to feel you out about it. You had to express clearly your intentions before allowing me to mention the possibility of the caretakers being interested. This you have just done. It is the opinion of both your guardians and the judge that transfer of the property to the caretakers would be beneficial to both you and to them. How do you feel about it?"

"Well sir, from what the Hassels wrote about his

disability, it sounds like they couldn't pay much for it," Delmar began. "I don't feel exactly right about just giving it away. Daren didn't strike me as a man that would accept charity. I think they should have it because of all the work they've put into it, but I'm not sure how to do it so I don't insult him," Delmar finished.

"The judge mentioned that the liaison officer told him about a fund the troopers in Daren's unit started to help him," Buckner said. "If anybody could give him help without hurting his pride, it would be those guys. You're already learning about the bonds that hold troopers together. We never abandon our own. If you agree to release your interest in the property, Mr. Hassel and the judge will see to it that it's handled correctly for all concerned."

"It sounds good to me, sir," Delmar replied. "What do I need to sign?"

Buckner pulled out the forms the judge had sent him. "Sign here and I'll witness it," Buckner said, pointing at a line. Delmar did so.

"I'll keep a copy in your file for safekeeping and dispatch the original to Erdinata tomorrow," Buckner said as he gathered the papers. "If there isn't anything else, you're dismissed."

"There's not, sir," Delmar said as he rose. "Thank you, sir," he said as he exited the room.

Buckner watched him go. *There*, he thought, *goes the making of a fine trooper.*

The doctor came out to the waiting room where the young wife and an older couple waited.

"Well, folks," the surgeon began, "the cloning went well. He should be in his room shortly." They thanked him and walked together to Daren's room. He had been here a month after the amputation. Rosemary was anxious to see Daren and glad that things were going smoothly. Entering his room, Agnes pulled out the letter that had come the day before. With the need to be here, there hadn't been time to read it until now.

Deagle>gss.3703.775.fwtb
HasselFarm>gss.bv.er
Subject: re: News from home

Dear Mom and Dad,

Sorry for the delay. We've been on field training exercises and just got back last night. DI Buckner was so pleased with our performance that he gave us the whole afternoon off today!

By now, you should have received the release I signed on the property. I want you to know that it is my desire that it go to the Sabetis in such a way that he doesn't feel like it's charity. DI Buckner said that Dad and the judge know a way to do it, so go ahead. I'll leave the details up to you and Dad.

How is Daren doing? Did his surgery go okay? I've wondered about it often since your last letter a few weeks ago. I hope they're happy. I already think of the farm as being theirs, and hearing about the new nursery was great. And I can't think of anything at the house I want that Dad and I haven't already gotten.

You asked about Stan. He's doing great. The DIs announced that he's the most improved trainee of our flight! He and I are both studying preliminary electronics together in the technical training. We each have a training station at the tech building to run our experiments and exercises on. The tech building averages one burned-up bench a week, and boy do they stink!

One of the trainees in our room caused the building computer to get caught in a loop cycle (it's supposedly impossible, but he did it). The instructor was about to crash the whole computer when Stan asked if he could try something. The instructor figured he had nothing to lose, except maybe a burned-up bench, so he let Stan go ahead. They're still trying to figure out what he did (so am I), but he restored the main computer from his training bench! Since that time, they've called on him to fix other problems that crop up. He and I have fun designing new circuit ideas together. He's a real whiz at it!

Well, I better close. You all take care and say hi to Daren and Rosemary for me.

All my love,
Delmar

PS—Less than six weeks to go!

Agnes smiled as she finished the letter. She already knew the plans the liaison officer and Robert had made to surprise Daren and Rosemary.

Three weeks later the Hassels and Rosemary picked up Daren at the hospital to take him home. The weather was starting to turn to spring and all that reminded them of winter were piles of dirty snow.

Although happy to be going home, Daren seemed somewhat reserved. When they pulled into the driveway, all his eyes could see were the chores needing attention. Robert helped Daren up the steps and to the front door. Daren was wearing a brace system on the cloned leg. Robert held back and let the young man enter the front door by himself.

As soon as he entered the front room, it exploded with people shouting and cheering. Rosemary came up close behind Daren to steady him while his eyes took in the host of troopers and friends surrounding them. Willing hands helped Daren to his chair while Agnes skirted the crowd to the kitchen to help with the refreshments. Robert stayed in the front room and watched Daren while he greeted and talked with the men from Daren's old unit.

When Agnes interrupted their conversations by announcing that cake and punch was ready in the dining room, several friends helped Daren up and into the adjoining room. On the table was a large slab cake with "Welcome Home, Daren" written on it. Propped up in the center was a small envelope.

At the urging of several troopers, Daren picked up the envelope and read the front: "From the guys of the 437th." The room became very quiet. Opening it, Daren extracted a single page. As he read it, his eyes grew wide and glassy. Rosemary became worried and went to him. He just handed the page to her and sat down heavily in a kitchen chair. She read it and soon mirrored her husband's expression. As one, they turned toward the Hassels.

"Is it true?" Daren asked in disbelief.

"Yes, it's true," replied Robert with a grin, handing the legal title to the couple. Rosemary shrieked and she and Daren hugged each other in an embrace of joy. Robert noticed that Daren had to reach farther around to avoid Rosemary's growing belly. The room became noisy again as friends congratulated the couple on their new home. Two troopers hauled out a wooden sign that read "The Sabeti Farm" and gave it to Daren and Rosemary.

Walking shakily with the help of friends, Daren returned to his chair in the living room. Rosemary sat on the arm, her right hand resting on her husband's shoulder. Plates with pieces of cake, along with cups of punch, helped liven the party. Daren and Rosemary answered a bombardment of questions about the farm and coming baby. Robert and Agnes held hands and watched the happy couple.

HasselFarm>gss.bv.er
Deagle>gss.3703.775.fwtb
Subject: Title to the farm

Dear Son,

Daren came home from the hospital yesterday. The doctors attached the new cloned leg three weeks ago, and he's doing well. To their total surprise, when we got to the house, the troopers from his unit had a welcome-home party waiting on them and presented them with the title to the farm. Of course, Rosemary knew about the party since it was at her house, but not about the deed to the farm. You helped make a young couple very happy!

The escrow account the judge set up for you now contains the proceeds from the sale. It's not as much as we'd hoped for, but with the interest it will draw over the next several years, it will give you a nice little nest egg for when you do decide to settle down.

The bank will send the statements here unless you direct otherwise. Dad felt that it was better this way so you don't have to lug around all the extra mail they tend to send.

Spring has finally arrived. In another week or so, the fields should be ready to plow and plant, and Dad is anxious to get started. I think being cooped up in the house so much is starting to wear on him.

We were excited to read about your interest and training in electronics. Jake suspected that you might be inclined that way. He said you really enjoyed the science museum on Mica, especially the computer wing. Although your training will help you gain an overall knowledge in many fields, having an area of expertise helps quite a bit.

Well, I better go for now. I can see Dad coming in from the field and he's probably hungry. Take care and greet Stan for us.

Love,
Mom and Dad

Delmar received the letter shortly after the unit came back from weapons training. There had been some limited training in fencing, and then they moved on to the other weapons.

Puzzled at first by the need for fencing, their instructor explained that using a blaster, for example, did take out your enemy but it also took out the ship wall behind him. Swords were preferable on ship because they didn't damage the equipment. He remembered Jake Sender telling him about a sword fight somewhere.

Training on the blaster and long-weapon (why they didn't call it a long-blaster no one knew) was more fascinating. The trainees first received single hand-blasters—blasters altered to limit their power. A fully charged regular blaster could take out a wall and leave a deep crater beyond, but the altered units could only leave scorch marks on the concrete targets. Delmar quickly proved his accuracy to hit the target without undue power consumption.

The long-weapon was even more interesting. DI Buckner asked for two volunteers to come forward. He then lifted two long-weapons off the table, one in each hand, and handed one to each of the volunteers. Unknown to the trainees, each weapon had a small built-in antigravity unit controlled by a simple switch. As he released the weapons, Buckner flicked off the switches. The weight of the weapons forced each trainee almost to the ground, much to the delight of the other trainees watching. DI Buckner then went to each and single-handedly picked the weapons back up, flicking the hidden switches again as he did. The two trainees looked at him in utter amazement. Then he laughed and showed them the trick. He explained that it was one way to make it harder for an enemy to take it away from you and use it against you.

The firepower of the long-weapon was many-fold that of the hand-blaster, and at a much greater range. It was most effective against fortified positions and low-flying ships. Delmar enjoyed the feel of the long-weapon. It reminded him of a good game rifle, but without serious kick. The targets on the range started at one hundred yards and went up from there. Delmar was able to master it quickly and qualified as an expert marksman.

The weapons training was at the end of their fourth month of training. As he started writing an answer to the letter, Delmar found it hard to believe that it had been so long.

19

This training exercise was different from any of the others Delmar's training flight had been on before. They were well past the basic portion of their training, the part where they learned to march, make their beds, and fold their clothes. Now their training had moved to actively using live, full-strength weapons with the possibility of facing their actual enemy, the Red-tails. And although their instructors had taken every precaution to avoid contact with their enemy, anything was possible in space, thus the service's policy that the only good weapon was a loaded one.

Delmar remembered his one and only encounter with a Red-tail, an experience he was in no hurry to repeat. He had told his friends in his training flight about the incident on the *Malibu* when they had come under attack while on their way to Mica. Only a few of the other men had ever seen a Red-tail, and they all agreed they'd rather not encounter any ever again.

Although Delmar's flight had been on several training missions since starting their advanced training, this trip was a live-fire exercise that would carry the Alpha squad of Delmar's training flight 775 of the 3703 Training Squadron to a moon base only a day from Freewater. Beta, Delta, and Gamma squads were also on the exercise, but Alpha would be the aggressor this time. Their instructions were to think of and refer to the other squads as the enemy. Their mission: to seek out and destroy an enemy communications relay station on the second moon of the planet Melanor. Beta, Delta, and Gamma would defend under the command of DI Buckner.

DIA Stoddard was leading Alpha squad; a man Delmar believed could handle himself in a combat situation. Stoddard knew his equipment and his men, and was technologically sound. Delmar had learned that Stoddard was actually a combat veteran, having served in almost a dozen Red-tail incursion campaigns before becoming a training instructor. Delmar felt safe in his hands.

The ship Alpha squad was on was ancient, which meant it was almost a hundred years old—well past retirement age for most military transports. Noise reduction dampeners were never installed on this ship because it was originally used as a cargo transport, so the whine of the ship's drive could be heard even through the ship's repulsion field. The seating on the ship was nothing more than canvas web strapping attached to the bulkheads, not the comfortable seating enjoyed by the other squads in their ship.

It didn't take long for Delmar to realize that service with the troopers didn't promise to always be comfortable. The most uncomfortable aspect of the seating arrangement was the shoulder strap that chafed unmercifully at Delmar's neck.

Another aspect of irritation for Delmar was the fact that his friend, Stan Shane, had been transferred to the Gamma squad and assigned the task of systems analyst, which meant he would be monitoring the enemy squad's communications network. Delmar cringed at the thought of having to try to get past Stan. He knew Stan was an expert computer analyst and had even been called on at the training school to debug the school's computer system and workbenches. Getting past him was going to be very difficult, if not impossible.

The ancient transport ship made its way into the Melanor system. The pilot set his directionals toward the second moon. Their landing zone would be in the northern hemisphere, where they would set up camp. The communications array being protected by the enemy squads was in the southern hemisphere, which meant Alpha would have to fly shuttlecraft or low-gravity flitters to reach their target. *That's one thing about being the aggressor*, Delmar thought. *Someone is always watching out for you.*

After the pilot made his announcement for all trainees to remain strapped in, he started his descent into the moon's limited atmosphere. Delmar could hear the rush of the atmosphere against the outer hull of the large transport. He knew the ship's repulsion field would keep them from overheating, but just the thought that only a layer of hull plating separated them from two thousand degrees of friction heat was unsettling to Delmar and the Alpha squad.

After what seemed forever, the friction noise ended and everything became silent. With exception to the firing of the retro rockets, the great transport settled down onto the moon's surface.

In the southern hemisphere, Stan Shane monitored the communications array the Gamma squad was tasked to defend. Beta through Gamma had already been on the surface for over a week. And although the moon had limited gravity and atmosphere, Stan was growing tired of the supplemental oxygen mask he was required to wear. *Well*, he thought, *at least they didn't make us wear the whole suit.*

When Stan had taken over the duties of communications analyst, he was amazed at the condition of the comm equipment. He doubted if any of the systems had undergone any kind of an upgrade for at least a decade, maybe two. The monitors were still green screen, not even color, and the keyboards weren't even the easy-touch pads common in any elementary school. What was worse, none of the systems had voice responsive command functions, which greatly limited their usefulness in case of an enemy attack.

Stan went to work upgrading the systems. First, he installed voice responsive command functions, which required replacing the motherboards on more than a dozen systems. This upgrade did not sit well with their supply officer since it required requisitioning every motherboard except one out of their War Readiness Spares Kits (WRSK).

Next came the upgrade on the incoming tracking arrays. Stan discovered that the arrays were completely out of alignment. He figured in their present condition he couldn't have monitored a fleet of invading Red-tail ships if he could have seen them out the window. And if he knew Delmar and the other guys in Alpha squad, especially DIA Stoddard, they would be working on some way to counter any precautions he would set up to ward them off.

Stan pried open the panel on one of the ancient consoles and looked inside. *How could Axia equipment have gotten into this kind of shape?* he wondered. He ran his fingers along the solid-state circuitry and could feel gaps in the circuits and components removed. He doubted if this equipment could intercept a clear signal from any kind of enemy transmission in this condition.

Next came the antenna array itself. The first thing Stan noticed was that it listed sharply to one side, completely out of alignment with the poles of the planet. *It's a good thing this is just an exercise*, he thought. *I wouldn't want to depend on this thing in an actual combat situation.*

Using the equipment available to him from their transport ship, and calling on every member of Beta, Delta, and Gamma squads, Stan was able to realign the communications array. At the objections of the transport captain and the supply officer, Stan even requisitioned every spare bedsprings rod from the limited WRSK to create an amplified transponder array. This, he hoped, would give them a fifteen-minute warning in case of enemy attack. DI Buckner didn't understand Shane's theory but he assumed it would work. After all, he had saved several work-benches at the school from the salvage after systems crashes. *Improvise, adapt, overcome,* he thought.

Stan looked at the chronometer on the console and realized that he had been working for fifteen straight hours without a break. He stood up, stretched his aching back, and tried to rub the soreness out of his hips and legs. *This is going to be a long exercise,* he thought. "Another hour ought to do it," he muttered to himself. "Then it's chow and some shut-eye."

Two hours later, Stan Shane crawled back out from under the communications console. "Give it a try," he instructed Trooper Trainee Thomas Bigga. Bigga, or Big'un as everyone called him, was the largest man in Flight 775. Buckner had assigned Big'un to work with Stan on the communications array, but the truth was Big'un wasn't very technically adept. Stan figured Big'un would end up in the infantry where he would carry large weapons into combat against the Red-tails.

Big'un pressed a series of buttons on the console. Lights on the panel began to blink, and Big'un heard a fan rumble and begin to whirl. He stepped back away from the console. Stan stood up and examined the console. "Looks good," he said.

"Now if you'd be kind enough to call us a taxi, we'll go get something to eat," he kidded Big'un.

Big'un suddenly reached out, grabbed Stan around his waist, hefted him up over his head, and laid Stan across his shoulders. "You wanna ride, hot-shot?" he said. "You got it!" Then with absolutely no effort at all, Big'un ran with Stan on his shoulders across the compound. The limited gravity of the moon created extra long strides for the large man, allowing him to leap twenty feet at a time through the air with Stan laughing and yelling all the way. In only a moment the two men were in line at the mess tent. Stan didn't realize how hungry he really was. Big'un had no misconceptions whatsoever.

Back at Alpha camp, Delmar and several of the other members of the aggressor squad were busy preparing for their attack on the communications array. "You don't understand," Delmar emphasized to the group, "I know the report says that relay station is defunct, but Stan Shane has been there for over a week. I promise you he's had time to fix it."

"Impossible," replied Tulie Greenwood, one of Alpha's shuttle pilots. "That relay is so far gone it would take a month of winters to fix it."

"He's right, Delmar," interjected Joquax Tip, Alpha's quartermaster. "I saw the report. All they have is a limited WRSK. It would take a complete overhaul to get that array up to speed."

"I understand what you're saying," answered Delmar. "But I've worked closer with Shane in the electronics lab than any of you guys, and I'm telling you that he will figure a way to patch that thing back together and they'll be ready for us."

"Not a chance. Nope. No way," answered the other men.

"DIA Stoddard, sir," Delmar said. "What do you say?"

Stoddard looked up from where he had been studying the reports on the communications relay. "It looks like it's in pretty bad shape, Eagleman," he answered. "But I agree with you that Shane knows his way around this kind of equipment. If anyone can jury-rig, it would be Shane."

"Then how are we supposed to attack that array if they'll know we're coming, sir?" Tip asked.

"That's all part of combat strategy," Stoddard answered. "You must expect the enemy to expect you, and then you work around him. If they know we're coming, and you can rest assured they do, then we'll simply not go."

"Huh?" everyone asked in unison.

"We'll just sit right here in camp, enjoy the view of the stars, and let them come to us," Stoddard answered.

"But sir," Delmar said. "Our mission is to take out that communications array. How are we supposed to do that if we stay here?"

"We're not," Stoddard answered. "You are."

"Me sir?" Delmar asked.

"Yes, you," Stoddard said. "Let me ask you this. Do you really believe Shane will have that communications relay up and running?"

"Yes, sir," Delmar answered.

"Long range or short range?" Stoddard asked.

"With the limited supplies he has, probably short range," Delmar answered.

"That's what I figure too," the DIA said. "So what we'll do is send out a series of short-range pulses declaring an emergency. We'll lure Beta and Delta squads away from their base camp. Then with only Gamma there to defend the array, you and a few others will attack and destroy the array."

"Sir, isn't that playing dirty?" Greenwood asked.

"Do you think for one minute that a Red-tail will care if he plays fair or not, Trainee?" Stoddard asked.

"No, sir," Greenwood answered. "Guess not."

"The only thing he wants to do is kill you and eat you, and not necessarily in that order," Stoddard said. "So stop thinking like a human and become the aggressor."

Alpha squad spent the rest of the afternoon preparing for an attack they knew the other squads were expecting the next day. Except this attack would not come the next day, or even the next. Instead, they would let the enemy sit and wait and hopefully become lax or even start to worry about them.

In the meantime, Delmar, along with Greenwood and Tip and a few select others, would take a shuttle, travel by stealth to the southern hemisphere camp of the enemy, and wait. Getting there shouldn't be a problem, Delmar reasoned. Greenwood was an excellent pilot, having served as a merchant pilot before enlisting in the troopers. As pilot, Greenwood was naturally in command of the mission after they were underway.

On the morning of the fourth day at first light, the shuttlecraft containing Greenwood at the helm, Delmar, Tip and a half dozen other men lifted off from the aggressor base camp and headed off at low altitude toward the southern hemisphere. Greenwood knew he would have to hug the surface of the moon in order to avoid detection by the enemy outpost they were going to attack. DIA Stoddard had instructed them to maintain communications blackout, but to monitor all transmissions. Tomorrow morning they would hear the emergency broadcast of the Alpha squad.

DI Buckner and the squad leaders of Beta, Delta, and Gamma squads gathered in the command center at the communications array. "They should have attacked by now," Kenji Toopka said. "We know they left Freewater and should have landed at their base almost a week ago."

"Maybe something happened and they didn't make it," Ronwell Brittin interjected. "What if they were attacked by Red-tails?"

"We would have heard by now," Buckner said. "Don't expect the enemy to play by your rules. It doesn't work that way."

"So we just sit here, sir?" Stan asked. "Just sit here and hope to pickup something on the array?"

"That's right, Shane," answered Buckner. "We wait. Stoddard isn't going to play into our hands. He's a cagey old veteran that knows what he's doing."

"Toopka, you and Brittin make sure your men are ready," Buckner instructed. "Don't let your guard down. We know the enemy is out there somewhere. Be ready."

"Yes, sir," both men answered as one.

"Shane," Buckner continued. "You and Big'un stay on that console. Let me know if you hear anything. And I mean anything."

"Yes, sir," Shane answered.

A day passed, then another. Stan Shane and Big'un took turns monitoring the comm console. Nothing. Not a sound for four days. Then on the morning of the fifth day, static began to crackle from the console speaker.

"Stan!" Big'un exclaimed. "Come here," he called.

Stan was lying on a pallet he had spread on the floor behind the communications console. Sleep had eluded him the more he thought of Delmar and the rest of Alpha squad possibly missing from the training exercise.

"Crash landed…injuries…declaring emergency," were the only words Stan could understand coming from the speaker.

"Go get DI Buckner," Stan ordered. Bigga ran from the communications center. His long strides carried him quickly across the compound to the command center. Within only a few minutes, he and Buckner were back at the comm center. Stan was lying on the floor with his hand up inside the console making an adjustment on a circuit board.

Stan reached his free hand up above the console. "Hand me that modulator," he said. "This one isn't responding."

Buckner handed Stan the piece of equipment while Bigga monitored the console. After a moment, the static began to clear and a faint, distant voice crackled from the speaker. "Need medical assistance … Red-tail attack. Axia independent freighter *Constance* declaring … mergency."

Bigga picked up the microphone and started to answer the distress call when Stan placed his hand on Bigga's arm. "Not yet," Stan said.

"But—" Bigga started to say.

"Could be a trick," Buckner interjected. Stan nodded.

Stan flipped several switches on the console. They heard the transponder come to life. He knew the transponder would recognize the incoming identification beacon of any ship in the solar system, particularly any which could be in close enough proximity to put out as weak a comm signal as the *Constance* seemed to be doing.

Buckner, Stan, and Bigga watched the console monitor come suddenly to life as it began to display the schematics for the independent freighter *Constance*. It showed her relative position to be only two hundred miles north of their present position. According to the readout on the screen, she had crash-landed in a dense mountainous region where the only access would be by taking the transport directly to the site.

"*Constance*, can you hear me?" Buckner asked into

the microphone. "This is Trooper-First Buckner from Freewater Training Base. Do you copy?"

"Freewater?" a voice asked. "We just left Freewater. How are you picking us up?"

"We're not at Freewater," Buckner responded. "At the moment, we are approximately two hundred miles south of your position on a training exercise. Do you have casualties?"

"That's affirmative," the voice answered. "Our captain is dead and our pilot is seriously injured. We have multiple injuries among the crew…hull breached. Can you help us?"

Buckner leaned back in the comm chair and looked at Stan and Bigga. Toopka and Brittin, the other squad leaders, as well as a number of the other men had joined them.

"What's up?" Toopka asked Bigga.

"We're receiving an emergency distress call," Bigga answered. "It's very faint."

"Is it real?" Brittin asked. "Could it be a fake?"

"I don't see how," Buckner answered. "The transponder positively identified the *Constance*."

"The *Constance*?" asked Brittin.

"Yes, why?" answered Buckner.

"Because, sir," Brittin answered. "I saw the *Constance* just before we left Freewater. She had put in for repairs when I was at the Ops Center for guard duty. She was scheduled to depart Freewater yesterday."

The thought that this could be an elaborate hoax crossed Buckner's mind. The probability that an Axia ship had actually crashed on this particular planet at this particular time seemed to be a bit of a stretch of the imagination. Then again, if this really were a true emergency, it was his duty to rush to the aide of the crew of the *Constance*. He would have to rely on his instincts, and right now they were telling him it was time to act.

Buckner stood up and stretched. This little training exercise had unexpectedly become a rescue mission. He just hoped the same Red-tail incursion that had apparently attacked the *Constance* hadn't also destroyed the Alpha squad on its way to the moon. If so, that would explain its failure to complete its part of the training mission.

"All right, men," Buckner began. "This exercise has turned real. Beta and Delta squads, prepare for emergency evacuation. Toopka, inform the transport pilot that we're going active and will require him to fly us to the emergency site."

"Yes, sir," Toopka answered, and then turned to leave.

"Just a minute, Toopka," Buckner said, stopping the man from leaving. "Also inform the transport medical staff to be ready for casualties."

"Yes, sir," Toopka answered. He left the command center and headed off toward the transport staging area.

Stan stood up and inquired of Buckner what he and the rest of Gamma squad should do. "You men stay here and monitor this equipment. Try to contact Alpha squad and fill them in on the emergency."

"Yes, sir," Stan answered. "But what if they don't respond?"

"Then assume they've also come under attack and are most likely already dead," Buckner answered. Stan nodded. Buckner turned to leave. "I know Eagleman is your friend, Shane," Buckner said. "But don't let this cloud your mind. Stay sharp."

"Yes, sir," Stan answered. "We will."

An hour later Beta and Delta were loaded onto the transport. The transport comm officer tuned his emergency directionals to the signal emitted by the *Constance*'s emergency beacon. He fed the coordinates into the navigational computer and relayed them to the pilot. A moment later, the transport lifted from the surface of the moon and headed north toward the downed freighter.

Watching from a bluff only a half-mile from the enemy camp, Delmar, Greenwood, and Tip could not believe their eyes. It looked like the entire enemy contingent had fallen for the trick and were evacuating the campsite. Delmar was certain DI Buckner would not take everyone, so he fully expected to find at least Stan and a few others still in camp.

They watched the transport ship gain altitude then vector off to the north, soon to disappear from sight. "That's our cue," Delmar said. "Come on. It won't take them long to get there."

"And get the surprise of their lives," Greenwood laughed.

The three men made their way back to the shuttlecraft that Greenwood had piloted at absolute ground level the last hundred miles of their trip. The trip reminded Delmar of a rollercoaster he had once been on, dipping and elevating over the rough terrain. Nevertheless, Greenwood sure knew what he was doing, and only once did the shuttlecraft skim the surface. "Sorry about that," was all Greenwood had said, as if bouncing off the surface was supposed to be a normal part of flight.

Greenwood guided the shuttlecraft around behind the enemy position and landed behind a low ridge opposite the main communications array. It was their mission to attack the array and destroy it. Nothing fancy. It was Delmar's hope that Stan and whoever else was in the comm center would be monitoring the emergency broadcast beacon and identification transponder and would not be watching the parameter for an invasion force.

The communications array looked like a super-sized satellite dish. Its base was set in concrete and steel, and Delmar could see what looked like bedsprings rods attached to it. *Must be some of Stan's handiwork*, Delmar thought. Cables unlike any Delmar had seen in the schematics of the array ran from the array back to the comm center and through an open window. "More of Stan's jury-rigging," Delmar said to Tip. "That guy could make a subspace radio out of two soup cans and a piece of string."

Tip agreed and then pointed at the comm center. Coming out the door was Bigga. He stopped to stretch a kink from his back and was just taking a bite from a large red apple when he looked up and saw Greenwood attaching something to the antenna array. Bigga took a couple more steps forward, then realized what was happening. "Holy cow!" he shouted, then turned and ran back into the comm center.

Without a second thought, Greenwood set the timer on the explosive he had just attached to the communications array then hurriedly began to climb back down the frame of the array. Delmar, Tip, and the rest of the attack force bolted through the door of the comm center only a moment after Bigga had disappeared inside. They caught Stan and Bigga still trying to unpack their weapons from the locker they had secured them in after the emergency evacuation.

A moment later, a loud whoomp sounded outside. Dark black smoke enveloped the communications array. Of course, Greenwood had not used an actual explosive charge, but only a smoke bomb. At the same time, Delmar reached over and threw the power switch on the console, shutting down the array. "Seems like you guys are out of business," he said to Stan and Bigga. Then he looked over at two other men from the attack crew. "You Red-tails hungry?" he asked. "We got a couple of hotdogs here fresh off the grill."

"Yeah, and one of 'em has an apple in his mouth," Greenwood said. Big'un opened his mouth and let the apple fall to the floor where it rolled over next to Delmar's foot.

Stan and Bigga looked back and forth at each other, then at the weapons pointed at them. A moment later, other members of Gamma squad were marched into the comm center and seated on the floor along with Stan and Bigga. "How?" Stan started to ask.

"We don't answer questions from our food," Delmar quipped. "So you boys just sit there, be quiet, and enjoy the show."

At about the same time the communications array was going up in smoke, the Beta and Delta transport was homing in on the emergency beacon of the *Constance*.

"Do you see her anywhere?" Buckner asked the pilot.

"No," he answered. "According to these readings, she should be right here."

"Can you set us down in that clearing?" Buckner asked, pointing at a large clearing a hundred yards from their current position.

"Sure thing," the pilot answered. "But unless they crashed behind that ridge and their transponder was thrown clear of the wreckage, we should be able to see them by now."

"I know," Buckner answered. "That's what I'm afraid of."

The pilot set the transport down in the clearing. Buckner, Toopka, and Brittin exited the ship and started making their way back to the supposed crash site. They surveyed the area and could find no trace of a crash. Buckner and the other men walked back into a box canyon of the rocky terrain. Using his wrist transmitter, Buckner called back to the ship. "Are you sure this is the place?"

"According to the signal, you are standing about ten feet from the crash," the comm operator on the ship answered.

Buckner looked around but there was no sign of a downed ship. Suddenly Toopka called out, "Over here, sir." Buckner walked to where Toopka was standing over what appeared to be a large ice chest. Attached to the chest was a note. Inside the chest were three bottles of soda pop and the emergency broadcast beacon and transponder of the *Constance*. The note read:

> You're busted, boss. Please bring this chest and the transponder back to camp with you. My friend on the *Constance* will need it when we get back to Freewater. By the way, we've already destroyed the communications array. Stoddard.
>
> PS—Get Toopka and Brittin to carry the chest. You're getting too old for this stuff.

Toopka and Brittin read the note and turned toward Buckner. Suddenly Buckner began to laugh, which caused the two trainees to join in with him. "Well, don't just stand there," Buckner said. "Open up those sodas and let's drink a toast to the victors."

Buckner reached down and started to grab one of the handles on the ice chest. *What am I doing?* he thought. *I have my orders.* He turned and started back toward the transport. "You've got your orders," he said. "You guys bring that chest."

"Yes, sir," both men answered. So, with a soda in one hand and the chest between them, Toopka and Brittin followed their drill instructor back to the transport ship.

That evening all of the squads were together again. Stoddard declared Alpha squad the victors. "More importantly," he said, "I'm taking your nice transport ship as spoils of war. Beta, Delta, and Gamma are welcome to use our old ship for their ride home."

Both a cheer and a moan rose up from the assembled forces. Alpha was cheering because they were going to ride home in comfort. The other squads were moaning because they had lost their position, their focus, and now their comfortable ride home. It was going to be a long flight back to Freewater.

20

Deagle>gss.3703.775.fwtb
HasselFarm>gss.bv.er
Subject: Almost finished

Dear Mom and Dad,

Only two weeks to go! I can't believe I've been here four months!

Yesterday we returned from a series of training flights. I already told you about our last exercise where my squad wiped out the communications array and captured DI Buckner's transport ship. This time they took us out on a transport to another nearby moon that has an atmosphere. Enroute, they drilled us on the suits and we got our time down to ten seconds! Then in the middle of the night, the alarms went off, and by the time I opened my eyes I was already suited. Several of the guys thought it was just another drill until their ears popped and their faceplate snapped shut. After five minutes, the all-clear light came on and DI Buckner came in and told us to take our suits off and service our equipment. Later we found out that it really was a drill, but done with hard vacuum as an incentive!

Once we arrived on the moon, we had to set up our camp from scratch. We had it assembled and operational in a day. It was that or live in our suits for another day, and none of us could stand the smell! We drilled in low-gravity maneuvers. It was interesting! The motion of the unit as we tried to march was really something. We finally got the hang of it and almost managed to stay on the ground. It wasn't as much fun as when we took out the communications array last month, but we enjoyed ourselves nonetheless.

Then we went to a firing range set up in a giant crater. They allowed us to use full power blasters, and boy can those things make a hole! Next they gave us the long-weapon. After working over the targets a quarter mile away, they catapulted boulders overhead and had us shoot them, or at least at them. It was like skeet shooting, only the targets were as big as trucks! I hit three out of five and was able to qualify as marksman on this range. DI Buckner was pleased.

The next exercise involved trying to overrun another emplacement of trainees. Stan monkeyed with our main transmitter and used it to send out a scrambling signal that confused the other unit. We surprised them completely!

Well, that's about it for now. We'll be going out on our final training trip soon, this time to a small planet farther out. I've enjoyed your letters because they are so newsy with just everyday stuff. Take care, and I'll write when we get back.

Love,
Delmar

Early summer finally arrived. Agnes made her daily vigil to the computer. Robert found her standing in front of the fireplace reading the letter from Delmar. Looking over her shoulder, he was able to read it, and when they finished they hugged each other. They were just beginning to prepare lunch when the phone rang. Agnes answered and was soon talking excitedly. She hung up and turned to her husband.

"That was Daren!" she said excitedly. "Rosemary has gone into labor!"

"Well then, let's go!" Robert replied. The two of them put the perishables away and ran for the ground car.

Arriving at the Sabeti farm, Agnes hurried into the house with Daren, who had been watching for them from the front porch. Minutes later, they came out with Rosemary between them. Robert saw that the baby had dropped since he had last seen her and was causing her difficulty walking. As soon as she was comfortable in the back seat, Robert turned the ground car onto the gravel road and raced for town.

At the hospital, aides helped Rosemary inside and generally took over. Agnes was glad that she and Rosemary had visited the hospital the previous month and learned what would happen. Daren hurried to a changing room where he scrubbed and put on a sterile gown. A male nurse escorted him to the expectancy chamber to be with his wife. Agnes and Robert made themselves comfortable in the waiting room.

As usual the magazines were, in some cases, years out of date. Robert even found one issue that was older than the hospital itself. He wondered where it had come from. Agnes went back out to the car to get her extra knitting bag and brought it inside. Taking a seat opposite her husband, she took out her latest project, and the click of needles soon filled the room.

Agnes was halfway through her second piece, and Robert was considering a career reciting the articles he had been reading, when a nurse came into the waiting room.

"Mr. and Mrs. Hassel?" she asked.

"Yes?" they both replied in unison.

"Rosemary just delivered a healthy baby boy!" the nurse announced. Agnes squealed with delight and hugged Robert.

"How are they? Are they okay?" Agnes asked.

"The mother and baby are fine," she answered. "But we thought there for a while that we were going to lose the father," she finished with a chuckle.

"When will we be able to see them?" Robert asked, amused by the nurse's comment.

"They'll be in their room in about half an hour," the nurse replied. "I'll come get you."

The Hassels thanked her and returned to their seats. Agnes tried unsuccessfully to resume her knitting while Robert just stared out the window.

Time seemed to stop while the seemingly eternal half-hour crept by. Eventually, the nurse returned and led the Hassels to Rosemary's room. They entered quietly and saw Rosemary propped up in bed holding a little bundle while Daren knelt beside her. Both parents were misty-eyed, and the signs of fatigue were obvious in Rosemary's features.

Peeking inside the blanket, the Hassels saw a little pink wrinkled face. The baby cracked a tiny yawn for their benefit and then snuggled down deeper into the blanket. Robert and Agnes voiced their congratulations to Rosemary while Daren saw them to the door.

Later that evening Agnes again sat at her desk and gathered her thoughts for what she would say to Delmar.

> HasselFarm>gss.bv.er
> Deagle>gss.3703.775.fwtb
> Subject: re: Almost finished

> Dear Son,

> We received your latest letter today. Just after we got it, the phone rang and we ended up taking

Rosemary and Daren to the hospital. She delivered a healthy baby boy! Daren is staying in the guest quarters at the hospital tonight, and we will take them their car when we visit them tomorrow.

Summer is finally here, and the crops are growing well. We have a new colt since I last wrote to you and another one due any time. Dad is getting around without a limp now, and it's good to see him strong again. A group of neighbors are coming by later this week to help put a new roof on the equipment shed. I'm glad Dad isn't going to try to do it by himself.

Your training trip sounds like it was quite an experience. When I had my training flight, one of the girls accidentally disabled the food synthesizer. As a result, we had nothing to eat except compressed meat product for a week! We had a contest between us girls and a flight of men trainees on the firing range. They were good, but we beat them by two shots.

Well, I better go to bed. Tomorrow is going to be busy. I'll send you pictures of the baby as soon as they are ready. Let us know when your graduation is scheduled. We want to be there. Take care and write soon.

Love,
Mom and Dad

PS—Daren and Rosemary named their son Del-Robert.

The transport was barely clear of the atmosphere when Buckner had the unit circle up so he could address them.

"Okay, listen up," he said to the assembled trainees. "First off, I want to tell you that we are going farther out on this training flight than we told you." A groan went through the unit. "Instead of the small planet in the Freewater system, we'll be landing on an uninhabited planet a few systems over. It should take us three days to get there, so make yourself useful on this ship or DIA Stoddard and I will exercise our creativity."

A hand went up in the back. "Yes?" Buckner replied.

"Sir?" began the trainee. "Why did they change our destination?" Buckner thought for a moment.

"The reason for the change," Buckner explained, "is because of recent incursions by Red-tails near Freewater. The service needs to use our usual training planet as a staging area for the combat troopers. We were transferred away from the incursions so we could train safely."

The compartment had grown quiet at the mention of Red-tails. "Any more questions?" Buckner asked. The group remained quiet. "All right, I'll brief you shortly before we land. Dismissed." The trainees got up and moved off toward their berths while Buckner and Stoddard went forward.

Two days later the trainees assembled around their drill instructor. "All right, listen up!" Buckner said as the hubbub died down. "We're going to be landing this afternoon, and I want you guys to be ready. This exercise is a practice deployment on the surface. Have you been going over your equipment?" he asked. A chorus of "Yes, sirs" greeted him in response. "Good," he replied. "On this maneuver you are going to be using field-strength weapons. Be careful. I don't want to have to fill out no paperwork on anyone."

The tension eased as laughter broke out. "That's better," Buckner said. "I don't want you too tense for this one. I want DIA Stoddard to go over your squad assignments."

Buckner moved to the back wall and let his assistant take over. "Okay, here we go," Stoddard began. "Squads one and two will secure a perimeter around our landing zone. Squad three will create a defensive fence around the ship while squad four sets up the communications and field command. You will have ten minutes before the ship lifts. If you aren't ready, tough. Each man will carry his own field rations and supplies. An enemy force will be trying to breech your position fifteen minutes after landing. Any questions?" he asked.

Before a hand could go up the emergency klaxon sounded. At first, the trainees did not know quite what to do. One glance at the surprised look on Buckner's face prodded them into action.

The compartment speaker blared to life: "This is not a drill! I repeat, this is not a drill. All hands to battle stations!" Buckner and Stoddard herded the trainees out of the way of the regular crew racing for their duty positions.

The trainees struggled into their pressure suits. Delmar whispered a silent prayer to the Unseen One, thanking him for the unending hours of pressure suit training they had received. Suddenly, the ship lurched sideways when something impacted hard near the stern. The faceplates on the suits snapped shut when the cabin pressure fell. Stoddard kept the trainees still while Buckner raced forward. In a minute, he was back, his face ashen.

"Okay men, listen up!" he announced through his suit speaker. "We've come under attack by a contingent of Red-tail ships. One of their torps has damaged our drive system, and the pilot is trying to bring us down. Squad leaders, take two men each and bring your gear forward. The rest of you get it on fast and prepare to exit the ship quickly. It looks as if your training is going to get a little more serious."

The ship lurched twice more. The inertial dampeners failed and they could feel the effect of inertia leak through the weakening drive field of the ship. Designated trainees raced to the equipment lockers and soon returned with the supplies.

Buckner again slipped forward and was soon back with another report. "We've taken two more hits, and the drive is failing," he said in a rush. "There are casualties up front, and both the pilot and captain are injured. One of the troopers is attempting to land us, but the ship is starting to buckle. Unless he can straighten this thing out, we're gonna hit hard, so get prepared. Assume crash positions!"

The trainees squatted low and braced against the bulkheads and support structure of the cabin. The ship lurched again when something exploded outside. They could hear the cry of tortured metal around them. Seconds crept by at a snail's pace, and they could hear the shriek of air outside the ship as it plummeted through the planet's atmosphere.

The crash was more of a glancing skid than a straight vertical impact. The trainees felt the ship bounce once, then again, then slide as it plowed into a field. Finally, the motion stopped and there was silence for a few seconds. Almost immediately, Buckner and Stoddard stood up on the leaning deck and ordered the trainees to move out.

The hatch was partially buckled, and it took Buckner and two trainees to force it to open part way. Immediately, there was the zing of a shot near the hatch. A Red-tail energy beam burned through the hatch torching through the chest of one of the trainees helping Buckner. Delmar recognized the man as Justus Beesder, their communications specialist. A medic tried to save the man's life but he was already dead.

Stoddard and Buckner both drew their weapons and fired through the opening to provide cover for the trainees. The young men tumbled out amid the dust and smoke from the crash and hit the dirt.

The first squad out fired toward the direction of the incoming shots and allowed the rest of the unit to scramble safely clear of the ship. Buckner and Stoddard ordered the trainees forward to establish a safe perimeter around the crash site. Following Stoddard's example, the trainees used low power settings on their blasters to gouge out trenches and then tumbled in.

The firing stayed steady and several enemy shots hit the ship. Delmar witnessed one crewmember get hit as he came out of the hatch and saw willing hands drag the wounded man back inside. The man's severed left arm lay twitching on the ground. Buckner also saw it and ordered Delmar's squad to go back and assist the crew in getting out safely.

As they ran for the ship, Delmar's squad leader and another man were hit but both managed to roll safely behind an embankment of the dirt plowed up by the ship. Delmar and the rest made it into the ship just as the intensity of the hits on the hull increased sharply.

The rest of the crew was inside the hatchway. Several were badly injured, and the ship would provide them with very little safety. One of Delmar's squad mates began to worry aloud and was quickly hushed.

It was then that Delmar had an idea. Remembering the weapons range demonstration about the blaster, he set his weapon on a higher setting. Aiming at the hull where it touched the ground, he squeezed the firing stub. White light filled the compartment as the ray bored a hole through the steel and into the rocks below. Delmar released the stub and surveyed his work. The hole burrowed only about ten feet below the ship.

Delmar grabbed a fire extinguisher and expelled the foam down into the hole he had just created, effectively cooling the sides. He eased himself down into the hole, trying to avoid any hot rock sidings that may not have cooled. He reset his blaster and aimed it at the still-cooling wall. He fired again, this time angling slightly upward toward the surface. He could hear Stan above him yelling at the DIs outside to clear an area.

Delmar fired twice more to lengthen his tunnel. Just as he was about to fire a third time, the roof began to cave in near the end of his last blast. Daylight streamed in through the hole, and Delmar could see that his tunnel had come up behind a wall of rock.

The enemy weapons sounded terribly close as he emerged into the light. Several trainees had formed a series of trenches and pits to provide cover from enemy fire. Ducking down into the tunnel, he called back to Stan at the other end to bring out the crew.

With the last of them lifted out into the trenches, an explosion ripped through the air. Delmar turned around to see that the central section of the ship was gone. Pieces of hot metal began to rain down around them, causing them to seek shelter. He shuddered to think that he had been in that section of the ship only a few minutes ago.

Darkness fell and the firing slackened until it became quiet. Buckner and Stoddard crawled around and checked on their trainees, even though Stoddard had been hit. Wounded men filled the main pit where the ship corpsman provided what emergency medical treatment he could. Of the sixty trainees, two were dead and eleven wounded. This was going to be a long night.

Among the crew of the transport ship, the worst injuries were both the pilot and the captain. Neither would survive the night. The trooper who had brought the ship in had been killed on impact, which left Buckner as the ranking able-bodied trooper on the scene. Buckner learned that three Red-tail ships, one of which had been destroyed, had attacked them.

Stoddard believed the planet had become a forward staging area for the Red-tails. He asked if the bridge had managed to get out a distress call, only to learn that the transmitter array had gone dead with the first hit. The news that their plight was unknown was not heartening.

Delmar overheard the conversation and approached Buckner with an idea. "Sir," he began, "what if we salvage the transmitter from the ship and jury-rig some power for it?" The drill instructor looked back at the ship and thought for a minute.

"Do you think you could do it?" he asked.

"Yes, sir," replied Delmar. "Stan and I should be able to drag out the transmitter if some of the other guys can get us some power."

"How do you plan to approach the nose of the ship?" the drill instructor asked. "It's badly exposed to enemy fire."

"The same way we got here, sir," replied Delmar, "by tunneling." Buckner thought about it for another minute and then nodded his approval. He knew Eagleman and Shane worked well together and that each knew how to improvise. Both had proven themselves on the exercise when they'd been assigned to the communications array on the Melanor moon. Eagleman had been the aggressor and Shane the defender.

Delmar moved out and found Stan. Explaining the plan to Stan, the two men were soon at the bottom of the pit Delmar had blasted beneath the ship. Now, instead of pieces of burning steel hull, light from the planet's smaller moon bathed them in a golden glow. It hardly seemed possible that they could be fighting for their lives under such a beautiful moon.

Delmar aimed to one side to avoid creation of a trench beneath the long axis of the wreck and fired his blaster in short bursts. The flash attracted a volley of enemy rounds but none came near them. Stan could hear another team led by Buckner behind them in the pit tunneling toward the aft section of the transport to reach the fusion power boxes located there.

Soon Delmar and Stan were far enough forward to change direction and tunnel under the remains of the control room. Two short blasts brought them underneath the steel hull. Aiming carefully, Delmar fired at the steel. It quickly evaporated and they found themselves looking up into the control room.

Climbing aboard, they found the room nearly demolished from both the attack and the crash. The body of the trooper who had brought them down was still strapped into the control seat. His head, savagely torn from his body, was nowhere to be seen. Delmar almost became sick, but a shake from Stan helped him come around.

Leaving the grisly scene behind, they moved toward the communications board. Fortunately, it was relatively undamaged. Stan found the service toolkit stowed nearby and quickly removed the access panels.

It didn't take long before they had the transmitter safely on the floor between them. Delmar scooted the heavy transmitter toward the hole while Stan repacked the tool-kit and attached it to his belt. He then reached inside the hole in the wall and yanked free several feet of fiber antenna cable. Stuffing this into his shirt, Stan helped Delmar lower the bulky piece of equipment down into the tunnel.

The sizzle of a heat ray on the outside hull of the ship encouraged them to hurry, and after they were again in the tunnel, they heard the muffled explosions of a Red-tail ray connecting with a piece of volatile component.

They met the other team at the pit. They had also come under attack and Buckner and one of the trainees were wounded. Buckner and the trainee crawled up the tunnel while the two teams struggled with their prizes. Soon extra hands arrived and carried the precious equipment out into the main pit.

Stan jury-rigged the transmitter while Delmar helped run connections for the power source. Delmar noticed they still lacked an antenna for the unit and looked around for something that would work. He spied a scattering of loose rods from the bedsprings drive on the back of the transport. He told Stan where he was going.

Delmar made use of the tunnel to get to the remains of the ship but would have to crawl in the open for several yards to retrieve one of the rods. The enemy was still taking occasional shots at the hulk of the ship. Delmar was afraid he would have to crawl out there unaided when he heard Stoddard call out for the trainees on the perimeter to give Delmar covering fire.

Under the cover of blasters and long-weapons, Delmar slid toward the rods. He had made it most of the way when an enemy sharpshooter spotted him. Immediately, the ground and wreckage around Delmar stirred violently by the unrelenting onslaught of projectile slugs. Pieces of seemingly indestructible equipment evaporated by ray blasts. Delmar stayed as low as he could and belly-crawled toward safety.

Just as he reached the edge of the pit with the rod, the night was lit up and Delmar felt himself spinning through the air. His last image was the brightly lit edges of the crater as the concussion drove consciousness from him.

21

"Are you sure this is the location we were given?" asked the captain as he peered downward at the planet.

"I'm sure of it," came back the reply from one of the other ships. "Do you see any sign of the transport?"

"Not yet," the first captain replied.

"Hey! I see something over there near that ridge," said a voice from the third ship. The path plowed by the crashed transport extended several hundred yards. When they drew closer, they could see the flashes from weapons fire surrounding the shattered remains of a crashed ship.

"We'll take care of this," one of the other ships said as they peeled off and dove toward the enemy positions. "You keep us covered." The first captain clicked his mic button twice in acknowledgment while he watched the other two ships peel away from the formation and attack the enemy ground forces and gun emplacements.

The superior firepower of the ships made quick

work of the limited Red-tail positions. As soon as the entrenchments were clear, one of the ships set down near the wreckage while the other two kept watch from the air.

What the rescuers found was a sorry sight indeed. The ship was little more than twisted wreckage, around which trenches and pits were dug by the defenders. All told, eleven trainees and eight of the ship's crew died, including the trooper Delmar and Stan had seen. Of the survivors, most were wounded to some degree, several critically.

The captain of the rescue ship surveyed the situation and called for a medical ship and extra escorts. Thanks to the distress call, the secret Red-tail staging area was searched out and destroyed. There were still a number of pockets of resistance to be dug out, but time and manpower would take care of it.

The rescue captain took stock of the defenders while they waited, noting that except for the two drill instructors and the surviving crewmembers of the transport ship, they were all basic trainees. Buckner had been wounded a second time in the same attack that got Delmar. Both now lay side by side, unconscious and seriously wounded.

Stoddard assumed command of the unit and directed the squad leaders from where he lay with both legs fractured. The captain examined the smoking remains of the makeshift transmitter destroyed by an enemy shell. They had managed to get the distress call out just before the shell hit it and wounded the alternate operator, also a trainee.

Radiating out from the crash site was a circle of destruction where the trainees had laid waste to anything that moved. Later investigation would reveal that there were the bodies or indications of more than 250 Red-tails slain or wounded by the defenders.

An hour later, the hospital ship was able to land near the crash, and the evacuation began. The most critically wounded were taken immediately into the surgical units where the process to restore them to health began. Those with lesser injuries were treated and sent to the waiting berths deeper in the ship. A mortuary detail recovered the bodies of those killed in action and took them to the ship morgue for the trip home. With everyone accounted for, the hospital ship captain gave the word, and the rescue ships lifted into space.

The Hassels were just sitting down in the living room when a service flitter settled onto their driveway. Robert looked out the window and saw a trooper coming to the front door. Answering his knock, Robert opened the door and greeted the man. Agnes saw the black uniform and stood beside her husband.

"Mr. and Mrs. Hassel?" the trooper asked. When Robert nodded, the trooper handed him a sealed envelope. "I was ordered to bring this to you. I'm sorry," the trooper said and then stood by silently. Robert and Agnes stood unmoving with the terrible paper weighing heavily in Robert's hands.

His hands trembling, Robert opened the envelope. In his years as a trooper officer, he had delivered many similar notices to other families—a duty he never enjoyed.

Major G. Gizdavich
Freewater Training Center

Dear Mr. and Mrs. Hassel,

This letter is to inform you that your ward, TT Delmar Eagleman, was wounded in enemy action and is now hospitalized at the Freewater Medical Center. Three Red-tail ships attacked his training unit while enroute to a field training exercise. They crash landed on a hostile planet and came under immediate enemy fire. The trainees performed well, and several of the trainees, including Trainee Eagleman, were instrumental in the rescue of the transport crew and defense of their position.

TT Delmar Eagleman is expected to fully recover from his wounds and resume active service in a few weeks. His medical report lists several broken bones and internal injuries, along with a severe concussion. He remains unconscious but is expected to come around soon. I request that you come to Freewater as your presence may aid in his recovery. The trooper delivering this notice will provide you with transportation to Jasper Station where a ship is waiting. The liaison officer can help you arrange your affairs.

Major G. Gizdavich
Commander
Freewater Training Center

Agnes packed while Robert quickly called the Sabetis and the liaison officer. Satisfied with the arrangements, he helped Agnes finish packing, and they climbed into the backseat of the flitter.

Wandering around in a thick fog, Delmar could not figure out where the booming was coming from. Searching, he finally saw a lighter area ahead and realized the noises seemed to come from the same place. Approaching the light, Delmar suddenly found himself lying on his back under bright lights while medical personnel discussed his condition. He groaned and felt pain course through his body. Delmar wished fervently that he could go back into the fog.

"He's coming around," one of the nurses announced. "I'll go get his parents." Delmar couldn't find the strength to speak and say his parents were dead, but then he remembered the Hassels. He tried to sit up but something weighed him down.

"Take it easy, Trooper," a deep voice ordered. "You got busted up pretty bad by that shell." Delmar tried to remember anything about a shell, but his mind refused to cooperate. Someone mercifully turned down the lights, and Delmar opened his eyes.

Everything was blurry and tried to spin or dance around the room. He closed his eyes again to calm the antics of the furniture. Someone gave him an injection and the pain eased. Delmar lay still trying to make sense of it all when he heard footsteps enter the room. Taking a chance, Delmar opened his eyes again. This time the surroundings were more cooperative and he noticed two blurry forms leaning over him.

"Hi, Delmar," Agnes said. "Dad and I are here." Delmar felt the touch of a familiar hand on his shoulder and figured it was Mr. Hassel. He opened his mouth to speak but was only able to croak.

"Don't try to talk, son," Mr. Hassel's voice said. "The doctor said you need to rest. We'll be back tomorrow when you're more awake."

Delmar wanted to say how much he loved them but couldn't figure out how to use his mouth. He felt the touch of Agnes' hand on his cheek, and someone gave him another shot. Delmar drifted off into a peaceful sleep.

Delmar's recovery progressed rapidly. He was soon able to get about in a wheelchair and visit the other patients. While visiting DI Buckner, he learned that eleven of his fellow trainees had perished in the Red-tail attack. The rest of the injured and wounded were recovering and most would be out of the hospital within the week.

He also visited DIA Stoddard, who told him that the graduation ceremony had been delayed at the request of the unit. They wanted to graduate with all of their surviving members present. A few of his buddies, including Stan, came to visit and presented him with a black armband embossed with the number eleven and their flight number. Delmar proudly wore it and noticed that Buckner and Stoddard wore bands as well.

A month passed, and Delmar was able to leave the hospital proper for a convalescent facility. Except for a hip injury that kept him confined to the wheelchair, Delmar had fully recovered.

The Hassels and his unit friends came to visit regularly and kept him posted on what was happening. Shortly after entering the facility, the unit had a memorial service for their fallen friends. Delmar was able to be present while the unit mourned its loss.

After the service, DI Buckner and DIA Stoddard came to visit Delmar. They inquired about his condition and how he felt about attending graduation in the chair. Delmar was disappointed not to be able to march with his squad, but did not want to delay the rest of his unit.

Finally, they agreed on how to handle the situation. Buckner said some of Delmar's flight mates would be over early on graduation day to help him get ready.

Graduation day arrived a week later. As promised, two men from his flight, TT Thomas Bigga and TT Marlon Hadde showed up to help Delmar slip an oversized pair of pants over the casts. Delmar was glad for the help. His regular dress jacket fit without any serious modification. After helping him with his boots, Bigga pushed Delmar's chair out of the facility while Hadde held the doors open.

Going up the walkway toward the parade ground, Delmar noticed that there seemed to be an unusual number of people headed there as well. He had

attended several graduation ceremonies while stationed at Freewater, and he knew these ceremonies
were usually only attended by the families of the
graduates. *I wonder what's going on?* he thought.

As they approached the parade ground, Delmar
saw that the stands were nearly filled to capacity, and
that many of the training units currently on base
were at parade-rest nearby. He looked from Bigga
to Hadde but their expressions never changed.
"Big'un," Delmar asked. "What's going on here?"
Bigga didn't answer, he just shrugged his shoulders.

Big'un wheeled Delmar into a hangar where
his flight was forming up. DI Buckner was there,
although he still moved stiffly. DIA Stoddard was
also present and was using a cane to steady himself.
His casts had only recently come off, and the wob-
bly instructor had visited Delmar a few days earlier.
Delmar suspected that the cane would disappear
when it came time to march.

Stan walked over to Delmar. He looked
resplendent in his dress uniform in spite of the
full cast on his left arm. Delmar knew that Stan
had received several shrapnel wounds when the
enemy destroyed the makeshift transmitter. The
doctors rebuilt the bones in his left arm from the
shattered remains left by the slivers of metal that
had riddled him. Stan told him that the cast would
come off in another month.

DI Buckner called the unit to form up, and that's
when it really hit Delmar that eleven of his friends
would not be there to graduate. Eleven black rib-

bons, each embossed with the name of one of the fallen, hung from the unit standard. All of the graduates wore black armbands edged in white to contrast it against their black uniforms. Delmar found his sense of elation about graduating tempered by the grief they all shared.

DI Buckner addressed them. "All right, Trainees. That's the last time I'll ever address you as such," he said. A quiet murmur of cheer ran through their ranks. "Today you graduate and become full troopers, and I want to tell you before all the hoopla that you guys made DIA Stoddard and me very proud. There's quite a crowd out there, so step lively and with pride. You've earned it. I want Eagleman and Shane in the front rank behind the standard bearer along with Eagleman's rather large friend there." He indicated Trainee Thomas Bigga pushing Delmar's wheelchair.

Delmar, Stan, and Big'un moved to their assigned places while the ranks reformed. "Remember now, we will march out and stop on my command. We will then salute the reviewing stand, and I will call you to open ranks. Ranks not under inspection will stand at parade rest and will come to attention at my command. The reviewing officers will then inspect you. From that point on, listen closely for my commands, as I understand there may be some added ceremonies. Afterward, we will pass in review and then be dismissed to the reception hall behind the reviewing stands. Are there any questions?" No one said a word. "Standard-bearer, remember what I told you to do when we open ranks for inspection," Buckner added. The standard-bearer acknowledged Buckner's instruction.

They could hear the Galactic Axia anthem begin to play outside. From the corner of his eye, Delmar saw DIA Stoddard toss his cane into a corner and take his position at the right rear corner of the unit. Delmar also noticed that two of the strongest men in his unit were behind and beside their assistant drill instructor. Buckner called the unit to attention and gave the forward march order as the doors leading to the parade ground swung open.

They marched onto the parade grounds and Delmar was amazed at the size of the crowd in the stands. As they marched around the perimeter of the field, he counted twenty-four training squadrons formed up in the center of the grounds. He still could not figure out why they were getting such a reception until they came to a halt in front of the reviewing stand.

When Buckner called them to salute, Delmar saw who the reviewing officers were—Empress Ane of Axia and Captain Mophesto, her consort! He'd heard on the news that she was making one of her "Grand Tours" but never expected to even see her, much less this!

The empress was dressed in a gray uniform similar to the ones worn by the ladies of the fleet. Her husband was dressed in Mican blue and wore a sash denoting his place as consort. Both wore Spacer Plates, which indicated to Delmar that they qualified in other areas besides being royalty. They returned the salute of the unit, their right arms horizontal across their chests with palms down.

When the empress and her consort came down from the reviewing stand, the standard-bearer knelt on one knee and lowered the standard. The empress removed her hair ribbon and tied it around the standard pole beneath the eleven black ribbons.

Just as she finished, Delmar saw her gently stroke the black ribbons with the tips of her fingers. He thought he saw a tear trickle down her cheek. She turned to Buckner, and he ordered the flight to open ranks for inspection. Stoddard ordered the rear three echelons to parade rest while Buckner joined the empress and her husband as they prepared to inspect the first rank.

Stopping in front of each graduating trooper, DI Buckner introduced him to the reviewing officers. Delmar was glad to see that Empress Ane and Mophesto seemed pleased with the inspection. After completing their examination, they both spoke to the new trooper and then moved on to the next.

Delmar also noticed that their comments amplified through a loud speaker for those in the stands. It wasn't often that a flight with actual combat experience and casualties graduated at Freewater. The royal couple soon came to Stan, who was standing next to Delmar. Again, they approved of his appearance. The empress then took a case from an aide that seemed to have magically appeared behind her. She removed a glistening commendation medal and pinned it to Stan's uniform. She then smiled at him, produced a pen, and signed his cast. Stan looked so proud he could bust.

Next, they stood in front of Delmar. He tried to stand, but Mophesto put his hand on Delmar's shoulder and pushed him gently back down into his wheelchair. His heart stopped while they inspected him and his chair. He could hear them murmur their approval, and when they returned to the front, Delmar noticed what looked like a miniature video camera hanging by a ribbon from the empress' neck.

Again, the aide appeared and handed a box to the empress. Opening it, she removed a commendation medal along with a second medal with a small eight-pointed star. She pinned the second medal to his uniform and announced that it was for exceptional bravery in the rescuing of the transport crew.

Delmar was dumbfounded. The empress then looked him in the eye and spoke quietly to him. "Delmar, you sure caused me a lot of paperwork," she said. Delmar blushed. He didn't know how to respond. The empress continued, "You will go far, Delmar. And remember, we have our eye on you."

Delmar murmured a thank you and heard two clicks from the video box hanging from the empress' neck. The empress smiled when she realized that Delmar had heard it and looked up at her husband. Mophesto looked at Delmar and gave him a knowing wink. "Mary says hello," he said. Delmar did not know who Mary was, but nodded his acknowledgement to the royal consort.

The rest of the inspection went by course as the

reviewing party inspected and addressed each graduate. Delmar heard several other friends receive medals, along with both Stoddard and Buckner. For taking command of the deadly situation on the planet, Stoddard received an on-the-spot promotion to trooper-first and full drill instructor. It took a lot of effort to keep from cheering.

The empress and her husband returned to the front, and Buckner again called for the lowering of the standard. As it was lowered down in front of her, the empress attached a unit citation to the flag. She then returned to the reviewing stand.

DI Buckner called Flight 775 to attention and ordered them to pass in review. With pride, the graduates strode forward past the stands while the Galactic Axia anthem played and the crowd cheered.

Once they had returned to their starting place, Buckner called them to parade rest. He stood there beaming at them and finally found his voice. "I'm proud to address you as troopers!" he said with choked emotion. "Dismissed."

Flight 775 broke up with a cheer and surrounded the two drill instructors. Several minutes later, they followed the rapidly disappearing crowd toward the reception hall.

EPILOGUE

A month later, Delmar and Stan were released from their plastic casts. Robert and Agnes had returned to Erdinata a few days after the graduation ceremony. They had managed to meet the empress before the graduation and personally expressed their thanks for her intervention in Delmar's custody case.

At first, Delmar and Stan both had difficulty retraining limbs long immobilized by inactivity. They managed to arrange the same therapy time and motivated each other in their drive to recover.

When the therapist finally released them, they reported to the duty office on the base. Passing the training area, they saw both Buckner and Stoddard drilling new training flights.

They reported in at the duty office and the trooper on duty handed each of them their assignment envelopes. Waiting until they were outside, they eagerly tore the envelopes open and removed the assignment sheets.

Trooper Delmar Eagleman,

You are ordered to report to the travel office for three weeks' leave to Erdinata where you will report to Major (Ret.) Robert Hassel. Upon completion of your leave, you will report for extended computer studies at the Mican Training Institute.

Major G. Gizdavich
Commander
Freewater Training Center

Delmar looked up at Stan to see his friend staring at him. "Here, read this," Stan said and traded assignment sheets with Delmar. He quickly read the sheet and saw that it was identical to his own, except for granting unspecified leave.

"But why don't they send you to see your family?" Delmar asked.

"Because I don't have a family," Stan replied. "I've been an orphan for many years."

Delmar looked at his friend and then at a familiar old pocketwatch, then slung his arm around Stan's shoulder. "Come on," he said as he pushed Stan toward the travel office. "I've got a family for you!"

Watch for Delmar and a host of other characters in upcoming adventures in the Galactic Axia Series by Jim Laughter and Victor J. Bretthauer.

Meet the Authors

Victor J. Bretthauer and his wife, Niki, are both ordained ministers working with small, struggling congregations throughout the western United States. They have started and led several support groups dealing with domestic violence, adult and childhood abuse, and bereavement and personal counseling. The Bretthauers live in Port Angeles, Washington, near their adopted son, Stan, his wife, Dawn, and their granddaughter. They have one surviving daughter, Rachel, who lives in Arizona.

Jim Laughter served in the US Air Force for twenty years and retired as a Master Sergeant in 1991. He and his wife, Wilma, traveled the world with tours of duty in Texas, Louisiana, the Philippines, Japan, and England. After retiring, Jim founded a non-profit organization to support missionaries around the world, focusing on raising funds to grant educational scholarships to worthy national students in missionary seminaries. Many thousands of people benefit daily from Jim's vision of educating national students to evangelize their own nations. Jim and Wilma live in Tulsa, Oklahoma, close to their three sons, Sam, Ben, and Jon (their wives too), and their three grandchildren.